LETHBRIDGE-STEWART

THE FORGOTTEN SON

ANDY FRANKHAM-ALLEN

CANDY JAR BOOKS · CARDIFF
2022

The right of Andy Frankham-Allen to be identified as the
Author of the Work has been asserted by him in accordance
with the Copyright, Designs and Patents Act 1988.

The Forgotten Son © Andy Frankham-Allen 2015, 2022

Characters from 'The Web of Fear'
© *Hannah Haisman & Henry Lincoln, 1967, 2022*
Lethbridge-Stewart: The Series
© *Andy Frankham-Allen & Shaun Russell 2015, 2022*

Doctor Who is © *British Broadcasting Corporation, 1963, 2022*

Range Editor: Andy Frankham-Allen
Editor: Shaun Russell
Editorial: Will Rees, Hayley Cox & Keren Williams
Licensed by Hannah Haisman
Cover art by Richard Young & Will Brooks

Published by Candy Jar Books
Mackintosh House
136 Newport Road
Cardiff
CF24 1DJ
www.candyjarbooks.co.uk

ISBN: 978-1-915439-04-8

Printed and bound in the UK by
Severn, Bristol Road, Gloucester, GL2 5EU

All rights reserved.
No part of this publication may be reproduced, stored in a
retrieval system, or transmitted at any time or by any means,
electronic, mechanical, photocopying, recording or otherwise
without the prior permission of the copyright holder. This book is
sold subject to the condition that it shall not by way of trade or
otherwise be circulated without the publisher's prior consent in any
form of binding or cover other than that in which it is published.

PROLOGUE

IT ALL STARTED WITH A ROAR!

On TV, Doctor Omega and his trusty aide, Captain Borel, were exploring a dark corridor of an empty house. The flickering flames from the fireplace threw their shadows against the walls, creating shapes that made young Jonathan 'John' James' skin crawl. He sat back on the sofa, trying his best to squeeze himself between the cushions, his eyes riveted to the television screen. He knew they were going to find something in the kitchen. The Shadow Beast, a creature that lived in shadows and fed off the darkest thoughts of men. Doctor Omega had done some horrible things on his adventures, as had Captain Borel. The Beast was going to have a feast.

The screen went black.

For a moment John sat in the darkness, the only light in the front room having been the TV itself.

A roar!

He jumped, his eyes darting around the room looking for whatever it was that could make such a sound. It definitely came from inside his house. He swallowed. He was all alone and something was in his house!

His mum wasn't in; she had popped out with Danny, his little brother, over the road for a cup of sugar from Mrs Setchfield. Said she'd only be a few minutes, but John knew that really she'd be a lot longer. His mum was never only a few minutes when she went to see Mrs Setchfield. He'd asked his dad about that once, and his dad had simply shaken his head and said 'women!', as if that answered everything.

The roar came again. It seemed further away this time. Outside maybe.

John looked at the black television screen, listened to the gentle hum. The TV was still on, there was just no picture. He took a deep breath, knowing he had to find out what the roar belonged to. Doctor Omega would.

It didn't take too long to realise the sound had come from the outside toilet, and so he tip-toed out into the garden, the evening already becoming dark. He didn't like to go into the garden at night; there were too many shadows that hid things he couldn't see. Like in the story Robert had told him about the dead finger he'd found in his garden a couple of months ago. Tooting Bec wasn't a dangerous place, at least not in the day, but night-time was another thing. At least as far as Jonathan James was concerned. He liked to play *Doctor Omega* with his friends. Robert tended to be Captain Denis Borel and William would be Fred, investigating strange goings-on at the Lido, but when it came down to it John realised he wasn't as brave as he liked to pretend.

The moon appeared over the tip of the grey clouds, giving John the only illumination by which he could see. Some of the neighbours had outdoor lamps, but they weren't cheap, and his dad insisted they had better things to pay for, like a new car. His old Audax Hillman Husky was a bit of a death trap, apparently. John hesitated, peering through the shadows, and then crept down the central path, careful to stay in the moonlight as much as he possibly could. There was the roar again. He paused mid-step at the sound. It seemed familiar, almost like the flush was broken and the water was having trouble going down.

He called out to his mum. She could have come home without him knowing; Saturday evenings were the only time in the week he really got hooked on the idiot box, as his dad often called television, so if she had come home John wouldn't have noticed unless she entered the front room and tapped him on his head. And if Danny needed to have a wee, then it would have been much quicker for their mum to take him straight to the outside toilet than run into the house and up the stairs.

Yes, that's what the roar had been. Not some creature, but rather the sound of the outside toilet, the pipes rumbling in protest at the flush. Convincing himself that he was being silly, he called out to his mum again.

She didn't answer.

But the roar did.

Perhaps it was one of those ill eagle aliens? John wasn't quite sure what one of those were, but his dad was always talking about them and how they took things that didn't belong to them. Although why an ill eagle would want to use a toilet... Well, if it was some alien then it was in for a shock. Doctor Omega knew how to take care of monsters, and so did Jonathan James!

He reached down and picked up the Little Snoopy pull toy which Danny had left in the garden the other day. Wasn't much, but if applied properly it'd leave a bump or two.

'You'll pay the Fisher Price,' John quipped, fortified by the feel of the wooden dog in his hand, and feeling oddly proud of his little joke in the face of such dread. Robert would have thought him crazy... and brave.

He crept close to the shed-like structure that contained the outside toilet. He was just about to reach out for the latch and open the door when the roar stopped him dead.

And it *was* definitely a roar.

He fell backwards, the Little Snoopy falling from his hands. Something large and shaggy emerged from the toilet. Eyes glowing from its large head, it lumbered towards him. John loved reading about explorers visiting strange lands, and knew an abominable snowman when he saw one. But what was it doing in Tooting Bec? And why was it hiding in his toilet?

Questions that would never be answered if he didn't scarper. But Jonathan James found he simply couldn't move. All he could do was look up, feeling an odd calm wash over him as the Yeti lurched towards him, a clawed-hand reaching down.

A loud bang and the creature staggered backwards. For a moment John could do nothing but blink, his ears ringing from the unexpected sound. Someone else was in his garden. He slowly turned his head.

Standing a short distance behind him was a tall soldier, a gun in one hand, still aimed towards the Yeti. The soldier looked down at him. He looked a little like Captain Borel, with his clipped moustache and revolver, but his hat was different. Not like the beret found on Captain Borel's head – more like a paper boat in shape, royal blue with a tartan band around it, a silver thistle at the front.

'Come on, son, let's get you out of here,' the soldier said. He didn't sound Scottish. John thought only Scottish people wore tartan – like those skirts highlanders wore.

John shook his head. There was only one question that really mattered right now, and it wasn't anything to do with Scotland. 'Where's my mum?' he asked, taking the soldier's hand as he offered it.

Pulling John up, the solider looked around briefly. 'Climbing into the truck out there, I suspect, like you need to be.'

John looked back at the Yeti, which was slowly climbing to its feet. 'What's going on?' he asked as the soldier stepped forward. Despite everything, John found himself smiling. He felt like Doctor Omega being rescued by Captain Borel. 'Who are you?'

'Colonel Alistair Lethbridge-Stewart,' the soldier said and aimed the gun again. 'Now cover your ears.'

John did as he was told. This was adventure!

The soldier fired.

CHAPTER ONE
The New World

DEAD LONDON. IT WAS A SIGHT COLONEL ALISTAIR Lethbridge-Stewart would never get used to.

He had been travelling from his little flat in Pimlico to the London Regiment offices in Battersea from where he was co-ordinating the re-population of London. It was a mammoth task, and one of the least enjoyable roles of being a colonel; he preferred to be out in the field, but after the last few weeks he had seen enough good soldiers die in London that for once he looked forward to returning to the office.

Nowhere was the evacuation more obvious than Carnaby Street. The centre of fashion for London, the street was usually full of young people; boys in their bell-bottoms and double-breasted jackets, and girls in mini-skirts and white go-go boots. Lethbridge-Stewart was far too conservative to fall into the latest trends, but he did admire the vibrancy of young people. And now, as he stood next to his car on that deserted street, he felt the lack of that vibrancy keenly.

It was simply wrong. All around him the city was still, despite the slight breeze. Barely a sound, not even the distant rumble of a dustcart. London was a city made to be loud, to be full of noise, of people. The lack of it was eerie.

Young people were emerging as the dominant presence in the city, overshadowing the more serious and less 'fab' gentry that were once the face of London. Lethbridge-Stewart felt a little depressed by the sight around him. The shops, usually open and full of life, were still closed. But now even the red and blue sign of *Carnaby Girl* seemed lifeless above the darkened windows, the colourful outfits in the windows of *Irvine Sellars* next door seeming almost drab and unwanted. Above the street Union flags blew gently in the breeze, as if even they couldn't work up the enthusiasm anymore, and on the corner of the street where usually an ice cream cart stood, was nothing.

Things were going to change, though. Friday 14th March would forever be remembered as the day that public life returned to London. Already the first trains were en route from the outer cities and towns, from the country, from wherever people could go after the unexpected and very abrupt evacuation last month. The London transport system was, after days and days of false starts, once again underway; getting the buses back on the streets, and the Underground moving, was not as simple as flicking a switch. Businesses, the lifeblood of London, were slowly getting ready for the upcoming deluge; workers and business owners had been among the first to return to London, ahead of the millions of others that were only now starting to be herded back home. Of course, most still did not know why they had been evacuated, although a D-notice had since been issued it seemed the reason behind the evacuation was to remain a secret, muddied by politics and rumour. Just like the Great Smog of '52 all over again, only worse this time. So many more lives lost. Only a select few knew the real reason: top civil servants, a few government officials and high-ranking military officers. And Lethbridge-Stewart. He knew because he had been on the front line, one of the last men standing in Central London.

He still found it hard to entirely accept what he'd

witnessed. But he was a practical man, of course, and a pragmatic one at that. He had been there right to the end in Piccadilly Circus Station, had seen with his own eyes his men butchered by the indefatigable onslaught of Yeti, the foot-soldiers of an alien intelligence. There was no getting around it. Just as, now the Intelligence had been defeated, there was no getting round the unenviable task of restoring London to its usual glory.

First there were all the dead bodies to account for; hospital mortuaries all through the city filling up with hundreds of dead soldiers, and then they had to surreptitiously remove all evidence of the alien presence – the Yeti, the control spheres, the pyramid device that had exploded and killed the last receptacle of the Great Intelligence. So much work, more than anybody would ever know about, all to ensure that normality returned. Where all the Yeti and control spheres went was anybody's guess; once they left London they seemed to disappear, no doubt taken to some top-secret vault, the location of which a normal army officer like Lethbridge-Stewart would never learn. This suited him just fine. He was quite happy to forget all that had happened, but he knew that he never would. Pragmatic to the last. He had seen too much, and as the commander in charge of restoring London he was being kept in a position of easy surveillance. His superiors were watching him closely, determining what they needed to do next.

It seemed nobody had anticipated this attack. Not even Professor Travers, who had encountered the Great Intelligence and its Yeti way back in 1935. But nobody was talking about that; both Travers and he had been debriefed on that score, and Miss Anne Travers, the professor's daughter, had been sent off wherever the Yeti had been taken. A brilliant scientist, it seemed the Powers That Be still needed to pick her brain. As far as his superiors were concerned the two events formed one sustained attack, which had now been dealt with. Lethbridge-Stewart wasn't convinced.

He had it on good authority that the Intelligence was still *out there*, whatever that meant. But such a warning was too ambiguous for the brass, and it was decided that they would cross that bridge should they ever come to it. For his part, Lethbridge-Stewart wasn't convinced that dealing with such potential attacks on an ad-hoc basis was a practical or wise strategy, if he could even call it such.

It was out of his hands, of course. He was merely a colonel in the Scots Guards, and he had his orders. Get London back up and running. Though if it was up to him he'd have made damn sure London would never end up like this again.

To that end, it was time to be on his way. He climbed back into his car and turned on the radio. The sound that greeted him made him smile. Not to be defeated, Radio Caroline was back on the air, and with it the music that helped make London the city it was, even if there was hardly anybody around to listen. Small Faces were a far cry from the music he enjoyed – he'd have preferred to listen to Scaffold's *Lily the Pink* – but, as his car continued on its way to Battersea, he found himself developing a fondness for *Tin Soldier*. It gave him hope. It was his job to make London vibrant once again, and he was going to do just that.

'Now that's a sight I never thought I'd see,' said Lance Corporal Sally Wright, as soon as Lethbridge-Stewart entered his office. She was standing behind his desk, looking out the window at the street below.

'What is?' he asked, not bothering to question her unauthorised presence in his office. He really should have a word with his assistant and remind her that no one but he was allowed access to this office without his express permission. There were top secret documents contained in the filing cabinets, not to mention the reports still open on his desk from a late-night session. Not that Corporal Wright would ever look at such reports without permission, but that was hardly the point.

'Buses on the streets of London.' She glanced back at him as he put his briefcase on his desk. 'We may yet get to have our party,' she said, offering him the kind of smile she knew he could not resist.

But resist he did. Lethbridge-Stewart turned away and walked back to the open door, poking his head into the ante-office where Lance Corporal Bell sat at her own desk. 'Lay on some tea for me,' he said, and glanced breifly back at Wright. 'Make that two cups.'

Bell smiled pleasantly. 'Yes, sir,' she said.

Lethbridge-Stewart narrowed his eyes and let out a *hmm*. Discipline was a bit too lax. He supposed he could put that down to two things: an exhaustive week and the early hour of this particular Friday. Not to mention how much work was bound to come their way over the next couple of days. They anticipated at least half a million flooding into the city over the weekend, and with them at least twice that amount of problems and complaints.

'Are the telephone staff in yet?' he asked, just as Bell picked up her own phone.

'Yes, sir. They started to arrive an hour ago. The switchboards are being set up all over London as we speak.'

'Good. We don't want two million phone calls coming to this office, especially not if one of them is the BBC.'

'Still complaining about not being able to film on the Underground, sir?'

'One of many complaints, Corporal. Evacuating London wasn't good for television programming, apparently.' That all said, Lethbridge-Stewart returned to his office and closed the door.

'What brings you here, Corporal?' he asked, once he had shooed her from behind his desk.

'Orders from General Hamilton.' She reached into her jacket and pulled out the orders. Lethbridge-Stewart took them, but he needn't have bothered opening them, since Corporal Wright proceeded to tell him what they said. 'He's reviewed your request, and has granted you full authority to initiate martial law until you see fit to rescind it.'

Lethbridge-Stewart raised an eyebrow and sat down. 'Anything Hamilton doesn't tell you?'

Wright smiled, her eyes twinkling. 'Everything, I imagine. And he didn't tell me; I sneaked a peek.'

Upon checking the orders Lethbridge-Stewart noticed that they had already been unsealed. He glanced at the open reports on his desk. 'Anything else you have "sneaked a peek" at?'

'Don't be such a prig, Alistair. You know you'd tell me anyway.'

That was debatable. 'Corporal Wright, I expect better from General Hamilton's adjutant, and when you're in this building I would remind you that you are on duty and, as such, I am your superior officer. And,' he added, lowering his voice, 'the walls of this building are awfully thin.'

She looked around, and nodded. 'Sorry,' she said, her voice also low. She cleared her throat and was about to speak again when there came a knock at the door. Bell entered, bringing their tea. Once she had returned to the ante-office, Wright reached out for her mug. 'So, martial law? Is that not a bit extreme? Sir,' she added, with a cheeky smile.

Lethbridge-Stewart rolled his eyes. What was he to do with her? Marry her probably. 'I would normally have thought so, but we've had workers striking already. Too much work, not enough pay, and right now we don't have time to negotiate with trade unions. Over eight million people need to be returned to this city in the shortest time possible; the longer it takes, the more it will cost everybody, including the tax payers who are now striking. Once the city is up and running again, then they can do as they like. It will no longer be my problem. I am not a politician, and neither do I intend to play the part of one now.'

'Thus martial law.'

Lethbridge-Stewart nodded. 'Easiest way. Work to your strengths, that's what my Uncle Archie always told me.'

'There could be riots at this rate.'

'Not if I have any say. This is not Paris, Corporal, and right now we have control of the streets, and we will continue to until it's no longer our problem.'

The conversation was over and for a few moments they sat in companionable silence. Then the intercom buzzed.

'Sir, Major Douglas is on line one.'

'Thank you.' Lethbridge-Stewart picked up the phone, but before he could press the line-one button, Corporal Wright spoke.

'Dougie? Why is he calling you?'

'Because I need a man out there I can trust, someone with enough clout to see that martial law is maintained with a firm and fair hand.'

Wright looked confused for a moment, then she grinned. 'You knew Hamilton was going to approve your request.'

'Well, of course.'

She narrowed her eyes. 'And you knew he'd send me.'

Lethbridge-Stewart pressed the button on his phone, enjoying the look of surprise on Wright's face. Of course he knew; indeed, he had asked if Hamilton would send the orders via Corporal Wright. If she was going to be his fiancée, then he had to find any way he could to spend time with her. Major General Hamilton knew this, and happily agreed.

'Major Douglas,' he said, once the call connected. 'Yes, yes, Sally is here. Yes, you would think I planned this. Orders for you, and a question. Would you care to be my best man?'

It had been over thirty years and once again he found himself returning to the area in which the 'accident' had occurred. He wasn't sure why; he liked to fool himself that Jack, his beagle, simply enjoyed the expansive area of Draynes Wood, but sometimes Ray Phillips wondered if there was some other reason he made the half hour walk from Bledoe every weekend. Wondered if there was something calling him back, never letting him get far enough away to forget.

He knew the risk of allowing Jack the freedom afforded him by Draynes Wood, but in all the time he'd brought the dog there, not once had they been near the area where Golitha Falls met the River Fowey.

There was a chill in the air. He wanted to say it was the weather, but he knew it was something more. He stopped at the edge of the woods, looking down at the gorge itself, the cascading water dropping to join the rest of the Fowey. The waters raged, and he remembered. The spring of 1938 and the day that changed his life. He shivered.

He looked around for Jack, and not finding him, for a moment worried that the small dog had jumped into the river. The current was especially strong at Golitha Falls, and Jack was old. He'd get swept away before Ray could even move. Fortunately, though, he spotted Jack a little way into the oak woodland, foraging through the bluebells that carpeted the ground either side of the gorge.

As he watched the dog snuffling away, a flash of light caught his eye. Ray placed his glasses on the edge of his nose and peered closer. He stepped back, overtaken by a sudden dread. In the far distance, just visible through the oak trees, was the old Remington Manor house. It had been deserted for thirty years, but now there was a light, a glimmer through one of the upper windows.

Ray shuddered. He was too old for this kind of nonsense, he knew, but deep down something in his gut turned.

He couldn't remain there any longer. He called Jack to him and walked back into the woods, in the direction of home. He'd get in his car, put on an 8-track, and take his dog as far from Golitha Falls as possible. There was loads of open land in Cornwall where Jack could roam free. He didn't need to walk through this woodland. He didn't need to be anywhere near the Manor. No, he would walk away from it all. He had dealt with his ghosts a long time ago.

But something made him stop. The same something that made him return there every weekend. He looked back up at the Manor.

The three boys who stalked Remington Manor were taking a risk.

Not that they would call themselves boys; they were young men, fast approaching eighteen years and, for Lewis at least, freedom from the suffocation that was Bledoe. Owain, twin of Lewis but often the polar opposite, blamed the third person in their little group, the intruder that was Charles Watts. He had returned to Bledoe (not that Owain remembered him ever being there before, but it seemed he used to often visit there when he was a kid) a few weeks previously, after being evacuated from London. He, along with the rest of his family, was staying with his nana. You couldn't have found a man less suited to country life than Charles; a city man if ever there was one. Like Lewis, Charles considered himself one of those 'lemons', as Owain had heard them called; a group of young men who found their solidarity in like-minded, working class men, with their tight jeans and Ben Sherman shirts and braces, their hair cut unfashionably short. Not that Owain much cared for fashion, but allowing your hair to grow was in some ways quite freeing. Something women had known since the dawn of time.

Lewis had taken to this new image quickly, to the point of permanently borrowing a pair of their father's braces and getting the local barber, Mr Bryant, to cut his previously long hair so it matched Charles'. He'd even removed his precious moustache; much to Owain's delight, since bum-fluff never looked good on anyone. Their parents had not been happy, of course, although their father had also found it oddly amusing, no different than when the twins had a cheeky pint in *The Rose & Crown*. Their mother was less amused and had attempted to ground Lewis, but with Charles in town that simply was not going to happen. They were seventeen and no woman was going to tell Lewis what to do.

That was the biggest change in Lewis. They had been brought up to mind their mother; her word was final. But in the past week Lewis had started questioning everything; almost every word she said. In his mind their mother was out of touch with the real world beyond Bledoe, and he had begun to talk more and more about London, about joining in the movement against the government there. 'We'll make it like Paris,' he said, although what he meant by that was beyond Owain.

Bledoe was their home, and as far as Owain was concerned what went on beyond was of little interest to him, unless it was football, of course. French,

Londoners... what did any of them matter?

It had been Lewis' idea to explore the house, driven as he was by boredom, and Owain resented that he had to come along. He wasn't sure he trusted Charles to be alone with his brother, besides it was almost expected for Lewis and Owain to do everything together simply because they were twins. Like that secured some mystic connection. Certainly Charles seemed to think so.

'I would love to have been a twin,' he had told them the first day they met. Since then he hadn't stopped going on about it. 'If I hit Lewis, would you feel it?' As if Owain and Lewis was the same person!

Owain looked around. Both his brother and Charles had gone on ahead; they were already some way down the long landing, while he was only just mounting the final step of the large, dusty staircase. He paused, bored, and pulled out his pocket transistor radio. He was missing the league cup final for this. He looked up briefly, to make sure neither Lewis nor Charles were paying him any attention, and twisted the small dial that turned the radio on. He kept the volume low and tuned into the match. It was bound to be an uneven game, what with most of the Arsenal players still recovering from a bout of flu, and, not surprisingly, as the radio tuned in, Owain learned that the Gunners were being trampled all over by Swindon Town.

Owain must have got caught up in the game, because the next moment Charles was before him, snatching the tranny off him. 'What are you playing at?'

Owain sighed, bored again. He looked over at Lewis, who stood watching, his arms folded, carrying about him a look of disappointment.

'Can we go now?' Owain asked. 'There's no one here besides us.'

'That's the whole point, innit?' Charles said. 'The Whisperer isn't here, you can just hear him. Creepy, huh?' He grinned and pocketed the transistor radio. 'I'll keep that, see if we can pick up some reggae on it later.'

Owain was about to complain. He didn't listen to music on his radio; that's not why he had it. It was for listening to football matches when his mum wouldn't tune the TV in to the BBC, preferring to watch situation comedies like *Her Majesty's Pleasure* and, even worse, super-spy programmes like *The Saint*. Complaining would do no good; Charles wasn't the type to listen. Not unless Lewis had something to say.

'Do you both share the same bird when you have one?' Charles asked, breaking the silence.

Owain gritted his teeth.

Lewis laughed at this. 'Not at the same time.'

'Anyway, we're not exactly identical,' Owain mumbled behind them. Which was true, but they were obviously twins. Even a blind man could see that.

'That must be so much fun, man, imagine if—' Charles stopped abruptly. 'Did you hear that?' he asked, looking back the way they had come.

The three young men peered around. The long corridor was, of course, empty, the wallpaper bleached by the sun that came in from the tall windows that were bereft of any netting. Cobwebs lined the coving along the top of the walls, dust covering the table and candlestick holders a few feet away.

Lewis glanced back, smiling. 'The Whisperer?' he asked.

'Of course not, moron,' Owain responded, giving his brother a dirty look. Of course it wasn't the Whisperer, no such thing existed. Just stories told by parents to keep the kids away from a house that was slowly falling apart. Not that it worked, obviously. They had both heard plenty of stories about it over the years, about the household driven mad by the whispering of the walls, and how one day a visitor came by to find the house empty, devoid of all life, everything in place as if the household had simply gone for a walk and forgot to come back.

That was back in '39, and since then nobody had claimed the Manor. It remained as it had been left, albeit with the gates and doors padlocked shut. Padlocks that had been broken many times by brave and bored teens – much like his brother and Charles.

'Then what?' Charles was now having fun. 'Should we go and look?'

Owain knew he couldn't say no; if he did he'd never hear the end of it. 'Come on then,' he said and stepped forward, the forced smile leaving his face as soon as his back was to Charles and Lewis.

They walked behind him, Lewis once again taking to humming another of his favourite tunes.

Charles started mumbling the words of the song, encouraging Lewis to hum louder. *'Shirt them a-tear up, trousers are gone.'*

'Don't want to end up like Bonnie and Clyde,' Lewis joined in. *'Poooooor me, the Israelite!'*

Owain was all set to complain when he heard it again.

Was it a voice? He shook his head. No, that was stupid.

Lewis stopped, his body tense. 'Creepy. I definitely heard that.'

'Yeah, man, me too.' Charles looked up and down the landing. 'Creepy,' he added with a large grin.

Owain preferred it when Lewis didn't agree with him. Then it was just him being stupid, but if Lewis and Charles agreed then… there was something in the walls.

'Maybe we should just leave?' Owain suggested.

That was probably, looking back, not the wisest thing to say, as was immediately obvious by the cold look that swept across Charles' face.

'What are you, a Nancy-boy? There's nothing else to do, what with us not being allowed back to London. And we don't have ten-bob between us, so no chance of doing anything else.'

Lewis laughed softly. 'Come on, O', you're the cynic, remember? You don't believe in ghosts or any of that rubbish.'

'And you do now? Not exactly fitting for a bovver boy.'

'I knew it! You read about London, too.' Lewis nudged Charles. 'See, told you it wasn't just me. Anyway,' he continued with a smug grin that matched Charles. 'We're not bovver boys. We're not looking for aggro, just letting people know we're not going to be one of the destitute struggling to make a living when the government is...'

Owain held his hand up. 'Yeah yeah, we're all working class heroes.' He shook his head and looked around the corridor again. 'Reckon we're all going a bit mad anyway. No voices here, except ours.'

It has been years. How many it does not know. Trapped in the walls, hardly able to do anything but whisper, a bodiless voice, intangible. But now it can feel it, the soul it's been waiting for. Young, but strong. Strong enough to give it strength. This time, though, it will be different. It will plan, prepare, and do things properly. It will not be beaten again.

Lewis waited a moment, straining his ears. 'Yeah, bit boring after all.' He threw his arm over Charles' shoulders. 'Come on, let's see if Old Man Barns will serve us. Could do with a pint.'

'Now you're talking,' Charles agreed, and they both set off ahead of him.

Owain knew it would never happen. Henry Barns would sooner tell their parents, but Owain would rather try their luck than continue in the Manor any longer. Besides, he was looking forward to seeing his brother taken down a peg in front of Charles. Serve them both right. And once that amused him no more, he could go and see how Old Man Barns' son, JB, was doing.

Owain glanced down the landing, at the door at the far end. He should never have come here in the first place. Lewis could look after himself, after all he was a skinhead now (apparently), and they both hated the cliché of twins who did everything together. As sad as he'd be to see Lewis leave, at least once he was gone they could both rid themselves of that cliché once and for all.

As they reached the top of the grand staircase, he looked back one last time. He wouldn't tell Lewis or Charles, of course, but he *had* heard something. Still could, in fact, a voice whispering to him.

Telling him to return, telling him that he had to come back so they could be family once more.

It was a week later and Lethbridge-Stewart was back at Army Strategic Command near Fugglestone, meeting with Major General Hamilton. Ostensibly Hamilton wished to personally congratulate Lethbridge-Stewart on a successful command, but Lethbridge-Stewart had bigger things on his mind than congratulations.

'General, I think it would be foolish of us to consider recent events an isolated incident,' he said.

Hamilton consulted the papers on his desk. 'Yes, I am aware of Professor Travers' encounter with this Great Intelligence in Tibet, but as that essentially formed part of the London Event we're chalking it up to one attack.'

The London Event; even the name spoke to the assumption that the matter was self-contained, over and done with, case closed.

'One attack separated by over thirty years?'

'Quite so, Colonel.'

Lethbridge-Stewart allowed a silence to sit between him and Hamilton, before he played his trump card.

'What about the next time, sir?'

'Next time? Good lord, Stewart, do you not think you're being a little bit of an alarmist? As I understand it this Great Intelligence was defeated.'

'Yes, sir, but that is not to say it won't try again.'

Hamilton looked down at his papers. 'I see no such indication, Colonel.'

Lethbridge-Stewart conceded the point. 'No indication on paper, no, sir. But I was told by the Doctor that—'

'Yes, I read the report. I understand the extreme nature of your experiences in London. A lot of good soldiers lost their lives defending London, and naturally that would leave you wondering what more could be out there. But hearsay? Colonel—'

'It was not hearsay. Professor Travers can vouch for—'

'Colonel, *if* there was any proof then I'd be the first one to take this to High Command. As it stands what we have is one isolated incident, an attempted incursion by robotic Yeti and their alien master. Which has been taken care of.'

Lethbridge-Stewart wasn't to be beaten. 'Then there is no harm in going to the United Nations and…'

'Out of the question.'

Lethbridge-Stewart had not expected such a quick response. Nonetheless he had gone too far to step back now.

'Sir, I am aware that the United Nations began creating protocols last year to…'

Hamilton held up a hand to silence him, and rose from his chair and walked the length of his office to the nearest filing cabinet, on which sat a decanter and two glasses. He poured himself a small whisky.

'We are still suffering from the White Paper of '57, cut-backs continue, regiments are being amalgamated into new regiments. The way things are progressing many of the junior battalions will be disbanded in a few years.' He offered another glass to Lethbridge-Stewart, who accepted it carefully. 'NATO continues to sap our resources, and the United Nations are not going to offer us any help.'

It was as Lethbridge-Stewart expected, but he had another idea. 'Then perhaps an intelligence taskforce, as it were, something a little more… homespun? More domestic and less international.'

Hamilton shook his head, a grim smile on his face. 'What you are suggesting… It will require a great deal of manpower and money. Neither of which the British Armed Forces has a great supply of right now.'

'With respect, sir, I am not seeing much of an option. The whole of London was evacuated simply because of one alien intelligence, what is to say that…'

'Enough, Colonel, you have said enough.' Hamilton gathered the reports together. 'I'm afraid you will have to leave this with me. *All* of it.'

'Sir, we cannot…'

'Leave it with me, Colonel. You have made a good case, and it is something High Command has talked about on several occasions in the last decade. Something does indeed need to be done. I will look into this and get back to you.'

Despite himself Lethbridge-Stewart knew he had no choice. He had pushed his point far enough and could do no more.

'Your actions in London have impressed many,' Hamilton said. 'You have been noticed, Colonel, and that will count for something. I cannot promise anything, but I will do what I can. In the meantime, you should return to London and continue the incredible job you have been doing. Martial law was a very good call.'

Lethbridge-Stewart knew he would get no further that day. And he did still have much to occupy him in

London.

Only two million had been returned to the city so far, and already some less than savoury elements had made themselves known. Looters, opportunists…

Oh yes, he had plenty of work to do there yet.

CHAPTER TWO
Guided by Voices

AT FIRST SHE THOUGHT IT WAS THE SOUND OF THE wireless cutting into her dreams, but as her senses levelled out and she escaped the grogginess left over from sleep, Mary Gore realised that it couldn't be. She never left the wireless turned on when she went to bed.

She sat there for a moment, straining her old ears to pick up the voice again. It was no use, the voice was gone. Her memory wasn't what it used to be, but now as she sat up in her bed, her legs growing cold due to the cooling of the hot-water bottle, she recalled that she had heard it before.

A child's voice. But what it said she had no idea.

For the rest of the morning she found her mind constantly returning to the voice, trying to recall what it had been saying. Her regular trip to the local shop was interrupted by a moment where she almost had a name to put to it, but the inspiration didn't last. Mabel, her nearest neighbour in the village of Coleshill in Buckinghamshire, had given her an odd look, worried about her friend.

It was no mystery that Mary had been ill the last few months, old age and loneliness catching up with her. She soldiered through it, telling everybody that her son was due a visit soon, and that was bound to lift her spirits, but none of the ladies were to be fooled. They all knew that Mary hadn't seen her son in quite some time.

Still mithering, Mabel escorted her home, telling her own stories of her grandchildren, who she had seen over the weekend. Mary was feeling better by the time they arrived, and as she prepared the tea she found herself mooning over her own lack of grandchildren.

'It would have been so different if he had not gone into the military, you know,' she said, returning to the living room with a tray of biscuits and the teapot.

'It's not too late. He's still young.'

Mary nodded and fingered the crucifix around her neck. 'But he's never married, never even courted a woman since he was called up for National Service. Been far too busy.'

Mabel nodded. She'd heard the stories of Mary's son so many times. 'Your Gordon would be proud of him, God rest his soul.'

Mary sniffed back a tear. Talk of her late husband always made her want to weep. Over twenty years and still she missed him. She had never re-married, never even thought of it. Of course there had been the odd gentleman over the years who attempted to court her eye, but she had never done more than go on an occasional date. Ralph Cooper up near the commons would surely love to make an honest woman of her, and he was a decent man, a deeply religious man who had spent his whole life waiting for his perfect woman. He went to great lengths during their regular visits to *The Harte & Magpies* to explain how she was that woman. Perhaps she was; it made her heart happy to believe so, at the very least. But she had to think of her son.

How would he feel should another man take his mother's hand? It was something she wanted to ask, but unfortunately neither of them had ever been particularly comfortable talking about their feelings.

She and Mabel continued to talk over tea, covering a variety of subjects, from the latest developments in *The*

Archers to sharing reminiscences about their late husbands. They had similar stories, both being widows of military men, but the conversation soon returned to grandchildren and the lack thereof in Mary's life. Mabel suggested that Mary join them the next time her family took a break in Devon. Mary couldn't express how much such an offer meant to her, and Mabel cheekily added that they could also invite Mr Cooper. That had the two old women laughing.

It was a much happier Mary who said goodbye to Mabel later that morning, one determined to put all maudlin thoughts out of her mind. She would finish the scarf she had been knitting and then pay a visit to Mr Cooper, ask him over for dinner later in the week. It was not in her nature to be so forward, her parents had not raised her that way, but it seemed to be happening more and more with younger women these days. She wasn't sure she approved; men and women had their own places in society and she didn't think such things ought to be messed with. But the idea of asking Mr Cooper to dinner did give her a certain thrill that she found pleasant.

She did up her cardigan and checked her curls in the mirror before leaving the house. It wouldn't do to look anything but her best when she saw Mr Cooper. She reached for her coat, not caring for the sound of the wind brewing up outside, when it came again. The voice.

Find me.

For the first time the words were clear. A child calling for help. But whose child? And why was she hearing it?

She had never been a superstitious woman, never one to believe in ghost stories, but this voice… It came from nowhere. There was no one else in the house with her; just her and her memories.

'How?' she whispered, certain she should feel foolish for speaking to an empty house, but she needed to know. It seemed like the voice had been haunting her for a long time, and with it came a memory of…

She shook her head. She hadn't thought about that in a very long time. It had been a dark time for her, shortly after the death of her Gordon, and the reason she and her son had come to live in Coleshill. Why was she reminded of it now? What did it have to do with the voice?

A knock at the front door made her jump. She laughed at herself. 'Silly old biddy,' she said, as she walked to the door. Through the glass she could make out the shape of a man with a flat cap on his head. It had to be Mr Cooper; he always wore a flat cap. What a wonderful coincidence.

She opened the door with a smile, but the smile froze on her face the moment she saw the man standing there. She didn't recognise him; it wasn't Mr Cooper, that much was certain. This man was a lot younger for one thing, probably in his mid-thirties, wearing his hair down to his shoulders, the fringe peering out from the cap, almost meeting his eyebrows, and a moustache that looked like a sad smile.

'Can I help you?' she asked.

His answer came in a dull monotone, his expression not altering in the slightest. 'Gordon is waiting for you.'

He travelled across London, confused. He couldn't remember anything but a need to be… somewhere. He didn't even know where, but he knew he was heading in the right direction. London seemed oddly deserted, only a few people here and there, the streets and roads mostly devoid of traffic. He felt certain that this was wrong somehow, but he did not know how, or why he felt such certainty over it. He could remember nothing else, but there was a sense of wrongness about the empty streets. A sense of… danger.

Along the way he had periodically stopped, stepping inside red phone boxes to make calls. He had spoken to people he knew, used words and names that were at once familiar and yet totally unknown to him. It was as if he were speaking with a different man's voice, using knowledge that he simply could not retain. He had made arrangements to have the 'cargo' moved, although now he could no longer recall what the cargo was, or to where he had ordered it moved.

He eventually reached what he thought was his destination, but as soon as he read the words *Paddington Railway Station* above the entrance of the building, he just knew he was not there yet. He had a long way to go, and for that he needed a train.

He entered the building, keeping his head low so as not to be stared at by the multitude of people who crowded the station. Once again he got a feeling of wrongness, as if the train station was over-packed. So many people stepping off the trains and shuffling their way outside to waiting taxies and buses. Voices called out over the tannoy, directing people here and there. Barely seconds passed before another voice took over from the previous one.

He looked around.

Many people were dressed like him, in green uniforms, directing people to the various exits, keeping order. They were assisted by men in dark blue uniforms with tall hats. He knew them. There were words that went with the uniforms. Army and police. He felt sure he should know why this was happening, like he had something to do with it.

Perhaps he should ask? Or perhaps not. It was at that moment that he caught sight of his reflection once again.

Still his skin was black and scarred, although it was looking better than it had when he had first left the mortuary. He was doubly lucky; one, that he was healing quickly, and two, that the train station was so busy that no one had time to notice such a damaged man among them.

He looked up at the travel board. There was one name he was looking for, his next destination. Liskeard. He found it, and without further hesitation set off towards the designated platform. The call was getting weaker, and he had to get there before it was too late.

As he sat in his office surrounded by a sea of reports, Lethbridge-Stewart could feel a headache coming on. He was used to co-ordinating things – it was simply another part of his job as colonel – but the task he was currently involved in was proving to be more and more daunting with each day. So far they had been hard at it for two weeks, and now with a week behind them they had managed to see only two million people return to London. Two million of the over eight million that usually lived and worked there.

As much as he knew it was a horrible thing to admit, considering how many had died, he'd rather enjoyed the weeks in which London was held in the thrall of the Great Intelligence. He preferred to be out in the field, commanding men, going into battle, making split-second decisions that could change the tide. It was why he'd remained in the military after National Service.

He selected a report at random, and gave it a perfunctory browse. Those who felt like looting or striking had been taken care of, having no choice but to surrender to the martial law that had been in effect for the past week. There had been the odd spot of bother, of course, occurrences as far out as Kenton. Teething problems, Hamilton had called it, and Lethbridge-Stewart agreed. Returning the report to its pile he smiled grimly, regarding his surroundings. There wasn't a surface in the room on which reports and train timetables weren't stacked. He doubted returning the evacuees after World War II was half as bad – at least back then the entire city had not been evacuated.

Still, soon none of this would be his concern.

Tomorrow he began his week-long holiday to celebrate his engagement, after finally convincing Hamilton to let him go. Procedures were now in place that would ensure that re-populating London would run more or less like clockwork, and his replacement could manage for a week without him. It was a break he was looking forward to; Sally and he rarely got to spend much time together since they'd started courting, the last month especially. It wasn't exactly beach weather, but a week in Brighton was the best they could arrange at such short notice, and in his experience Brighton was not void of romance. All he needed now was to be relieved of his current duty so he could return home and begin packing. And, unless he was mistaken, Sally was already planning a quick engagement party in *The Unknown Soldier*, a pub not far from the London Regiment offices.

A brief rap on the closed door, and Corporal Wright poked her head through the gap. She was still in uniform herself, now acting as his assistant while Bell brought his replacement up to date.

'Yes, Corporal?'

'Major Douglas is here, sir.' She glanced back into the ante-office, and her voice took on a less officious tone. 'Two hours early.'

Lethbridge-Stewart smiled at this. That sounded just like Dougie. He was what the Americans called a 'quick study'. Lethbridge-Stewart shouldn't have been surprised that the major had finished his briefing so quickly. No doubt Dougie was certain he was all prepared for the laborious task ahead, a necessary step in his own soon-to-be-finalised promotion to lieutenant colonel. Well, Dougie would soon discover that staff work was less exciting, and more time consuming, than field work.

'Send him in.'

Douglas entered, his face beaming.

'Congratulations, Major Douglas,' Lethbridge-Stewart said, walking around the desk and offering Douglas his hand. 'Lieutenant colonel, eh? Are you sure the bath star won't be too heavy for you?'

'I'm sure I can bear the load, sir.'

'That's the spirit.' Official words done with, Lethbridge-Stewart dropped his formal posture and relaxed.

For a moment Major Douglas regarded him closely. 'I was sorry to hear about Old Spence. A good officer.'

Douglas didn't know Colonel Spencer Pemberton as well as Lethbridge-Stewart, but knew him well enough to feel the loss.

'Yes, a good man, too,' Lethbridge-Stewart agreed. 'But enough time to mourn all those lost in recent weeks once London is up and running.' He looked back at the desk and the reports upon it. 'Sure you're ready for this, Dougie?'

'Made for it,' Douglas said. 'Couple more years and I'll be after your job.'

At this Lethbridge-Stewart laughed. 'My dear man, you're more than welcome to it. In fact you can start right now.'

Douglas looked down at all the reports. 'Paperwork; my favourite.' His smile dropped. 'Anything I need to know that wasn't in the official briefing?'

'Need to know?' Lethbridge-Stewart shook his head. 'Unfortunately nothing I am permitted to tell you. Besides, I can't imagine how knowing will help you in the task ahead. You will have enough to occupy your mind with over the next week. Six million other things.'

Douglas whistled. 'Bit more than a couple of hundred soldiers to command.'

Lethbridge-Stewart raised an eyebrow. Douglas really had no idea, and probably never would. Unless General

Hamilton chose to reveal such information.

'Not to worry, once London is up and running again I'm sure you'll be assigned to your new regiment.'

'Lucky old me.' With that Douglas walked around the desk and sat in what was no longer Lethbridge-Stewart's chair. 'Enjoy your holiday, Alistair,' he said, the old mischievous glint appearing in his eyes. 'Want me to let Doris know you're on the way?'

There really was no answer to that, and so Lethbridge-Stewart chose to ignore it. Any other man and he would have issued a quick reprimand, but Douglas had earned a pass by virtue of a long friendship. Still, he did have a point, even if it was unspoken. Brighton was possibly not the best choice for a romantic getaway this time, after all that was the usual romantic rendezvous spot for him and Doris. Of course, that had been before he and Sally had started courting.

The door opened once more, this time without the prerequisite introductory knock.

'Yes, Corporal?' Douglas asked before Lethbridge-Stewart could.

'Excuse me, sir,' Corporal Wright said, no longer smiling or joking. 'A message for Colonel Lethbridge-Stewart, from St Mark's. Staff Sergeant Arnold has gone missing.'

'Missing? What the devil?' Lethbridge-Stewart was certain Wright was mistaken.

'Great time for one of your men to go AWOL,' Douglas said.

Lethbridge-Stewart turned to look at him. 'He wasn't one of my men,' he said, a frown creasing his forehead. 'But that hardly seems to matter now. Staff Sergeant Arnold died weeks ago.'

For a moment Douglas was stuck for words, his eyes moving from Lethbridge-Stewart to Wright and back again. He glanced down at the reports, the reality of his new position beginning to sink in. 'Are you sure there isn't more to know about this London Event, Colonel?'

'Probably,' Lethbridge-Stewart said. 'But if you wish to know more, I suggest you contact Major General Hamilton. But before that, can you get your assistant to lay on a jeep for me? Looks like I'm needed in Harrow.'

Mary had no idea why she had got in the car with the strange man, but get in she had. Soon they were leaving Coleshill and she sat in the back seat, not much caring for the cramped space of the Morris 1300, her handbag on her lap. She tried to engage the man in talk but he simply refused to acknowledge her.

He had said *Gordon*, that Gordon was waiting for her, but it couldn't be. She remembered receiving the letter informing her of his death in '45, she remembered the darkness that had followed and the… She shook her head. It had taken her a long time to come to terms with the loss, to accept that she would never feel his arms around her, never hear him complain about *Miss London Limited* again. She smiled. She may have accepted all that years ago, but she still missed everything about him.

It couldn't be her Gordon, then.

Only… No body had ever been returned to her. They said he was MIA – Missing In Action. Had they lied to her? Was her husband still alive after all this time?

Mary couldn't even begin to get her head around such an idea. It was impossible, the Royal Air Force would never put her through that.

And what of that child's voice. She refused to believe in ghosts, in anything mystical. She knew that young people today were all about meditation and all that new age mumbo jumbo, but she had no truck with it. Yet she couldn't deny the voice she had heard, the boy telling her to find him. And then there was the strange man driving her to God knows where. To this Gordon who was waiting for her.

It was nonsense.

'Do you have the time?' she asked the man. He didn't answer, of course. 'Must be about time for *Desert Island Discs* and I do so love that. Listen to it every week, and this week it's Lady Diana Cooper. Have you read her books? Her acting is better.' Nothing. She leaned forward and tapped the man gently on his shoulder. 'Can you please turn on BBC Radio 4?'

She didn't expect the man to respond, but he moved his hand to the radio and twisted the dial until it found the station.

'Thank you,' Mary said and sat back, feeling a little bit more relaxed by the soft sound of seagulls and an introduction she knew all too well.

'Each week a well-known person is asked the question, "if you were to be castaway alone on a desert island, which eight gramophone records would you choose to have with you?" As usual the castaway is introduced by Roy Plomley...'

She didn't know where she was going, or even why, but she at least had Mr Plomley's lovely voice to keep her company for the next three quarters of an hour. Something normal at last.

'Lady Cooper, how well would you endure loneliness?' Mr Plomley asked his guest, and Mary closed her eyes. It was a question she often asked herself, almost every day. And again she was reminded of Mr Cooper, wishing he were with her right now.

Mondays were always busy at the post office in Bledoe, which doubled as a little shop for those necessary supplies. George Vine usually didn't mind it – what was a little hard work? He had lived through a world war, served as a private for a spell, and was no stranger to hard work. Unlike his sons, it seemed. He wasn't keen on the way the world was changing for young people; too many opinions, ill-informed and outspoken with no real regard for the consequences. He had hoped living away from the main towns and cities would have kept his boys safe from such destructive influences, but it seemed he was now fighting a lost battle.

It had all started with Lewis and his mouthing off to his mother, something that would have once resulted in a slipper across the backside. But both George and Shirley had to concede that their boys were no longer... well, *boys*. They were becoming young men and at least one of them was ready to fly the coop. That Watts' boy wasn't helping matters, either, but George had no control over him; didn't seem like his own parents did, either. Not enough discipline in the big city for George's tastes. At least people were now slowly returning to London, which meant young Mr Watts would soon be gone, too; unfortunately he was taking Lewis with him. The boy had already told his parents that he was returning with his new best friend. Which, at least, left them Owain. Or so George had thought.

The last week the younger of the twins – younger by only five minutes, but legally that left them both with different birthdays – had been acting a bit strange. Owain had never been the most outspoken boy; even growing up he had been the quieter of the two, though always the most practical. Almost clinical in the way he thought and did things. But he had never been withdrawn, unhelpful. George knew his sons well, and he couldn't understand why Owain had taken to acting so oddly. Shirley had suggested that perhaps it was a bad reaction to Lewis' imminent departure, and she may have been right, but deep down George felt certain there was more to it.

Perhaps he'd found the files in the study...?

He called out to Owain again. Still no answer.

He poked his head through the doorway into the

kitchen and called out to his wife, who was busy sweeping the carpet in the living room.

She stepped into view, her hair in curlers under a shawl. She waved away the dust kicked up by the sweeping. 'Yes, my love?'

'Is he asleep again?'

Shirley glanced at the stair next to her. 'I haven't seen him all day. Are you sure he didn't go out with Lewis and Charles?'

George shook his head. Of course he was sure. 'Do you think I don't know where my boys are? Go and tell him to get his bone-idle backside down here. Greg Whittaker will be here soon.' His wife gave a long-suffering sigh but placed the sweeping brush against the wall and set to climbing the stair. George knew that between him and Greg they could easily unload the sacks of vegetables off his cart, but that was beside the point. If Owain wished to remain living under his roof then the boy needed to pull his weight.

Owain wasn't asleep, Shirley Vine knew. He was simply distracted, upset that his brother was soon leaving home. She could understand that – after all, her sons had done everything together since they were born. They had never been apart for more than a few days before.

She knocked on his door gently. There was no answer, as she had expected. Owain was unusually quiet, had been since at least a week Saturday back. She went to push the door open, even got as far as lifting the small black latch, when she stopped, listening to the voices inside. One was Owain's, the other she did not know, but it sounded like a small boy, probably around twelve years old if she was any judge of such things. Both were whispering so it was difficult to quite make out their words.

'I can't!' Owain said, his voice not especially loud, but

loud enough to make Shirley jump back in surprise by the sudden volume.

This time she didn't knock. 'Since when do you have people over without first asking —?' She stopped, barely inside his bedroom, and looked around.

Owain was lying across the width of his bed, his long legs dangling over the end, while his chin rested on his hands, looking out the window next to his bed. There was no one else in the room with him. Shirley was tempted to look under the bed, but there had been no time for anyone to hide from her.

For a moment Owain didn't move, but then he slowly craned his neck around, enough that his mother could see his raw, bloodshot eyes, purple shadows beneath them. He looked like he hadn't slept in months.

'Owain, who were you talking to?'

'What?'

Shirley looked around again. 'There was a boy in here, I heard you talking to him.'

Owain didn't move. 'It's just me here.'

'Yes, I can see that, but... I heard another voice. Unless I'm going mad.'

For a brief second there was a haunted look in Owain's eyes, but then it was gone. He swung himself around so he was sitting at the end of the bed.

'I was just reading.' He stood up abruptly and walked across the room towards her. 'I'm going out. Back later.' He carried on past her, and she stood there watching as he jumped down the staircase in two leaps, using the banisters for support.

Shirley wasn't stupid. And she wasn't going mad. She *had* heard another voice. She entered the room properly and looked around. It was tidy as usual, a copy of that new football magazine, *Shoot*, on the floor beside the bed. She supposed he *could* have been reading the magazine, except he had been facing the window, and the magazine was on the floor on the opposite side of the bed.

For the briefest of moments she felt a deep sense of panic rise in her. Perhaps it was Owain who was going mad? She shook her head. No, that was foolishness; he was simply upset that Lewis was leaving soon. Yes, she nodded, that had to be it.

Being at St Mark's Hospital showed Lethbridge-Stewart how much of an upheaval the evacuation had been, even to those on the outskirts of the main city. Even the ill and wounded needed to be moved to country hospitals, and now came the awkward task of transferring them all back to where they could get the best care. As a result, among so many other things affected by the evacuation, the NHS was now in a state of disarray. After the fallout from the invasion, St Mark's was one of many hospitals that had their mortuaries commandeered by the military. They were needed to house the many soldiers killed, until arrangements could be made for their bodies to be returned to families and proper burials (with honours in most cases) could be performed.

One such soldier was Staff Sergeant Albert Arnold. Lethbridge-Stewart hadn't known Arnold for very long, but in the short time they served together he had proven himself to be a dependable soldier, a no-nonsense senior NCO. Arnold had died at the hands of the Great Intelligence, not that it had actual hands, but not before he had been used by the Intelligence to kill several good men. It had taken over his mind, possessed his body, and lured them all into a trap in Piccadilly Circus Station. The Intelligence had been defeated by feedback from its own pyramid device, which it had intended to use to install itself in to the mind of the Doctor, and as a result Arnold died.

And now his body was missing.

Lethbridge-Stewart looked from the hospital

attendant, a man of Pakistani origin who could not be blamed, to Driver Gwynfor Evans, a Welsh soldier who could, and would be, blamed.

Lethbridge-Stewart had met Evans during the London Event. If Lethbridge-Stewart had his way, Evans would have been court-martialled for acts of cowardice. On several occasions he tried to flee the Underground rather than stand his ground; even McCrimmon was a better soldier, and he belonged in 1746. Evans could not be counted on. Who put him on guard at the mortuary?

'You popped out for a cigarette break?'

Any other soldier would have looked embarrassed, but not Driver Evans. He merely shrugged it off as if it was perfectly normal behaviour for a soldier to leave his post without permission.

'Well, I got bored, see? And the stiffs weren't going anywhere, were they?'

Lethbridge-Stewart raised an eyebrow. 'I see. Soldiers who died defending their country and you just left them?'

Again Evans almost shrugged. 'It's not my country, is it?'

'Quite beside the point, Evans.' Lethbridge-Stewart really didn't know what to do with the man.

With London filling up, the hospitals would once more serve the purposes for which they were built; people would be coming and going all over the place. Men who had given their lives to protect this city deserved to be left in peace, not disturbed simply because one Army driver could not contain his boredom. Lethbridge-Stewart had checked inside the morgue immediately upon his arrival, and was much relieved to find that only Arnold's body was missing. Spencer Pemberton's body still remained; resting peacefully.

'I will deal with you later, Driver Evans. In the meantime do *not* move from this position again, do I make myself clear?'

For the first time Evans looked chastised. He gave a half-hearted salute. 'Yes, sir.'

Lethbridge-Stewart nodded sharply and turned to the hospital attendant.

'What if I need the toilet, sir?'

Lethbridge-Stewart glared at Evans. 'Then hold it in, man!' He shook his head. Unbelievable. 'Mr Khan, do you have a phone I can borrow?'

'Of course. This way.'

The attendant led him up a corridor away from the mortuary and to a small office that still showed signs of being vacated in a rush. A phone sat on the table. The attendant excused himself and closed the door. Lethbridge-Stewart lifted the receiver and asked the operator to put him in touch with General Hamilton.

After Lethbridge-Stewart had finished briefing Hamilton on the situation, at least as far as he himself understood it, there was a long pause. He could almost hear the general's gears turning. Eventually, Hamilton broke the silence.

'Why would someone want a dead body?'

'Beyond me, sir. More to the point, though, *who* would want it? Someone aware of his close connection to the Intelligence would be my guess.'

Hamilton was silent for a few moments, his mind no doubt running through the various scenarios that implied. 'I suppose information was bound to slip through the cracks, Colonel. Very odd. And I've just received another very strange report from Major Douglas.'

Lethbridge-Stewart wasn't entirely sure he wanted to know. He knew enough already, knew where this was all leading, but he felt obligated to ask about the report.

'People at Paddington started acting in the most unusual way. Groups of them walking around in circles, quite literally. Concentric circles, so the report says, weaving in and out at one point. Lasted about half an hour, and then they all continued on their way as if nothing had happened. Caused quite a disruption, as you can imagine.'

He could. Every inbound train station in London was going to be jam-packed for the next few weeks.

'I suppose we're running with the assumption that it is connected in some way to the disappearance of Arnold's body?'

'I should think that is wise, at this point. We may have rounded up all the Yeti and those control spheres, but who knows what else the Intelligence left behind? So much for teething problems.'

Lethbridge-Stewart pointedly did not remind Hamilton that he had warned him of such potential danger. 'Do we halt our operation?'

'No, Colonel. After all, we're too far into it. Keeping the London Event out of the press is proving difficult enough as it is. Had to threaten Harold Chorley with criminal charges to keep him quiet, but it seems someone has got wind of what happened, or at the very least Staff Sergeant Arnold's connection to it. We can't afford to draw in any more attention.'

'Then what do you recommend, sir?' It was a question to which Lethbridge-Stewart knew the answer, and it was one that Sally wasn't going to like.

He didn't much like it himself, but the whole situation was fragile at best, and he knew he was needed.

The animated corpse in question was sitting comfortably on the train while it rushed through the countryside en route to Liskeard, Cornwall. From the outside he looked like any other old soldier returning home after a hectic tour of duty. His combat fatigues looked dirty, his skin and hair even worse. Several passengers noted this, and one young boy kept asking questions of his mother, while his sister wanted to go and poke the old man to see if he was dead. The mother was, for now, keeping her children under control. But such curiosity could not be sated for very long.

A ticket inspector passed through the carriage, checking the tickets of those who had boarded the train at Exeter St David's. Barely a handful had joined the train at Paddington – people were still returning there and those who had managed that feat were in no rush to leave again – and so the inspector was only now doing his first pass through the train.

He glanced out the window, absently clicking the ticket he had been offered, watching as the train came to a rest next to a field of cows. A common stopping point on this line, as the signal changed to red to allow a high speed train to pass by. Such a train rushed by, the tooting of its horn just audible over the rumble of the wheels on the tracks and the gust of wind squashed between the small gap separating the trains. The inspector was glad to not be on the other train – he would never have been able to walk one end to the other. There was barely any standing room.

'Tickets, please,' he said, passing by the old soldier as if he hadn't even noticed him.

The inspector stopped, blinked, and turned around. He walked back up the carriage and stopped at the door joining it to the previous carriage. He turned and started through the carriage again, like he'd not stepped on it before.

'Please have all tickets ready. All tickets, please!'

He received some odd looks from the first passengers whose tickets he had already clicked, but they still handed them back to him nonetheless. He didn't notice that they'd been clicked, for his eyes were on the field outside.

The cows were moving in circles, weaving in and out as if they were performing some strange ballroom dance.

All the while the soldier appeared to sleep, his lips moving as if he was whispering. Had the little girl been allowed to get close enough to poke him she would have heard the voice that ushered from his mouth.

A child's voice; a little boy saying, 'follow me, this way home.'

CHAPTER THREE
Mapping the Route

THE PAKISTANI HOSPITAL ATTENDANT PROVED TO BE very helpful in finding Lethbridge-Stewart the right people to interview. Mr Khan had explained that not much went on in the hospital without him knowing about it these days, since the building wasn't fully staffed yet. Lethbridge-Stewart expected a lot of it was due to Mr Khan's race, too; he was often invisible to most people. Just another dark-skinned man who was little more than a porter. Lethbridge-Stewart had served for a short time in India and found the culture there to be rich, and he expected no less was true of Pakistan. Unfortunately the layperson in Britain would never learn this, and so ethnic minorities like Mr Khan would never get their dues. Which meant Mr Khan saw and heard a lot. But not who had stolen the corpse, apparently. Still, the two men now in front of Lethbridge-Stewart seemed more helpful in that regard.

Alf and Ralf were two delivery men who had been unloading supplies around oh-one-hundred-hours that morning, the time the corpse had gone missing. They looked much alike, both dressed in dirty casual clothes, matching flat caps on their greying hair, and a peppery moustache setting off their deeply lined faces. Lethbridge-Stewart assumed they were brothers. They now stood next to the loading bay at the rear of the hospital, not far from the mortuary. They had just arrived with new supplies to unload when Mr Khan pointed them out. They stood to attention as soon as Lethbridge-Stewart approached, probably ex-Army men themselves.

'I was having a quick fag break with that taff,' Ralf was explaining. 'Nice fella, talks a bit too much, though. Bored of looking after stiffs, he said, reckons the bigwigs have it in for him.' He lowered his voice. 'Not one for the night shift, if you get my meaning.'

Lethbridge-Stewart nodded. Ralf was probably right; Driver Evans wasn't going to last long in the Army the way he was going. Didn't have the stones for it.

'That was when you were doing that funny walk, remember, Alfie?'

Alf looked away, puffing on his cigarette. 'Don't know what you're talking about, mate, never did. I was waiting for you and your lazy backside, I wasn't bloomin' well exercising.'

Ralf laughed at this. 'Excuse me brother, sir, reckon he had too much of the sauce last night. Bit of a black-out on our last run.'

Lethbridge-Stewart chose to ignore the implication that one of them had been drunk while working. He wasn't their supervisor, and besides they at least were working without complaining about the money. 'A funny walk?' he asked, warning bells ringing in his head. This sounded familiar somehow.

'Yeah, I came back and he was standing here walking in circles. Tried to talk to him but he ignored me, his own bloody brother, stone cold ignored me, then started walking in… Oh, what do you call them?' He moved his right hand around in a weaving loop. 'Figure of eight, yeah, that's it.'

'Weaving from one circle to another?'

'Yeah, guess he was.'

The report from Paddington Station came to mind.

'And did you see anybody at that time?'

'Well, the hospital was pretty deserted, especially down here, but...'

'The bloke in the army get-up,' Alf said, finally stepping into the conversation. 'Looked like he'd been in a horrific accident. Skin all burned. Thought it was just shadows at first, but it was definitely burned skin.'

Ralf was nodding along with his brother, then stopped, a thought coming to him. 'Hang on, come to think of it I think I spotted him just before, too, when me and the taffy were having a quick smoke. Down by the mortuary.'

Was it possible that Arnold had removed himself? Lethbridge-Stewart had to concede it was at least slightly possible after all the things he'd seen in the past month.

'How old was this man?'

'Hard to say, what with all the burns,' said Alf.

'Yeah, but I'd guess late forties, maybe early fifties? About this tall,' Ralf said, raising his hand just below his own height.

It sounded like Arnold.

'Thank you, gentlemen,' Lethbridge-Stewart said, already planning on taking an inventory of the uniforms removed from the dead soldiers. He would happily place a bet that the one uniform missing was that which had belonged to the staff sergeant. He also needed to place a call to Dougie again, to get Sally to double-check those reports about the odd events in London since last night. They started out in Kenton, and that was not too far from here. Something told him they'd find a trail leading to Paddington Station.

Intentionally or not, Arnold was leaving breadcrumbs behind him.

Lethbridge-Stewart left the two brothers to their bickering and went back inside.

He had been there in Piccadilly Circus Station, saw the blackened corpse of Arnold after that pyramid device thing went up in smoke. There was absolutely no doubt in his mind that the staff sergeant had died, the Army MD who arrived shortly after had even confirmed it. First robotic Yeti controlled by an alien intelligence, then possession and now this... How things had changed for him since being called in by Old Spence.

He stopped for a moment outside the office he had commandeered, overcome with a feeling that the strangeness was far from over.

Ray was considered something of a recluse by the people of Bledoe, although that had not always been so. Four years earlier he had published the last of his ghost stories after twelve years of relative success. He'd done well on those books, made enough to be comfortable for a few years, and Bledoe had embraced his minor celebrity. Now he helped out here and there, just enough to keep his small fortune topped up, but he was considered by most as reclusive, a man who liked to keep his own company while he thought up new stories.

Nobody knew the truth.

He was a haunted man. It was the source of his own ghost stories, a fact he had never shared with anybody in Bledoe, although there were a few people who actively chose to ignore what they, too, knew. He had seen things when he was a kid, things that had never left him.

He now sat at the bar of *The Rose & Crown* enjoying a quiet tankard of ale, trying his best not to listen in on the conversation George Vine was having with Henry Barns, the pub landlord. It seemed that one of George's sons was going through a rough patch. Everybody in Bledoe knew the Vine twins – two more helpful lads the village had never known – so it was a bit strange for Ray to hear George talk about them in such a way.

'They're young men now, George, they have to let go of the apron strings at some point.'

George nodded. 'That's not the problem, Henry. Lewis let go of those a couple of weeks ago, when the Watts' came back from London, but Owain... Something queer is going on with him.'

'Well, as long as he doesn't start winking at my son, he can be as queer as he likes,' Henry joked loudly and all the men at the bar laughed. Even George. Ray found himself laughing, too. 'No fairies in this village, and if they ever do come here, they ain't welcome in my pub.'

'Don't blame you,' George agreed.

'Always was a mummy's boy, that one,' Henry added, just to make it clear he wasn't completely joking. 'At least Lewis and that Watts boy are proper men, none of this long hair like they have in London. Proper short back and sides. What a young man should look like. Not surprised so few of them sign up for military service these days. They'd bawl their eyes out if they had to cut their hair.'

For a moment George considered this, and Ray could see the cogs turning in his brain. He was really considering the possibility. Ray doubted that was the way Owain was going, and he said so.

'Kids just like to fit in,' he added. 'We were all the same back in the day.'

All the men at the bar agreed.

'He's been like it ever since he went up to the Manor,' George said, once he'd taken a sip of his pint.

By contrast, Ray missed his mouth with his own ale. He wiped his chin with the back of his sleeve. 'The Manor? Last weekend?'

There were murmurs around the bar, everybody surprised by Ray's sudden question. Even Fred Murray, sleeping off his eighth pint, looked up from where he was resting his head on the bar. It was one thing for Ray to make a quick comment, but to actually get involved in a conversation...

George Vine narrowed his eyes – he'd never been Ray's biggest fan.

'Yeah, think so,' George said, his tone carrying a warning. 'Wanted to show the place to Watts. Lewis I can understand, but not Owain. Never seemed to be up for that kind of larking about, but then the boys have always done everything together.'

Ray tuned George out and let him and Henry continue to speculate. The light on at the Manor, it had been the Vine twins and the Watts' boy. Ray quickly finished his pint and left the pub, barely remembering to say goodbye. His mind was full of the same feeling he'd had when he noticed the light on. Something had happened at the Manor again, and now Owain Vine was caught up in it.

By the time Lethbridge-Stewart returned to the London Regiment offices in Battersea, Corporal Wright was hard at work mapping out the odd events reported in London since Arnold decided to go for his early morning stroll.

Pins were stuck into a map of London, detailing the trail from St Mark's to Paddington. Lethbridge-Stewart sat down on the edge of Douglas' desk, a welcome mug of tea in his hands. Wright stood next to the map, explaining the route taken.

'It seems that Staff Sergeant Arnold…' At this she paused, her face showing her disbelief.

'Takes a little getting used to, Corporal,' Lethbridge-Stewart said. The door to the office was open and more of Douglas' staff were in the ante-office; even though the only people in the office with him were his oldest friend and fiancée, Lethbridge-Stewart had order to maintain and spoke in his most official voice. 'But I am convinced that it is indeed Arnold who has moved himself. How…? Well, that is something we shall learn in time.'

'Hopefully,' Douglas said behind him.

Lethbridge-Stewart raised an eyebrow and glanced back. 'Quite so, Major,' he said, barely able to keep his smile at bay. 'As you were, Corporal Wright.'

'Yes, sir.' She turned back to the map. 'It would appear he moved on foot and took the longest route, although judging by the time he left St Mark's and arrived at Paddington we can assume he stopped a lot along the way. He took the A4088, some eight point seven miles, which would have taken a normal healthy person just under three hours. It took him almost the entire night, leaving St Mark's at approximately oh-one-hundred and arriving at Paddington Station around 11:50am.'

'Hours,' Lethbridge-Stewart said.

'What?'

'It's eleven-fifty hours.'

Wright just looked at him, blinked and returned to her map. She pointed to the pin nearest Kenton. 'The first report we have was on Grasmere Avenue, Kenton, around 2:20*am*...'

Behind her Lethbridge-Stewart folded his arms and raised an eyebrow at Douglas. The man smiled. Lethbridge-Stewart was reminded why it was never a good idea to work alongside someone with whom you were romantically involved. After this business was all dealt with, he would make sure the corporal returned to Hamilton's side.

'...Which matches the report given at Paddington and St Mark's; people walking in interweaving circles. What with London still relatively empty it has been difficult to track these instances. However, the second instance seems to have been on Elmstead Avenue around oh-five-hundred-*hours*, followed by a report some miles further away on the A4088 near Neasden Lane at 6:45*am*. Luckily, traffic is pretty thin so no casualties were reported, just massive disruption. Following that we had a report from Kensal Rise Underground Station at 9:10am, the last before Paddington itself.'

Lethbridge-Stewart waited a few moments to take it all in. This confirmed the link, although it left the answer to the most important question of all – why? – no clearer in his mind. Why were people walking in circles? And on top of that, what did this have to do with Arnold's resurrection, and just where was he going? That he was going in some specific direction seemed a reasonable assumption. Lethbridge-Stewart doubted it was random; nineteen years of military service showed him that very little happened by accident.

'Would it be safe to assume, taking into account the time it took him to reach Paddington, that the staff sergeant stopped at these places?' Douglas asked. 'Maybe it was his extended presence that caused these… disturbances?'

'A safe assumption,' Lethbridge-Stewart agreed. He turned to Wright. 'And there have been no further instances beyond Paddington?'

She double-checked the reports before answering. 'Not within London, no, sir.'

'So, Arnold has almost certainly left London. No doubt on a train from Paddington. Very well. Corporal Wright, please contact British Rail and see which trains left Paddington within the half-hour period during which the incident occurred. Then see if any further incidents happened along those stops. Get any help you need from Major Douglas' staff, but keep Bell free for Major Douglas. He still has a city to re-populate, after all.'

Wright nodded and left the office, closing the door behind her.

'Well, Colonel,' Douglas said, 'looks like I do need to know after all. You can't disrupt my operation without filling me in on this London Event now.'

Lethbridge-Stewart was inclined to agree, although now that his leave was cancelled he wasn't sure it could be called Douglas' operation. Still, since Hamilton hadn't reassigned Douglas, Lethbridge-Stewart was more than happy to share the load.

'Very well,' he said and nodded towards the decanter on the table. 'But a drop of scotch may be needed.'

Douglas couldn't very well deny him – after all the whisky was his.

Two small glasses poured, Douglas sat back in his chair and waited. Lethbridge-Stewart swirled the scotch in the glass before starting.

'As you know, London was evacuated at the end of last month, but what you don't know is that this all started a long time ago. 1935 to be exact, in Tibet of all places. Professor Edward Travers was an anthropologist back then and a member of the Royal Geographical Society to boot. Well, he had this fanciful notion of exploring Tibet and proving the existence of the abominable snowmen. By all accounts most of the RGS laughed at him, but his oldest friend, a chap named Mackay, joined him and off they went. Unfortunately Mackay died early on, and Travers happened upon a monastery called Det-Sen, although one suspects he probably wished he remained in old Blighty...'

As he neared the small town, passing through the Cornish countryside, Dingle Hill Wood in the near distance on his right, the old soldier could feel it. He was coming to the end of his journey, and he'd be able to rest again.

The train slowed as it crossed a small bridge over the A38. For a short while the train remained there, once again halted by a red signal. Around him the other passengers started preparing themselves for their arrival. A child, a girl, kept looking at him. He frowned, his cracked skin hurting as he did.

'You smell,' she said.

She was probably right. He had died, he knew that. He still did not understand how he was living again, since almost all of his memory was gone. All he knew was what he needed to do. Where he needed to go.

Something is wrong.

The child's voice came from nowhere. But he knew it was right. Something was tugging at him, pulling him away. Not his body, but his mind. Trying to empty him out.

People started crowding the right side of the carriage, peering out of the windows with exclamations of shock. He didn't move. He couldn't.

He closed his eyes, urging the train to move on. He had to keep moving.

He didn't even register the sounds of tyres screeching down on the A38, or the crunch of metal on metal as cars collided…

Somehow Mary had managed to drift off shortly after *Desert Island Discs* had finished; she was far too exhausted by the mental strain of trying to understand what was happening. Her dreams, such as they were, were haunted by a little boy. He was about twelve, dressed in grey shorts that reached just above the knees, a tank-top over a smart shirt. They were both standing in the woods, looking out across a gorge of cascading water. There was something familiar about it, as if she had been there before. The next minute he was on the opposite side, waving her across. She looked down at the rushing water. She couldn't cross that.

'You must. I need you,' the boy said.

'But I don't know who you are.'

The boy looked agitated by that, his eyes moving around quickly, like he expected something to jump out of the trees. 'You do, it's me. Gordon.'

'But I…' Mary shook her head. It couldn't be her

Gordon, he was too young. She had never known him as a boy, but... In death could her husband have been reduced to his innocence? Wasn't that the definition of Heaven: being free of all sin and evil influences?

Decided, Mary took a step forward. She would cross the gorge and be with Gordon again.

She snapped awake, disorientated by the suddenness of it all. Her dream was still very clear in her mind, more like a memory from the previous day. She looked around, hoping to see Gordon, but instead all she saw was the countryside rushing past her at great speed.

She was still in the little Morris, rushing up an A-road. She recognised the geography around her. Not too far away on her right was Dingle Hill Wood, which meant she was approaching Liskeard. Her destination was now obvious. She hadn't thought about the place in nearly twenty years. And it made perfect sense; where else would Gordon be waiting for her than where they had lived so happily together?

Only they were driving too fast. Up ahead cars were losing control, careering all across the A-road; those going the opposite way were crossing the verge. She leaned forward.

'Slow down, look!'

The driver didn't even flinch. His hands held the steering wheel tightly, the Morris not diverting from its direct course towards the cars that were even now crashing into each other. Mary tried to move across the man, to take the wheel off him, but there wasn't enough space. The man didn't blink; his eyes were glazed over, looking at nothing.

Ahead, like an albatross, a train waited on a bridge that ran across the A-road. Even as the Morris drove her to her death, Mary couldn't help but notice all the people on the train, faces pressing against the windows, watching with horror and ineptness at the carnage beneath them.

She wanted to scream out. Wanted to be back in Coleshill having a nice dinner with Mr Cooper. But it was too late. Much too late.

Owain didn't want to be back at the Manor, but he could feel the cold hand of the little boy leading him forward. He glanced down. There was no one there, of course, but still he could feel the smaller hand clasped around his.

He didn't even know what the boy looked like. But he could hear him; the voice hadn't changed since Owain had first heard it a week earlier in the Manor.

The Whisperer was real; a ghost, perhaps, but *real* nonetheless. And it wanted him. Wanted his help.

For the past week the boy simply wanted to talk, to tell him stories of all the things he had seen. The futures he had witnessed, the strange worlds. Owain wasn't sure he believed a word the boy said, but he felt such a need from the voice that he couldn't help but continue to listen.

It was nice to be wanted. To be *needed*. Lewis no longer needed him, of that Owain was sure, he didn't need the voice to tell him that.

Owain stopped, his hand free once more. He looked around to see if the boy was there. Nothing, just the woods nearby and the gate that was still open from when they had broken in last weekend.

Owain swallowed and walked towards the Manor. He passed through the gates and looked around. In the distance, just left of the house he saw what appeared to be an Army truck, but before he could question the oddity of such a thing, he spotted the boy.

For the first time Owain could see him. Not very clear, but definitely there. Dressed in clothes a good thirty years old: grey cap on his brown hair, grey shorts and tank-top, the sort of uniform he'd seen in old pictures at his school.

The boy looked worried.

Something is wrong. We need to go.

'Where?' Owain asked.

For a moment the boy did not answer, but then he spoke again. As he spoke he vanished and reappeared a split second later next to Owain, holding out his hand.

Liskeard, the boy said.

CHAPTER FOUR
All Roads Lead to Bledoe

We ran through the woods, joking and laughing, kicking the tin can between us, completely unaware of what trouble we were about to find ourselves in. How could we have known? Three boys not yet teenagers, ignorant to the dangers life could bring. But we soon learned.

Jimmy was the one who got the blame, but of course it was not his fault. How could he be blamed? Only children could be so mean. He kicked the can high over my head. I thought about jumping for a header but I didn't fancy the dent the tin can may have left in my head. So I let it fly past me. We all watched it as it flew in slow motion, like time itself was pausing around it. It stopped in mid-air. Moments later lightning erupted out of it. We stood there mesmerized.

We could only look on in shock as light crackled around us, like a thunderstorm at ground level. A man stepped out of the crackling light, a man from a bygone era, dressed as he was in the clothes of a Victorian gentleman, complete with top hat and cravat. He looked around, his steely eyes taking in the woods, the foreboding Carrington Lodge in the distance and eventually us. His cold eyes rested on us, a look that I can only describe as malevolent.

RAY LOOKED UP FROM THE BOOK, THE FIRST ONE HE'D EVER written. *The Hollow Man of Carrington Lodge*, just like all his other books, was inspired by real events, although none would believe it. Sometimes he didn't even believe it himself.

Sometimes he looked back and wrote it off as the disturbed imaginings of an insecure child. Except the events of late-1937 to early-1938 were real, and his life was not the only one affected by them.

Everybody had heard stories about the Manor, ghost stories he had turned into fiction, almost as a warning to the young boys who wanted to explore the place. Whether the books helped to keep the place closed, Ray could not say, but he liked to think they played their part. Of course most people just saw them as fiction; very few believed them to be embellishments of things he had personally experienced. Only a few could confirm the fact of the fiction, and two of them were gone, while the other hadn't mentioned it once in thirty years. The others who had been affected by the events, his family and his friends, had either left Bledoe or passed on themselves. Or simply forgotten. He was the only one left in Bledoe who would admit the truth. Who would accept that the Whisperer, as the locals called the ghost, had begun life as the Hollow Man who had appeared in 1937 and made that Manor his home.

Only a fool would go up there.

Ray looked down at Jack, who was curled up in front of the fire.

Only a fool like Ray.

He had to go to the Manor. The Vine boy was up there now, he was certain about it. He'd popped by the post office hoping to talk to Owain, but Mrs Vine said he'd not been back in hours. There was only one place he could have gone, as far as Ray was concerned. If the Hollow Man had got to him, then Owain would have no choice.

Which meant Ray had no choice.

He knelt down and ruffled Jack's fur. 'Material for a new book, eh?' he said, trying to sound more cheerful than he felt.

He stood up and took a deep breath. Time to get on with it. He'd put this off for thirty years. Now it was time to confront the Hollow Man and hold him to account.

*

People were still shaken when they disembarked the train at Liskeard, some of them worried that family or friends may have been in the accident on the bypass. But one person was unaffected. The dead staff sergeant didn't pause as he stepped out of the station, didn't blink as the small panda cars rushed through the town to help in the emergency.

He had expected to get transport from Liskeard, but the bypass incident had prevented that. Now he had to walk the rest of the way. Due north to Bledoe. What should have been a journey of no more than twenty minutes would now take him over an hour.

The delay was bad. The boy's voice kept telling him this.

The boy could not reach Liskeard. He could barely manage to exist *in* Bledoe. The staff sergeant had to go further, to Golitha Falls. The boy was waiting for him, waiting for both of them.

Lethbridge-Stewart's vision blurred as he looked up from the reports. He'd been reading over them for what seemed like hours. Major Douglas had gone to deal with a little trouble in Greenwich, leaving him on his own to read the reports and co-ordinate the continual influx of people. It was almost six o'clock, but it seemed much later. The day was dragging, no doubt because he had expected to be well on the way to Brighton by now. When he'd woken up that morning he had prepared himself to turn off from work, hand over to Dougie and then go home, with no further thought of reports or logistics or recalcitrant privates crossing his mind for a week. And here he was, still at work, with no sign of going home any time soon.

'Come on in,' he called barely a second after the knock came. Tired he may have been, but Lethbridge-Stewart prided himself on keeping his reactions sharp.

Corporal Wright entered, holding a mug in one hand and a sheaf of papers in the other. 'Thought you could do with a cuppa,' she said, walking across the office and placing the cup on the desk before him. He took it gratefully as she closed the door and took a seat opposite him. She placed the papers on the desk and leaned down to remove her shoes. 'So much for our break, Alistair.'

So, she was in Sally-mode. Lethbridge-Stewart wasn't keen on that while at work, but he was too tired to resist.

'Yes, can't be helped,' he said, and walked around the desk. He took one of her stockinged feet in his hands and began to massage the sole. 'Better?'

'Much,' she said, trying to smile around a rising yawn. 'Sorry. Hamilton rarely keeps me on my feet this much. Is it always like this for you?'

'Most of the time, yes. You don't reach colonel after eighteen years by sitting around. Rank has its privileges and all that.' He smiled laconically. 'Any luck with British Rail?'

'Oh.' Sally pulled her foot away quickly, and handed him the sheaf. 'Sorry, that's why I came in here. Got distracted.'

Lethbridge-Stewart stood up. 'It's quite alright, no one but us noticed.' He looked down at the papers in his hand. The top one showed the timetable for the 11:15 to Penzance. 'This would be Arnold's train?'

'Looks like.' Sally also stood. Removing the papers from him, she flicked through them, her expression troubled. 'Incidents in Exeter St David, Newton Abbot and Plymouth. All around the times the train stopped at those stations.'

'Why would he be heading to Penzance?'

'Perhaps he fancied a mid-death skinny dip?'

Lethbridge-Stewart allowed a smile.

'Something at sea, maybe? It is on the coast.' Sally blew out air and sat back down, still studying the papers in her hands. 'I really have no idea. I'm still trying to grasp the idea that there is a living corpse travelling across country.'

'Stranger things have happened,' Lethbridge-Stewart pointed out.

'Well, since I am not cleared for such things, I shall have

to take your word for it.'

'Quite right, too.' He offered her a smile, but knew it lacked conviction. He sat on the desk, suddenly even more tired than before. 'At least that gives us something to work with. I believe there is a regiment of Green Jackets stationed near Penzance.'

'Is there? Off the top of my head, I wouldn't know.'

'Hmm. I think it may be D Company.'

'Want me to alert them?'

'Yes, arrange for a platoon to meet the train at Penzance. Tell them…'

He was interrupted by another knock at the door. A cadet doing on-field experience poked his head through the gap and saluted.

'Sir, another incident reported just near Liskeard.' He handed Lethbridge-Stewart a sheet of paper. 'A pile up on the A38 bypass. I double-checked the time, and it occurred approximately the same time as the Penzance train paused there.'

'Thank you, Cadet…?'

The cadet looked down at the floor and mumbled in embarrassment. 'Constable, sir.'

'Cadet Constable, I see.' Lethbridge-Stewart cleared his throat. 'Unfortunate. Very well, Cadet, dismissed.' He waited until the cadet had left the room, then glanced at Sally. 'Perhaps we should make it a new rank?' he said, unable to resist the smirk.

Sally rolled her eyes at this. 'It's not his fault. Brave of him to join the Army, considering.'

Lethbridge-Stewart raised an eyebrow. 'Yes, considering.'

He looked at the report from Liskeard. It told him little more than the cadet had reported, save that emergency services were already attending.

'Contact the Green Jacket Battalion stationed near Plymouth; have them deploy a unit to the A38 Liskeard bypass. I shall take command as soon as I can get there. I'll get on to RAF Northolt, see if they can airlift me there. I don't really have another four hours to waste on travelling by car.'

Corporal Wright stood, official mode engaged. 'Yes, sir. And the Penzance train?'

'I want a platoon there at the ready. Arnold needs to be stopped before anybody else is hurt.'

It felt strange to be walking along Golitha Falls without Jack by his side. He rarely reflected why he continued to visit this area; he reasoned that Jack liked freedom to run, but as the previous weekend proved there were plenty of other open areas around Bledoe. Indeed, neither Bodmin Moor nor Lanyon Moor were that far away in the car. But now, as Ray trekked the path that led towards the Manor, now overgrown through lack of use, he began to realise the truth.

He had been unconsciously watching over Remington Manor, like a caretaker making sure no one got too close. He hadn't done a brilliant job of it.

Granted, there had not been many instances in the last fifteen years or so, other than the usual youngster breaking their way in, and nothing that involved the Hollow Man. Until now.

He couldn't be absolutely sure, but his gut told him that somehow the Hollow Man had been woken by the Vine twins' trespassing last weekend. Now it was up to him to stop it.

He paused for breath, feeling a tightness in his chest. He wasn't unfit by any means, but this walk was taking it out of him.

He carried on, but as the Manor became clearer through the branches he found himself stalling. He felt cold, sweaty...

He stopped again. Darkness was falling around him, and with it came shadows and strange sounds in the woods. Something was out there watching him.

The Hollow Man.

Ray glanced around, his eyes playing tricks on him, no

doubt, for he could have sworn he saw a large shape moving through the trees, a creature of fur. He closed his eyes and shook his head. No, he had to go on, he had to end this once and for all.

But he couldn't. His breath became laboured, the sweat now showing on the back of his hands. The anxiety was too much.

He couldn't do this.

He opened his eyes. There was nothing there but the trees.

'I'm sorry,' he muttered, knowing full well that no one could hear him.

Raymond Phillips turned and walked away.

Inside his head he was that child again, that scared child who could do nothing but stand by helpless.

It just wasn't possible. The walk to Liskeard would have taken him almost two hours, and it wasn't like Owain hadn't tried. Gordon, the boy, could have asked him to do anything and he would have. As he sat in the Manor, arms wrapped around his knees, he could not believe that earlier in his bedroom he had been stupid enough to deny Gordon, to resist returning to the Manor where Gordon lived. This was where he belonged. He knew that now. But it just wasn't possible.

Everything had all made sense as soon as he stepped back inside the dusty old house. The door had closed behind him, he'd looked down at Gordon and saw a set of brown eyes looking back up at him. Eyes that felt so safe and warm. Telling Owain that he was needed, that only he could help. Then, like a mist of ash, Gordon had fallen apart. At first Owain had felt a rise of panic, but that soon subsided when he realised where Gordon had gone.

Owain hadn't been left alone. He could feel Gordon in every nerve, every muscle, every pulse. Gordon and he had become one.

Everything became clear to him. Who Gordon was, what

he needed, and why only Owain could help him.

And he had tried to help. Together, Gordon was sure, they could get to Liskeard, but it hadn't worked. They had barely passed Bledoe when Owain felt Gordon's presence fade. It was a feeling he could barely describe, like a hole had appeared in his centre, growing bigger with every step. Never in seventeen years had he felt so alone. And he couldn't be alone, Owain knew that now. So he turned and walked back to the Manor, feeling Gordon's strength surging through his body once again, the black hole shrinking into nothing.

So now he sat in the Manor, just him and Gordon. They had to wait. Parts of them were still missing, but they were drawing closer. All they needed was one more part and then they'd be strong enough to find the final piece.

The woman – Mary.

All emergency services were present by the time Lethbridge-Stewart's helicopter arrived at the site of the bypass pile-up. The police milled around without any purpose now that the Green Jackets had arrived to take over. A few soldiers helped the firemen where they could, finding ways to safely remove passengers from the more seriously mangled vehicles, while ambulancemen took care of the minor injuries and ambulances carted off the more seriously injured to the closest hospital. Lethbridge-Stewart ducked and rushed towards the grass verge, holding on to his cap, while the helicopter took off behind him. He stopped at the edge of the road, and looked around.

Both sides of the A-road were blocked off, with soldiers and police directing traffic back the way it had come. A soldier walked over to Lethbridge-Stewart and saluted, no doubt spotting him a mile off, what with the tartan band around his cap.

'Colonel Lethbridge-Stewart? RSM Bevan, sir.'

'What's the situation, Sergeant Major?'

The man was older than Lethbridge-Stewart, as was often

the case with staff sergeants, but he didn't miss a beat in relinquishing command. Superiority had very little to do with age in the Army.

'Hard to say, sir. Seems to be some confusion from the statements we've been able to secure. No one can recall what happened; some kind of group blackout it seems.'

'Sounds about right.'

They walked into the melee. The civilians didn't appear to be too responsive to the administrations of the ambulancemen, most looking around in a daze. But Lethbridge-Stewart had seen much worse damage in his lifetime, and although many had life-threatening injuries, luckily no one had actually died. He supposed they should be grateful it was a Monday and not a weekend. Very few families travelling this time of the evening.

A train rumbled by over the bridge ahead.

'Any news from Liskeard?'

'No, sir. We have some men there now, questioning passengers from the train, more witnesses, although so far there's nothing important to add. The train stopped at a signal, and moments later every car down here went barmy.'

'Just after the train stopped?' It was as they had surmised. Whenever Arnold stopped for a given amount of time, people nearby were affected. 'And no disturbances in Liskeard?' There wasn't, which meant that either Arnold didn't stop there for any length of time, or he had gone on to Penzance. He would have to contact Corporal Wright to find out if anything had occurred further down the line, but first he wanted to speak to the injured here. At least one of them had to remember something. 'How many casualties, Sergeant Major?'

'One second, sir.' Bevan called out to a constable, who came over with his pad open. 'Casualty list,' Bevan said, and the police constable handed the pad to Lethbridge-Stewart.

He glanced down at the list. No numbers, just names. He blinked, and looked closer. It couldn't be! Of course it could have been another Mary Gore, but…

He pointed at the name. 'Where is this woman?'

The constable checked his list. 'Miss Gore? Taken to the hospital in Liskeard,' he said. 'Red dot means they've already been moved.'

'Thank you, Constable.' Lethbridge-Stewart returned the pad, then turned to Bevan. 'Do you have a jeep I can borrow? I want to talk to some of the casualties taken to Liskeard.'

Bevan saluted. 'Sir! If you'd like to come this way, I'll assign Rifleman Bishop to you.'

Lethbridge-Stewart followed the staff sergeant through the crash site, his mind elsewhere. Coincidences were something he did not believe in.

En route to Liskeard Hospital, Lethbridge-Stewart received a report from Corporal Wright via RT. The platoon at Penzance had found no sign of Arnold on the train, which meant he had to have disembarked in Liskeard. Lethbridge-Stewart asked Wright to liaise with the local authorities and find out if there had been any further disturbances, in the hope that Arnold continued to leave his breadcrumb trail behind him.

At the hospital he was greeted by Nurse Bidwell, a woman of Caribbean origin, one of the thousands that staffed British Hospitals, a result of the cheap labour solution of the last two decades which was needed to help out the NHS. He asked to be taken directly to question Mary Gore. The nurse nodded, looking harassed.

'Poor dear was delirious, mumbling incoherently,' Bidwell said, her Caribbean accent softened by many years living in England. 'Her wounds weren't as severe as they looked, no bones broken, just cuts and abrasions. Could have been a lot worse.'

'Yes,' Lethbridge-Stewart agreed, having seen some of more critically wounded on the bypass. 'How long will she be kept here?'

'That's up to your lot,' Nurse Bidwell said, cutting her eyes at the soldiers who guarded the ward. 'Is all this necessary? It's not the first crash we've dealt with.'

Lethbridge-Stewart didn't respond, his face as grim as his thoughts. He was relieved to hear that the woman in question wasn't among the more critical, but he still felt a jump in his heart at the knowledge that she was somehow caught up in all this. 'You said she was mumbling? About what?'

'Was difficult to hear, but at one point at least she mentioned how she had to find someone called Gordon.'

Lethbridge-Stewart stopped.

'Are you all right?'

He blinked and looked at Nurse Bidwell, who was now standing by one of the curtained-off beds, her hand ready to pull back the curtain.

'Yes,' he lied. 'Quite alright. If you would…?'

Nurse Bidwell eyed him for a moment, clearly not convinced. She shrugged and pulled aside the curtain to reveal… an empty bed. She immediately called out to the ward sister, who didn't have any idea of where the patient had gone. They went to check the toilets, leaving Lethbridge-Stewart to stand over the empty bed, his mind rushing through what he'd been told.

When he had seen the name on that list he hadn't wanted to believe it. His private life and work life did not, through necessity and design, interact. It was the way it had always been, but recently… First Sally, and now this.

He had tried to reason that there could have been another Mary Gore, but to hear she had been mumbling about finding someone called Gordon… He remembered her talking about using her maiden name, but he didn't know she had actually started doing so. Mary Gore, or as he had always known her, Mary Rosina Lethbridge-Stewart.

His mother.

'I believe she was brought in with a man?' he asked, once Nurse Bidwell had returned.

She checked the clipboard in her hands. 'The driver? Yes.'

'Take me to him.'

'I don't think he's going to be able to answer any…'

Lethbridge-Stewart wasn't interested in her opinion. He brushed past the nurse. A few moments later the sound of her shoes clicking on the polished floor told him that she was following.

Gordon was asleep. At first Owain thought the boy had gone again, but he didn't feel any sense of loss or emptiness, but rather a calming presence. Soothing almost. The kind of peace he often saw on Lewis' face when his brother slept.

While Gordon had been awake, he and Owain had continued to talk, sharing stories of their lives and experiences. It seemed Gordon had lived a long life, one that belied the youth of his voice and his child-like appearance. But now Owain found himself at something of a loose end. At first he had taken to exploring the house, but had soon tired of that. There was only so much to be seen in empty rooms full of dust and cobwebs. He had thought to look for clues as to why the house had become vacant so suddenly in '39, but it seemed easier to simply ask Gordon later, since obviously he was at the heart of that story.

So instead he stepped outside into the dark grounds of the Manor.

Owain remembered the Army truck he had spotted before. The truck hadn't moved, it was still parked left of the house, now mostly in the shadows, but still on easy view to anyone entering by the gates.

He crept up to it, and noticed that the tarpaulin covering the back wasn't strapped down. He was about to pull the flap up, to see what was contained within, when he heard a sound. It sounded like a scuffle, as if someone was shuffling in the gravel, and it was coming from the front of the truck. Curious, he walked to the front cabin and put his foot on the step beneath the door. Using the open window for leverage, he lifted himself up and peered inside.

There was a man in Army uniform. He was leaning to one side, his head seeming to rest on the window of the other door.

'Hey, mate, you okay?' Owain asked.

There was no answer, so Owain climbed down again with every intention of walking around the cab and checking on the soldier. But there was the noise again, behind him now.

He paused, the hair on the back of his neck rising. It sounded like a deep growl, a noise unlike any Owain had heard before today. He turned slowly, carefully, so as not to alarm whatever had made the sound. Not that he imagined he would be any kind of threat to something that sounded like that.

He was right.

The creature that stood before him, towering over him, its eyes seeming to glow, was a shaggy beast with long arms and powerful looking claws. Owain swallowed, unable to take his eyes off the beast. It reminded him of something he'd seen in picture books when he'd been a kid. Only that book had been about mythical creatures. The thing before him was no mythical creature.

It was real, very large, very fierce and probably very hungry.

It was an abominable snowman!

CHAPTER FIVE
Homecoming

LETHBRIDGE-STEWART LOOKED AT THE UNCONSCIOUS figure in the bed before him. He had hoped he would recognise the man; that whoever had brought his mother to Liskeard was someone known to him.

It was true that he didn't visit Coleshill very often, and there were almost certainly many people in his mother's life that he did not know, but he couldn't quite understand why she would be in the car with someone so young. Well, young compared to his mother. Despite the injuries, and the long hair and trendy moustache, Lethbridge-Stewart could tell that the man wasn't much younger than him.

'Do we have any idea who this man is?'

Nurse Bidwell consulted the clipboard hanging at the end of the bed. 'No form of ID on him. Perhaps you can find out from the officers at the pile-up?'

Lethbridge-Stewart decided to add that to his list of things to do. He shook his head. 'And he arrived in this state?'

'He was awake when he arrived. Was disturbed about something, but we couldn't understand him. Speaking some foreign language.'

'Which?'

'No idea. None that any of us has heard before.'

Lethbridge-Stewart turned and walked out of the ward, glancing at the two Green Jackets on guard. The nurse followed him, and they walked a short distance down the corridor. For a moment they looked at each other, her steely gaze drilling into him. He chose to ignore it. He'd withstood worse looks in his time, and from bigger men than Nurse Bidwell.

'Have you travelled far?'

If Bidwell was surprised by the question she didn't show it. 'Well, if you consider moving from Barbados to England fifteen years ago as far, then yes.'

'And you don't know any foreign languages?'

'Just your English,' Bidwell said, smiling honestly for the first time since she'd introduced herself.

'Of course. You were a Bajan speaker?'

'Way I raised,' she replied, putting her Barbadian accent on thick.

Lethbridge-Stewart nodded. He spoke a few languages himself, but unless the man in the bed woke up, such linguistic skills were of little use.

'If you had to guess, what language did it sound most like?'

Bidwell shrugged. 'Perhaps Latin?' She laughed. 'Don't be so surprised. De longer yuh live, de moreyuh does hear.'

'Yes, quite.' Although he'd spent some time in the Caribbean, he still had a little trouble understanding Bajan English, but he found if he listened carefully the meaning usually became clear enough.

A scream dragged them from their conversation.

It came from the same ward they had just left.

Lethbridge-Stewart got there before Bidwell, but not soon enough to stop the attack. Another nurse was on the floor, looking around dazed. The bed was empty; the man who had accompanied his mother was gone.

Lethbridge-Stewart looked at the Green Jackets who had entered the ward ahead of him.

'You remain here,' he told the one who was helping the nurse to her feet. 'And you —'

Lethbridge-Stewart didn't get to finish. The clatter of something hitting the floor alerted him. He pushed past Bidwell and dashed through the side door, which led into the adjacent ward. People were looking around confused, nurses and doctors trying to calm the patients lying in their beds. At the end of the ward a man was scrambling to his feet, a trolley knocked over next to him, petri dishes and other instruments now scattered on the floor.

Lethbridge-Stewart called out to the man. He looked back, crazed eyes peering out from a deeply scarred face, wounds re-opened by his collision with the trolley.

The man managed to get to his feet and ran. Lethbridge-Stewart reached down for his revolver, and remembered too late that he was in his regular uniform and was thus unarmed. He shook his head in irritation. He turned back to the Green Jacket who'd followed him into the ward. He could take the soldier's rifle, he supposed. But no, the man may well need it. Lethbridge-Stewart would manage without.

'Go that way!' he ordered the soldier, and pointed to the side exit. The Green Jacket saluted and set off. Lethbridge-Stewart continued through the ward to the door by which the man had left.

He had to know why that man had been driving his mother towards Bledoe.

She wouldn't miss Bledoe, of that Mary was certain. It had been her home for many years now, where Gordon and she had settled after their wedding in '25. Twenty years and now she had to leave. But it was too difficult to live there anymore. Too much pain, too many bad memories. And then there were the shadows.

She simply could not take any more. Her sister had been such a help, and had sent her husband all the way from Lancashire to take her and Ali away. Even now Thomas was packing the boot of his car, with the assistance of Ali and

Raymond.

She was going to leave so much behind. Isobel, her sister, had insisted that Mary keep the house on, rent it out perhaps, since it would be such a shame to simply lose so much. Mary still wasn't sure about that, but she had agreed – after a fashion.

She did not wish to rent out her house, after all she was never going to return, so she instead gave it to Eileen Phillips and her family. Eileen, alongside Maureen Barns, had been her best friend for many years, and her own house had suffered after a Spitfire had crashed into the village after a mechanical fault while it was returning to St Eval, twenty-seven miles away down the coast. No lives had been lost, even the Spitfire pilot had managed to parachute to safety, but Harold Phillips had been badly wounded after rushing into the ruins to save Patrick, the evacuee from London who had been billeted with them. Mary's house was too big for just her and Ali, especially after their own evacuees had vacated the spare room and returned to London, so with nowhere to go, the Phillips' had moved into Mary's home.

It seemed only right that they should have the house now. England was recovering from the war, the economy ruined. There was no way the Phillips' would be able to fix their own home, and otherwise they would almost certainly be forced out of the village eventually. This way they could remain in the only home they had known.

She peered out of the kitchen window. Many people were outside her house, gathering to say goodbye. Jemima Fleming and Henry Barns stood nearby - hovering, really, something awkward between them. Ali and Raymond were leaning against Thomas' black Humber Sixteen Saloon, the boot tied with rope to prevent the suitcases from falling out. The poor car had seen better days, but who had the money to buy a new one? Mary was simply happy that Thomas was here and pleased that Ali seemed to be excited that he would be sitting in the front seat with his Uncle Tommy for the journey. This was something Gordon would never have allowed. Mary didn't mind. She would be quite content to sit in the backseat on her own, wrapped up in her memories and thoughts of the new life she was heading towards.

Ali and Raymond both seemed happy enough, but Mary knew better. Ali was sixteen now, almost a man, and he deserved better than to be uprooted from his home. He was older than his years, forced to grow up by recent events, not least of which was the death of his father earlier that year. The boys had been friends their whole lives, especially after the loss of James, and she was separating them. She had promised Raymond that they could see each other during the holidays, and both he and Ali had taken that on the chin. Ali was off on an adventure, and they'd have much to tell each other when they next met. Perhaps at Christmas. If Eileen allowed Raymond to visit them in Lancashire, of course. Mary was never returning to Bledoe, and neither would she be bringing her son back. He, too, needed to be free from the painful memories.

She turned from the window to face Eileen and Maureen, who were still talking. Mary had lost track of the conversation again. She did that a lot, her mind distracted by the presence she always felt around her. She glanced sideways, certain there was someone standing next to her. A sadly familiar child, trying to talk to her. But as usual there was nothing there but a shadow.

Almost twenty-five years later, Mary slept as the taxi carried on into Bledoe. She was still sore from the crash and had fallen asleep almost as soon as the taxi had left Liskeard Hospital. This time, though, her dreams were not haunted by the ghost of her dead husband; instead she was reliving the darkest period of her life. It was as if her mind was trying to tell her something, to remind her of why she had left Bledoe, and why it was not a good idea to return.

She may not have noticed as the taxi's headlights cast their beams on the police box that sat on the grass verge, blocking the signpost that indicated Bledoe was less than a mile away, but the taxi driver did. And he was a little confused.

He had driven into Bledoe several times, occasionally taking Tremar Lane rather than going the long way, and not once had he noticed a police box before. He knew that the police were slowly moving from the need for the telephones inside the blue boxes, so he reasoned that perhaps London were passing the old boxes onto other places in England, those that might benefit from a better communication system for the local constabularies. Bledoe certainly fit, since it was served by the police station at Liskeard and didn't have its own constabulary to speak of.

He dismissed it moments later, and chuckled to himself. Not at his clearly aging memory, but at the drunken man he'd seen sleeping in the grass next to the police box.

An old soldier, by the look of it; having imbibed a little too much brandy, no doubt.

It seemed to be bigger on the inside.

As he continued to chase the man through the hospital, Lethbridge-Stewart couldn't help but be surprised by how much was contained within the externally misleading building. He had passed through several departments already, causing chaos in the X-ray Department where a poor woman was having her chest X-rayed. As soon as the pursuant burst into the X-ray room, failing to notice the red light above the door, the woman had reacted in shock, sitting up abruptly. Lethbridge-Stewart had to avert his eyes to spare the woman any embarrassment, but didn't have time to apologise before he continued to give chase.

He really wished he had his revolver to hand. One well-placed shot and the man would soon stop running.

Lethbridge-Stewart hadn't thought to count the floors as he approached the hospital, but he felt sure he must have been nearing the top by now. He was on the fourth floor and the sound of children crying could be heard at the end of the corridor. He glanced around, trying to locate his prey, and his eyes alighted on the signs that indicated the two departments that took up the fourth floor. Maternity and the Neonatal Unit. Expectant mothers and newly born babies. Not the place for a confrontation.

At the far end of the corridor, just beside the double doors that led to Maternity, a side door crashed closed. The sign above the door, swinging in the breeze that wafted through the corridor, told Lethbridge-Stewart that the door led to the roof.

'Perfect.'

He dashed down the corridor, grabbing a fire extinguisher off the wall as he passed, and bolted up the metal stairs leading to the roof. The cold air hit him as soon as he stepped outside.

Liskeard was not a particularly crowded town and thus not very well illuminated; what light there was on the roof was mostly provided by the moon above.

He looked around, expecting the man to be hidden somewhere. Perhaps behind the shed-like structure that housed the workings of the hospital lift. But instead the man just stood there, out in the open, his back to Lethbridge-Stewart and his head tilted to one side, much like a dog listening out for something.

Feeling a little foolish, Lethbridge-Stewart lifted the extinguisher and pointed the nozzle at the man. He doubted he'd do much damage with just CO_2, but it would be enough to startle the man, and allow Lethbridge-Stewart close enough to put him down with his hands.

'Turn around slowly,' Lethbridge-Stewart said.

The man gave no indication of hearing. Lethbridge-Stewart stepped closer, his hand squeezing the trigger mechanism.

'I said...'

The man turned slowly. For a moment they stood looking at each other. There was something familiar about the look on the man's face; an expression Lethbridge-Stewart had seen before, except he couldn't place it.

The man spoke, but the words were gibberish to Lethbridge-Stewart's ears. They certainly weren't Latin, nor were they any language he'd heard before. The man stopped and waited, an expectant look on his face.

'Sorry, Johnny, I can't understand you.'

The man spoke again, now clearly agitated. He moved forward. Lethbridge-Stewart wasn't taking any risks. He released the CO_2. The man threw his hands up to cover his face and Lethbridge-Stewart struck him in the gut with the heavy cylinder. The man staggered back.

'What did you want with my mother? Where were you taking her?'

The man lowered his hands. Red rings encircled his eyes, burned slightly by such close exposure to the CO_2. He stepped backwards.

'Who are you working for?'

Lethbridge-Stewart could feel the anger rising in him. In his time he had used such anger on the battlefield, but this was something different... It was personal. This involved his mother, and he was intent on getting answers.

'Why is she looking for my father?'

The man tilted his head once again. But still he spoke in words that meant nothing to Lethbridge-Stewart.

'Damn you!'

Lethbridge-Stewart struck with the extinguisher, straight at the man's face. With a sickening crack, the man's nose exploded. For a second he stood there, and then he was gone.

Lethbridge-Stewart looked down. He hadn't realised they were so close to the edge of the roof. Four storeys below the man lay dead, his body splayed out on the concrete forecourt of the hospital. Women screamed, men looked around confused, some embracing the women and hiding their faces from the horrific sight. A couple of Green Jackets, including Rifleman Bishop, looked up.

Still Lethbridge-Stewart could feel his anger pulsing. Why was his mother being taken to Bledoe? How could she possibly believe his father was alive? It made no sense.

He needed answers. And the only place he knew that might hold them was the place of his birth; Bledoe.

It had all come around so quickly. Charles' family had received news that they were able to return to London the next day. When they'd been discussing the idea of it down the *The Rose & Crown*, Lewis had been all up for going to London with them, for finding a flat with Charles and some of his friends. But now it was just around the corner...?

Lewis knew he needed to talk to Owain about it. He wasn't having second thoughts exactly, but the dream was about to become a reality, and he found it more than a little daunting. He returned home with Charles to find his parents sitting in the living room watching one of their favourite television programmes, *Hugh and I Spy*.

'You're starting to spend more time here than home,' Lewis' dad said, looking up as the front door closed.

There was no creeping into his house. The front door led directly into the living room. You had to walk through the room to reach the staircase that led to the bedrooms. Even the corridor from the backdoor led into the living room before it reached the staircase. The only way in without being detected by his waiting parents was to use the post office entrance, but he didn't have keys to the shop.

'My home is London, Mr Vine,' Charles said pointedly, but politely.

Mr Vine let out a harrumph at that, and turned back to the television, which sat next to the bay windows that looked out over the large garden.

'Actually he's received notification that his family can return home tomorrow,' Lewis said, and immediately regretted as a look of alarm crossed his mother's face.

He knew he shouldn't care, that he deserved his own independence now and, as Charles often reminded him, his parents couldn't do anything about it. But Lewis did care. As much as he wanted out of the village, Bledoe was still his home, and his family... Was he really ready to leave it? To leave them?

'Anyway, we're just going to tell Owain,' he said, and they continued towards the staircase.

'He's not here,' Mr Vine said, his eyes not leaving the television screen.

Lewis stopped. 'What? Since when did he leave the house in the evening?'

His mother got up from her comfortable chair. 'He's been gone for hours,' she said, and walked into small dining area just off the living room. She stood by the window, and looked out towards the dark road and the fields beyond. 'He could be anywhere.'

His mother was worried, and Lewis knew she was right to be. Owain never left the house after dark, unless he had to go into Liskeard with their dad to pick up some last minute supplies for the shop. He would spend the nights in his room listening to his tranny or reading the latest football magazines. He never visited any of his friends, not that Owain had many in Bledoe – the few he did have lived in Liskeard near their old school.

A horrible feeling came over him. In the past week

Owain had talked a lot about the Manor. Nothing concrete, just the odd comment here and there, so vague that Lewis hadn't really paid much attention to them. But now...

He shook his head. No, Owain would never go up there on his own.

'He'll be back when he's back,' Mr Vine said, finally getting up from the sofa. He passed a look of annoyance at Lewis and Charles. 'Look what you've done, worrying your mother over nothing.'

'What did I do?' Lewis asked before he could stop himself.

'You didn't go with your brother, for one thing!' his dad snapped. He glared at Charles. 'Isn't it about time you went to your gran's house? Before your mother starts worrying about you.'

'They don't worry about me,' Charles pointed out, his tone aggressive. 'They never do, 'cause I can take care of myself.'

'Can you now?'

Lewis had seen that look in his dad's eyes before. He was spoiling for a fight, casting his anger at the wrong place as usual.

Lewis stepped between his dad and Charles, looking over at his mother. 'Why don't you make mum a cuppa or something? Charles and I will go and find Owain.'

His dad turned on him. 'Who the hell are you to tell me what to do in my own house? You're leaving tomorrow, remember? You don't get to order anyone around.'

'I wasn't...' Lewis shook his head.

'George, just stop,' his mother said, moving from the window. She looked defeated by her worry. 'I'll make us all some tea.'

'To think we fought for twerps like you,' Mr Vine said. 'No respect, none of you. Thought *you* would know better.'

'Fought for us? You were a *private*, Dad, that's all, and that's only because you had no choice. Hardly a hero of the war!' Even as he spoke Lewis knew he had gone too far, as proven a second later when his dad's fist struck him in the jaw. Lewis staggered back, dazed a little.

A split second later Charles was there, pushing Mr Vine away, while Mrs Vine turned and screamed at Mr Vine for hitting their son. Lewis stood there, rubbing his jaw as the three of them shouted, none listening but all with things to say. Lewis had much to say, too, but he knew there was little point. Nobody was in the mood to listen.

He grabbed Charles by the arm and pulled him towards the front door. 'Come on, we'll find Owain ourselves.'

Charles was still shouting the odds when the front door closed behind them, while inside the house the raised voices continued unabated.

Lewis had to half-drag his friend up the short driveway and onto Caradon View. With each step he realised even more fully just how much he couldn't wait to leave Bledoe the next day.

Henry Barns had heard it all now. His family had owned the pub for over forty years; he had grown up in it, and so had his own children. And he had heard every story under the sun, not least about the old Manor up near Draynes Wood. He had even warned his own children away from the place, not that he believed half the stories told, but he knew enough... A distant memory. But this was a whole new slant on things, and that it was coming from Ray Phillips...

Henry didn't know what to make of it.

'And there's something in the woods.' Ray was slurring his words.

Henry should probably cut the man off, but who was being harmed? In a place like Bledoe everybody knew everybody, and everybody knew Ray. Some had even read all of his books, although most only the first one, and so they all recognised the tale he was drunkenly telling. Except now it was taking a new spin. Perhaps it was from one of the later books? Henry didn't know, he was one of those who only read the first book to support Ray. And he hadn't liked what he'd read. Way too familiar...

'I saw it today. A big hairy thing, like a grizzly bear, only bigger.'

Along the bar Fred laughed. 'Grizzly bears in Cornwall! You need to write that one down.'

The rest of the pub joined in the laughter, which only served to encourage Ray. Even Dr Jason Starling and Mark Cawley, the local vet, who were the furthest away from the bar, looked up from their conversation. It was not like Ray to be the centre of attention; he was the one who just liked to enjoy a quiet pint on his own, sharing the odd joke with whoever happened to sit next to him at the bar. But this was different.

This was a side of Ray that Henry had not seen since they were kids, before that terrible accident. Back then Ray had been a bright kid; funny, outgoing, just one of the boys who liked to hang out in the woods, building rope swings over the gorge. But after the accident he had changed, became withdrawn. He only had one real friend after that, despite the best efforts of Henry and the others.

To this day Henry believed it to be guilt, like Ray blamed himself. But now, seeing him like this, Henry had to wonder if perhaps Ray was simply a little cuckoo in the head.

'None of you really know what happened, what lives in Remington Manor. But I saw him, and I tried to warn you all. I wrote it all down, but none of you believed me.

And now look what's happened.' Ray's drunken gaze crossed the whole pub, and he pointed, his hand shaking.

Henry was unsure if it was due to anger or fear, or perhaps simply the drink.

'It's all your fault!' Ray hissed, melodramatically.

Pitying looks and shaking heads around the pub. Reverend Edwin 'Ted' Stone stood up from the table he shared with Ross Howard, but Henry shook his head gently, and after a searching look, Ted sat back down. Ray was losing his audience. Soon the pub was filled once again with the background chatter of many conversations. Darts resumed, and someone put a song on the jukebox. Ray still sat there at the bar, looking out at everybody, but no one paid him any heed.

Henry walked to Ray and tapped him on the shoulder. 'Perhaps you should go home, sleep it off?'

'You're kicking me out?'

Henry was stung by the look of betrayal on Ray's face. He laughed it away.

'Of course not. Since when have I ever kicked any of the old Cadets out? No, I'm just saying you need to sleep this off, stop making a fool of yourself.'

'A fool?' Ray snapped, then shook his head and looked down at the ale before him. 'Yes,' he continued, so softly that Henry had to strain to hear him. 'I'm a fool, all right, a fool for not doing something sooner. But you don't know, Henry, you just don't know.'

'Don't know what?'

Ray looked up at him, their eyes locking. Henry prided himself on being able to read people. After all, in his line of work it paid to see a mood change before it happened. And he knew that Ray was scared... No, he was *terrified*.

'I tried...' Ray swallowed. 'I tried to go back up there, to find the Vine boy, but I couldn't. There was something in the woods, a beast belonging to the Hollow Man. I couldn't go any further. Henry,' he said, grabbing Henry's arm and pulling him closer, 'the Hollow Man has Owain Vine up there at the Manor!'

It was at that precise moment, as those very words came out of Ray's mouth, loud enough to travel across the pub, that the door opened and in walked George Vine.

Lethbridge-Stewart felt a shiver shoot down his back. He glanced at Rifleman William Bishop, who sat beside him, driving the Land Rover through the dark lane which took them to Bledoe. The young rifleman didn't notice the movement, his eyes firmly fixed on the road ahead.

'One mile, sir,' he said. His accent was a strange mix of South London and something northern.

Lethbridge-Stewart's eyes flicked briefly to the signpost as the headlights brushed against it. Sure enough, Bishop was correct; they had only one mile to go before they were in Bledoe.

Lethbridge-Stewart was trying his best to recall details of the village, but he hadn't been back in almost twenty-five years, all of his adult life. The village was a distant memory, so much so in fact that even now when he thought of home his mind always went to Lancashire and to Coleshill, where he had spent most of his life when not studying or serving his National Service.

'Where to first, sir?'

That was a good question. He seemed to recall the village pub was in the centre of Bledoe and, if his memory was right, his parents had been on good terms with the people who owned it. Assuming the same family still ran it, then it seemed likely his mother would pay them a visit.

'*The Rose & Crown*,' he said, the name suddenly coming to him. 'If she's not there, then hopefully someone will have at least seen her. Bledoe is not a very large place, but we'll almost certainly need the help of the locals to find her. My own local knowledge is a little... sketchy.'

Bishop smiled politely. 'Still better than mine, sir.'

Lethbridge-Stewart had to give the lad that. He may not remember a great deal about the place, but he remembered something, and that was at least a good place to start.

The pub was not as far into the village as he remembered. They had passed a few houses on the way in, but had seen no one bar a couple of young men walking up a lane, and they'd been so caught up in their conversation that they had only stepped aside at the last minute, just quick enough to not be run over by Bishop. Other than that it seemed the village, the little they had seen of it thus far, was closed down for the day.

Lethbridge-Stewart checked his wristwatch, a present from Doris which he should probably stop wearing now he was with Sally. It was almost nine o'clock – no wonder the village was so quiet. He was reminded of his days in Coleshill, and how that village had always turned in by ten o'clock. Even the pub was shut by then, and he suspected it would be true of *The Rose & Crown*. The landlord would be calling 'time' soon.

'Hey up,' Bishop said, and nodded towards the front of the pub. 'Local bother, sir.'

Two men appeared to be scuffling outside the pub. Voices were raised, and emphatic gestures were being made, including a lot of shoving and pulling. Lethbridge-Stewart couldn't make out the words over the noise of the Land Rover, but he knew an argument when he saw one.

The Land Rover pulled up in front of the pub, and as Bishop put on the brakes, Lethbridge-Stewart jumped out to put an end to the public disturbance. He had no jurisdiction in Bledoe, really, but he doubted that there was a local police force, and as a member of the British Army he felt it was his duty to put an end to such activities.

'Now then, chaps, what appears to be the trouble?'

The two men stopped instantly, both looking at Lethbridge-Stewart in surprise. It was perfectly obvious that the younger of the two was drunk, his glasses crooked, while the other was quite sober. Bishop joined him.

'No trouble, General,' said the sober man. 'Just trying to get Ray here home before he causes himself a mischief.'

Lethbridge-Stewart smiled, realising what the scuffle really was. Two friends, one trying to be responsible while the other wanted to continue drinking and making a fool of himself. It was hard to tell if he knew either – after twenty-five years they had all grown a lot. He stepped closer to the drunk man, the one who had been named as Ray. Could it really be Raymond Phillips? If so he looked so different, drunk and haunted.

'What's your name?' he asked.

The drunk man tried to stand up straight, and gave a sloppy approximation of a salute. 'Raymond Harold Phillips, sir!'

Good Lord, it was him! Lethbridge-Stewart hadn't thought of his old childhood friend in many years, and this was not the reunion he would have expected. He smiled ruefully, remembering that *Harold* was not Raymond's middle name at all, but rather something a lot more uncommon. Oswald or something.

He looked over at Bishop. 'Rifleman, see this man gets home safely, then meet me back here.'

'Sir.' Bishop reached out for Raymond and gently guided him towards the Land Rover.

As the vehicle disappeared around the corner, the sober man reached out a hand. 'George Vine, General.'

Lethbridge-Stewart accepted the hand and shook it. He didn't recognise the name, and assumed from that,

that the Vine family must have moved into Bledoe after he had left.

'Colonel, actually, I've not quite got that far up in the world. Colonel Alistair Lethbridge-Stewart.'

Mr Vine nodded. 'Sorry, Colonel, I'm not very good at Army insignia I'm afraid. Did my National Service, of course, but never moved past private.' He looked around at the now empty lane. 'What brings you to Bledoe?'

Lethbridge-Stewart nodded at the pub. 'Why don't we talk about that over a pint?' he said, knowing full well he was on duty, but quite certain that Rifleman Bishop would not pass comment on it should he return before the pint was finished.

Besides, it had been a very long day and his holiday had been cancelled. And now he was back where he had begun, the place he had spent the first sixteen years of his life, who could deny him a quick pint?

CHAPTER SIX
Echoes of the Past

INSIDE, *THE ROSE AND CROWN* WAS YOUR TYPICAL English village pub, and was instantly familiar to Lethbridge-Stewart. He wasn't sure if that was down to the number he had been in, or if it was the result of some distant recollection. The ceiling had wooden beams, giving it a cottage look, while wooden chairs and tables littered the floor. There was a fireplace to his left, brass pots and pans hanging above it, and coal burning happily in its grate. Just right of the fireplace was a dartboard, where two highly inebriated men were attempting to play a game. Music was playing from a modern looking jukebox. Lethbridge-Stewart knew the song, and had to smile at the sentiment expressed in it: *We Gotta Get Out of this Place*.

Quite.

A few people looked up as he and Mr Vine entered, curious at the sight of a British Army officer in their village. But such curiosity didn't last long. Most of the men in the pub almost certainly had either military experience themselves, or knew people who did. Military men were ten a penny for those in their thirties.

He fancied that he recognised a few of the men, but then he was trying to recognise people, imagining how they all looked when they were kids, probably convincing himself of familiarity in the process.

The man behind the bar watched him approach,

glancing at Mr Vine with a look that asked, what's going on here then?

'What's going on here then?'

Lethbridge-Stewart smiled, but allowed Mr Vine to speak first.

'Just turned up outside. Thought they'd come to arrest Ray for a moment.'

The landlord laughed and turned to look at Lethbridge-Stewart directly. 'So, what can I do for you, Colonel? Bit late in the night for manoeuvres, isn't it?'

'The cover of darkness is often best for manoeuvres, actually, Mr…?'

'Barns, Henry Barns.'

He offered his hand and Lethbridge-Stewart shook it. The name sounded familiar, as did Lethbridge-Stewart's face it seemed, judging by the searching look in Mr Barns' eyes.

He narrowed them, and slowly opened his mouth. 'I know you, don't I? Only…' Mr Barns shook his head.

'That is very probable. I was born here, you see. Lived in… Oh, what was it called? Redrose Cottage, I believe.'

Mr Vine looked from Lethbridge-Stewart to Mr Barns. 'Up at Penhale Meadow? Hang about, that's where Ray lives. Thought his family always owned the cottage.'

'Only for the last, what, twenty-four years? They were given it just after the war by…' Mr Barns' face erupted into a huge smile. 'Well I'll be a monkey's uncle; you're Ali, aren't you? Ali Lethbridge-Stewart!'

'The very same. Although I haven't gone by Ali in a very long time.'

'Never thought I'd see you return after… Well, you know,' Mr Barns said, his eyes lowering for a moment, a look of uncomfortable sadness on his face. He stepped over to the ale pumps and began to pull.

Lethbridge-Stewart wanted to point out that he did not know, actually, that for some reason his memories of

Bledoe were vague at best. Now that he was here, in a place that seemed distantly familiar, looking at a man who he was sure he once knew, he realised how little of his first sixteen years he remembered.

When I became a man I put away childish things, he thought; never a truer word spoken. He didn't often think about his childhood. Nothing would be served by doing so. But now he was being confronted by it, he found he remembered so little of it.

'On the house,' Mr Barns said, putting a tankard of ale down before Lethbridge-Stewart.

'Many thanks.' He quaffed the ale, and wiped his mouth, letting out a breath of air. 'Ah, now that was needed. But I must ask, do I know you, Mr Barns?'

Barns looked disappointed, but shook it off. 'Well, I have put on a few pounds since the war, not to mention a bit of grey in places.' He laughed again. 'We were never really friends, but yes, I did know you. More friends with Ray and James, really, but you were always tagging along.'

Raymond Phillips he remembered, certainly more so than Henry Barns. But James... He did not recall a James at all. It didn't matter; he was not really here to take a trip down memory lane.

'Is this why you've returned? By my reckoning it must be the anniversary now.'

'Of?' Lethbridge-Stewart raised an eyebrow.

'Well, you know,' Barns said, quickly busying himself with some dirty glasses.

'I'm afraid not, no. But if you'll excuse me, I've been out and about for hours now and I do rather need to visit the gents'.'

George and Henry watched the colonel walk off to the toilets. George knew he was missing something, and judging by the look on Henry's face he was confused, too.

'Well, it's been an eventful day,' George said.

'Yes,' Henry replied, clearly distracted. 'How can he not know what anniversary it is? I mean, it's not a big one, I know, and he never returned last year which would have made more sense, but still. To come back now.'

'What anniversary is this?'

Henry swallowed. 'Haven't really thought much about it myself, really, but what with Ray earlier and now this…' He shook his head. 'When we were kids, there was this boy called James, used to pal around with me and Ray. Part of a gang, called ourselves the Bledoe Cadets. Ali was about three years younger, so he only came with us when we couldn't lose him.' Henry chuckled at the memory. 'Kids, eh? But there was an accident in, oh, '38…'

George nodded. He had heard something about the accident before, but the details were unknown to him. A boy had drowned at Golitha Falls, and Ray and… Of course, the other boy who had seen the accident was the colonel. And he was… George shook his head. Now he understood Henry's confusion.

Colonel Lethbridge-Stewart returned from the gents' and joined them once again at the bar. For a few moments they all passed out small talk, random jokes with little meaning, before Henry asked the question that was on both his and George's mind.

'So, what does bring you back home after all these years, Ali?'

Lethbridge-Stewart took another sip of his pint and said, 'My mother. She has returned here and I'm looking for her.' He went on to explain about the big pile-up on the Liskeard bypass, and her subsequent departure from the hospital. 'She's getting on a bit, and is not very well, I fear.'

'Dementia?' Henry asked, his own mother having fallen into such a few years back.

'Well, I didn't think so, but she does appear to be looking for my father.'

Henry frowned. 'Didn't he die in '45? Listed as MIA, as I recall.'

The colonel nodded. 'Yes, one of the last RAF casualties of the war, I'm afraid. Hence my concern.'

'Yes, I seem to recall talk of a breakdown after she left here. My mother was in touch with your aunty for a while.'

This appeared to surprise the colonel. 'A breakdown? I don't remember a… But that might explain why Uncle Tommy and I…' He nodded abruptly. 'So much for not taking a trip down memory lane. Very well. I had hoped she'd have visited here first, since I vaguely recalled she knew the owners. Your family,' he added, nodding at Henry.

'She did. Mum, Mrs Lethbridge-Stewart and Mrs Phillips, Ray's mum. Always met here for bridge night on Saturdays.' He smiled at the memory. 'Feels like a long time ago. But no, she's not been here today, sorry to say. I'm sure I'd recognise her. Even if I didn't, I'd notice a "stranger" in my pub.'

'Quite. Then where would she go? My recollection of the village is not very clear, unfortunately.'

The men were quiet for a moment, each of them trying to think of places to look.

'Redrose?' George finally asked. 'That's where you used to live, right? If she's confused, looking for her dead husband, makes sense she'd go "home".'

'Reckon you're onto something there,' Henry said.

Lethbridge-Stewart agreed. He finished the last of his pint. 'And here's my lift,' he said, as the pub door opened and Rifleman Bishop returned.

'Sir.' He saluted the colonel, his eyes dropping to the empty tankard in Lethbridge-Stewart's hand. The men all smiled at his look of desire. George was going to offer up a round, but the colonel beat him to the punch.

'Well, thank you for your help, gentlemen. And thank you for the ale, Mr Barns.' He turned to the rifleman. 'Bishop, you're taking me back the way you came. I assume you remember the way to Mr Phillips' cottage?'

'Of course, sir.'

'Excellent.' The colonel turned to George and Henry. 'If I have no luck there...'

'Then return here and we'll help you where we can. Cadets always look after our own.' Henry gave a fraternal smile.

Ali had been a long time gone, but once a Bledoe Cadet, always a Bledoe Cadet.

'Good, glad to hear it.' With a shake of hands, Lethbridge-Stewart and Bishop left the pub.

Once the door was closed George turned to Henry. 'Seems to be a night for missing people. Owain's not been home for hours.'

Henry couldn't help but laugh. 'Maybe Ray's right? Perhaps this so-called Hollow Man of Ray's does have him?'

George wasn't amused, but laughed it off anyway, remembering his wife at home, worrying needlessly. 'He'll return when he does. Now, how about another pint? No rush to be home tonight.'

Some distance away from *The Rose & Crown*, two young men were walking down Fore Street, the main road that passed through Bledoe. Lewis was getting worried now. He and Charles had checked everywhere in the village, their torches out. They'd even looked in the graveyard of Bledoe Parish Church, which had been empty but for an old woman. That was an unusual sight in itself; people rarely visited the graveyard at night, but it wasn't of any concern to either Lewis or Charles. Let the old dear do as she pleased; Lewis was more concerned about his brother.

They had moved on from there to the sports field, but still no Owain, and then to Bledoe School. It was hard to know where to look, since Owain was an indoors person. They were now walking back from park near the school, looking across at the fields that reached out on either side of the road. They passed by a couple of houses, most of which had all lights out.

'Still think we should try the Manor, man,' Charles said.

Lewis was beginning to agree. But there had to be somewhere else to look. Of course, as the night continued so the darkness got denser and the less likelihood there was of finding Owain in the village itself.

He sighed and stopped. 'Might be right.' Lewis shook his head. 'This isn't good, is it?'

Charles shrugged. 'So your brother is up at the Manor? What of it? Maybe he's not such a stick in the mud after all. Come on, Lew.' He punched Lewis lightly on the arm. 'It'll be fun either way, exploring the Manor in the dark. Maybe this time we'll find the Whisperer on our own.'

'If he hasn't already found Owain.'

Charles grinned at this. He put the light under his chin and opened his eyes wide, his face distorted by the sharp shadows cast by the torch. 'Spooky!'

Lewis forced a laugh. 'Okay then. To the Manor we go.'

Gordon had left him again, but this time Owain didn't feel the same emptiness as before, mostly because he could now see him. The boy, still little more than a spectral form, stood in the middle of the main hall of the Manor, directing the Yeti.

Owain continued to sit on the bottom step of the staircase and watch them. With every movement it seemed the Yeti were changing shape. They still looked much the same as when he'd first seen them by the truck, but now their legs were longer, their bodies more lithe, giving them much more dexterity. Which, he supposed, came in useful for the task they were performing.

There were putting together a pyramid made of metal. It was hollow, wires hanging down from the tip, to which they attached what seemed to be a small silver bowl.

'What is this for?' he asked, bored of just watching.

Gordon looked over at him. 'To complete the natural energy of the living entity.'

'Which means?'

Gordon was confused for a moment, then he nodded slowly. 'I am part of the ultimate sphere of reality, the unborn sphere of all phenomena. But all parts are needed and this device will bring them together.'

Owain wasn't sure what that meant, but he knew from joining with Gordon that other parts of them were returning. Them? Yes, Owain realised, he too was part of this ultimate sphere of reality; after all, he knew from their joining that Gordon was a past life of his.

He looked at the Yeti. 'And what about these?'

'Servants, soldiers, whatever I need.' Gordon laughed. 'They are not real, just robots controlled by an intelligence greater than any you have ever witnessed. But soon you shall. Soon you will experience the pure consciousness, that which is the original, natural energy of the living entity.'

'What living entity?'

Gordon spread his small arms wide. 'Everything around you. Every particle, every atom, everything that makes this universe.'

This sounded familiar to Owain. Something he had read somewhere, or maybe heard about on the wireless.

'But you're a ghost, a ghost of a little boy. What would you know of this entity?'

Gordon looked down at himself. 'Yes, I became part of the pure consciousness.'

'You mean you died?'

For a moment Gordon looked sad. 'Yes. Many times over. Died, reborn, died again. We are forever.'

Owain accepted this with ease. 'But what about the Yeti? How come they've changed?'

'Matter is malleable, subject to the ultimate sphere of reality. If you know how, you can change it.' Gordon turned back to the Yeti, all of whom were now standing by the pyramid, awaiting orders. 'It is complete, and I am too weak to join with you again.' He waved Owain over to the pyramid. 'You must sit inside the pyramid.'

Owain stood up. He had many more questions, things he wanted to understand, but one thing he did not question was Gordon. Trust was absolute or it was not trust. So he sat inside the pyramid, crossing his legs uncomfortably. A Yeti reached down and placed the metal bowl on his head.

'Close your eyes, and let your mind become one with the pure consciousness.'

Owain took a deep breath and did as he was told. A sound filled his head, a strange chanting. The vibration felt peaceful, relaxing. For the first time ever he felt nothing but contentment, a certainty that everything was as it was meant to be.

Penhale Meadow was only a ten-minute drive from *The Rose & Crown*, a road at the top of the village. They passed many homes along the way, and much more countryside to boot. There was something relaxing about driving through the village at night, Lethbridge-Stewart decided, and as they neared Redrose Cottage he felt a real sense of coming home.

It was a strange feeling to have when he considered he barely knew Bledoe. Yes, he had been born there, yes he had spent sixteen years of his life there, but that was the past now, and it was such a distant and disjointed past. He knew he should remember more; that as they drove from one end of the village to the other he should recognise the landmarks. But the church, which they drove around, could have been any old church to him, one of hundreds he'd seen in his forty years. He knew it should stir some kind of memory. His parents had always been God-fearing people, especially his mother, and they certainly would have brought him to Bledoe Parish Church almost every Sunday. But there was nothing.

The sense that he was missing something – not just any something, but great chunks of his past – was only magnified when Bishop pulled the Army Land Rover alongside Redrose Cottage. The place was alien to him; nothing sparked a memory of any kind.

He looked at the thatched cottage and shook his head.

'Are you okay, sir?'

He glanced at Bishop. 'Not especially, Rifleman. Have you ever visited a place you feel sure you should know, but can't recall a single thing about it?'

Bishop gave it some thought as the two men stepped out of the vehicle. 'Well, there was this park near my home when I was growing up; apparently I fell from the hut at the top of the slide when I was about six, but I don't remember that at all. Been back a few times, but nothing.'

'A feeling I can understand.' He stopped before the cottage. 'I was born here, yet it's like I've never been here before.'

Bishop nodded slowly. 'Traumatic childhood, sir?'

'Not that I recall. Come on, let's see if Raymond has had any visitors.'

Bishop followed him. 'Raymond, sir?'

Lethbridge-Stewart glanced back. 'How easy we fall into old habits. Mr Phillips used to be my best friend, by all accounts. At least I vaguely remember that much.'

There were no lights on, as far as Lethbridge-Stewart could see. 'Did you escort him inside?'

'Yes, sir,' Bishop said and reached for the door. He turned the doorknob and pushed. 'Not particularly security conscious in these parts.'

'I don't suppose they need to be.'

The two men entered the house, and Lethbridge-Stewart called out to Raymond. There was no answer. He flicked the light switch. They were standing in the living room, and there was Raymond, conked out on the sofa. Lethbridge-Stewart smiled, for the moment studying the man, trying to match him to the boy he vaguely recalled. Both had a head of thick black hair, a beaky nose, although the boy in Lethbridge-Stewart's memory was as thin as a rake, unlike the man sleeping before them. Not that Raymond was fat, far from it, but equally he would never be called slim.

Bishop moved around Lethbridge-Stewart and approached the small table on which sat an old Marconiphone Record Player. He hadn't seen one like that in a while; it looked almost like a suitcase, the lid open to reveal the turntable inside. A 33 was still spinning, the needle scratching in silence while it waited for someone to lift it back to its cradle. This Bishop did.

'You left music on for him?' Lethbridge-Stewart asked.

'No, sir. He was still awake when I left. Maybe the music made him sleep.' Bishop picked up the record sleeve. 'Gioachino Rossini? Would put me to sleep.'

Lethbridge-Stewart had to agree with that. 'Okay, you look around down here, see if you can find my mother. Take a look in the back garden, too. I shall look upstairs. And, Bishop?'

'Sir?'

'If you find her, don't alarm her. She's probably very confused.'

Bishop saluted casually. 'Yes, sir, no rude jokes.

Understood.'

Lethbridge-Stewart watched Bishop turn away, a slight smile on his lips. He would have to keep an eye on Rifleman Bishop; he was just the kind of soldier Lethbridge-Stewart might one day need on his team. Once this was all over, he'd speak to Hamilton, see about getting the young man transferred to his regiment.

He left the living room and found the staircase immediately. Without actually remembering, he just knew the layout of the cottage. Curious as to what he might find, he climbed the stairs.

There was very little of interest to see. A bathroom and airing cupboard and three bedrooms. The double bedroom was clearly where Raymond slept – not used much beyond that. It was too clean, too sparse. He moved on to the smaller room next to it and paused there. For the briefest of moments he remembered a glimpse of how it used to be. Toys everywhere, model planes, and a small boy sitting on a hard mattress of an old slim bed. The boy looked up from the plane and toy soldiers he was playing with, looked Lethbridge-Stewart right in the eyes.

They both smiled the same smile. It was him. It was his childhood bedroom.

He pulled away and closed the door gently, disturbed by the memory. Not by the content, since he felt a strange happiness about the place. There was another sense that came with it.

He looked down at his hands, certain they were soaked. They looked normal. He rubbed them together. Bone dry.

He turned from the single bedroom and walked a bit further down the landing to a slightly larger room. Inside was a study, books squeezed together on shelves to the point where the shelves looked ready to collapse under the weight. A desk sat at the end of the room before the window, a typewriter sitting on top of it. He walked further into the room.

Something was wrong. He walked over to the desk and without rational reason pulled it away from the wall. There, scratched into the wooden sill were two letters. 'G' and a… He wasn't sure, the letter was faded, but it looked like an 'I'. Suddenly overcome by a wave of dizziness, he sat back on the desk.

He had lived here during the war, when evacuees from London had been billeted in the countryside. The 'G' had to be his dad, Gordon, but the 'I'…? An evacuee? It was the only explanation he could think of.

He returned downstairs, troubled by unfamiliar feelings. His life had always been so certain, his mind always directed towards his future. He did not look back, never considered where he had come from. All his life experiences added up to the man he was today, everything from studying to be a math's teacher, to his National Service, to his abrupt career change afterwards; everything together had made him a colonel in the Scots Guards, had equipped him to defeat the Great Intelligence in London. But that's all the past was – had been, at least, until today: a path to the present, to the future, and a one-way path at that.

The sooner he left Bledoe the better.

'What's the time, Bishop?' he asked, just for something to distract him.

'Nearly half past ten, sir.'

'Very well. Let's take one more drive around the village, and if no luck then we'll return here. I don't think Mr Phillips will mind too much. After all, unless I'm mistaken, my mother still technically owns this cottage.'

Bishop walked towards the front door. He opened it and waited. When Lethbridge-Stewart did not move, he asked, 'And then, sir?'

'We begin a search at first light. Mr Barns said that they look after their own, so I'm sure we can count on the help of the entire village.'

'Yes, sir.'

Bishop left the cottage. For a moment longer Lethbridge-Stewart remained where he stood, his hand hovering over the light switch.

Except for the television set and the record player, he had a feeling the living room hadn't changed in twenty-four years. Every bit of furniture had once belonged to his parents. He placed a hand on the sideboard beneath the light switch and closed his eyes.

This was his home.

It took them longer to reach the Manor than usual. Lewis had never been there at night before, and by the dim light of their torches the path seemed to swerve and dip in ways he didn't remember from their trips in daytime. So focused were they on navigating, that they were only a few yards from the Manor when Lewis noticed that there seemed to be lights on; a first from what he knew.

Somebody was definitely home.

'Ergh!'

Lewis glanced back at Charles, who was shining his torch on his hand. 'What?'

'What is this?' Charles showed him the filament-like strands that had somehow attached itself to his hand. 'Some sort of cobweb?'

Lewis shrugged. 'Probably.'

'But it's so thick. Yuck!' Charles rubbed his hand against his Lee jeans. Once suitably free of the web, he joined Lewis and looked out at the Manor. 'Hang on, what's that over there?'

Lewis looked. There appeared to be someone standing by the gate. No, not someone, he realised, once the shape moved. Some kind of creature. Bigger than the average man, covered in hair. Lewis strained his eyes.

'Claws?'

'Looks like.' Charles made to move ahead. Lewis grabbed him back by the shoulders.

'What the hell are you doing?' he hissed.

'Going to investigate, what do you think? Last night in Cornwall and finally something interesting is happening.'

Lewis could hardly believe him. 'Interesting? What do you think that thing is?'

Charles shrugged. He really didn't care. 'A bear? The Whisperer?'

'You're mad. Come on, we should go and...' Lewis stopped. Twigs snapped behind them, crunched underfoot. He swallowed and looked back.

What he saw scared him more than any bear.

Two more of the beasts approached. Whatever they were, it was obvious they were quite capable of tearing Lewis and Charles apart limb by limb. That wasn't the worst of it, though.

Between them was a very familiar figure, whose eyes glowed with the same red fire as those of the two beasts.

It was his brother, Owain.

CHAPTER SEVEN
Out of the Woods

THEIR BRIEF TOUR OF BLEDOE BY MOONLIGHT HAD proven fruitless; the village would have benefited from the odd streetlamp, Lethbridge-Stewart thought. They had even searched the graveyard, but little joy was to be had there. It seemed to be empty, but there were so many nooks and crannies hidden in the darkness that such a search was almost self-defeating. It was fast approaching midnight by the time they returned to Redrose Cottage, and it was agreed that they should rest there for the night. It was unfair to return to the pub and turn Mr Barns' life upside down; he did, after all, have his own family to look after.

Bishop took one of the comfortable-looking chairs in the living room, although Lethbridge-Stewart doubted the young soldier would sleep much, while he went upstairs to sleep in the room that had once belonged to him – so many years ago.

Sleep was elusive; he was far too distracted by the huge gap in his memory. He remembered leaving Bledoe late-1945; he remembered how he and his mother had gone to live with her sister and brother-in-law. They had remained there for a couple of years, before finally settling in Coleshill, although Lethbridge-Stewart had never spent a lot of time there, too busy studying in college. But before '45 what did he recall? The death of his father early in the year, the letter his mother had received informing her that Gordon Lethbridge-Stewart was missing in action, believed dead. Neither he nor his mother had believed it, but as the months passed the reality settled in, especially after the memorial, which had seen his maternal and paternal families descend on the village. It had all led his mother to the decision to leave Bledoe, in an attempt to escape all the pain and loss she associated with the village.

But what of before? He had lived in this cottage for sixteen years, which meant he had gone to school in both Bledoe and nearby Liskeard. He had a life in Bledoe, sixteen years of memories, of experiences, of friendships... And yet he could recall almost nothing of them. Mr Barns mentioned something about tagging along, that Lethbridge-Stewart had not been part of the gang that included Barns, Raymond and some boy called James. So he must have had his own friends, surely?

Lethbridge-Stewart sat up. No, sleep was not going to be had. He checked his wristwatch. Half-past midnight. He really should call HQ, check in and find out the latest about Arnold.

He reached for his uniform jacket, reminding himself to go and pick up some fatigues from the nearest Army base tomorrow – he had the distinct impression he would be out in the field for a while, and his colonel's uniform did not suit such field work. Besides which, despite the rough material, he always felt more comfortable in fatigues.

He took the Land Rover back to the pub, leaving Bishop at Redrose to keep an eye on things. The lights were out at *The Rose & Crown*, so he did not knock the door. He supposed they would have their own telephone, but that didn't matter; he wasn't here to disturb the Barns'. There was a red phone box outside the pub. No doubt the only one in the village.

He had tried contacting the local Green Jackets via

walky-talky earlier, while he and Bishop had been driving around the village, but there was no signal in Bledoe. Too far from the nearest radio transmitter, no doubt. So the phone was the only alternative left to him.

He inserted a coin and pressed a button. It took a few moments for him to be put through to the nearest operator in Liskeard, and she seemed a little put out by being disturbed so late at night. He doubted there were many phone calls made at such a time usually. He asked to be put through to the London Regiment Office, and waited once more while she connected him.

There was no one on duty connected to the Arnold case: Major Douglas had found a bunk to sleep on, and neither Corporals Wright nor Bell were there. The sergeant asked if he wanted her to disturb Major Douglas, but Lethbridge-Stewart said no. Dougie had been working hard all day, and had many long days ahead of him. He should enjoy all the sleep he could get. But there was one person he didn't mind disturbing, even at this hour.

'Alistair, where have you been?' Sally asked as soon as she picked up the receiver. He felt a twinge of guilt at the concern in her voice.

'Did I wake you?'

'Of course not,' she replied, but the following yawn belied her denial.

'Sorry,' Lethbridge-Stewart said. 'I've been following a lead in a little village a few miles out of Liskeard.'

'It's fine. I've been waiting for you to call for hours.'

'Any sign of Arnold?'

'Well, no,' Sally said, a little put out by the officious tone of his voice.

He couldn't blame her. He had woken her and immediately turned to work. He shook his head, frustrated, and listened as she relayed the facts.

'The Green Jackets and local police force searched

Liskeard, but there was no sign of him. Inquiries are still being made, but nothing strange has been reported in the town, so it seems likely he's moved beyond Liskeard now.'

Then where would he have gone? Lethbridge-Stewart looked out through the Perspex windows of the phone box at the field beyond. There were many villages around Liskeard that Arnold could have gone to, but Lethbridge-Stewart didn't bother telling Sally to arrange a search. He felt certain that Arnold was heading this way.

He didn't know the connection between Arnold and his mother, but the odds of both of them coming to Liskeard at the same time was too high for him to write off as coincidence. Not that Lethbridge-Stewart could really tell Sally this; he doubted even she would believe him. He would talk to Hamilton in the morning.

'Dougie's really enjoying his new administrative role,' Sally offered to fill the silence while he thought. She was always good at that. 'We may get to Brighton after all,' she added.

'That would be nice.'

'Say it once more with feeling.'

'Sorry, distracted.'

'Did you know Arnold well?' Sally asked, not missing a beat.

'Barely at all, met him during the London Event. He seemed to be a good man. Dependable, knew his stuff. Captain Knight spoke highly of him. But…'

Lethbridge-Stewart couldn't blame the dead staff sergeant, really, but he did wonder just for how long Arnold had been an agent of the Great Intelligence. Perhaps they would never really know.

'Any idea why he'd go to Cornwall? We've been discussing that here, and there's the old Hope Cove Bunker in Devon that…'

'We?'

'Me and Dougie.'

'I see.' Lethbridge-Stewart should have expected that; Dougie and Sally had been friends for a long time, and both knew something of the London Event. It was only natural that they would speculate.

He sighed, suddenly feeling like he shouldn't even be in Bledoe. He should have insisted on taking his leave as planned. He preferred to leave the past where it belonged, behind him. This felt too much like running backwards.

They ran, heading deeper into the wood. Lewis knew the wood quite well, certainly better than Charles, but even he had to admit he was losing track of their position. Draynes Wood wasn't immense, but at night-time it seemed to go on forever.

They crouched down, trying to hide behind a large tree.

Charles looked at him, sweat on his forehead, a big smile plastered across his face. 'What are those things?' he asked.

It was the first time they had a chance to talk, other than panted instructions as they ran. Lewis poked his head around the tree and listened. No sign of them.

'I've seen them before,' he replied. 'In a book. Some expedition in the Himalayas in the '30s... Owain used to love all that kind of stuff. I think they're abominable snowmen. They look the same, even down to the...' Lewis stopped, the image of Owain rushing to the front of his mind. 'What has happened to Owain?' He shook his head.

'Seemed to be controlling them.'

'What? My brother? Come on, Charles, you saw what I saw. His eyes... That thing on his head!'

'Yeah, some kind of metal hat.' Charles slumped down on the damp earth. 'This is mad,' he said, smiling again.

'What are you so happy about?'

Charles waved his arms around. 'All this. We're in the woods being chased by... what did you call them?'

'Abominable snowmen.'

Charles frowned. 'Snowmen in Cornwall? In March? Abominable ones at that!' He laughed suddenly. 'Tell me you're not having fun? That this isn't more exciting than anything you've ever experienced?'

Lewis couldn't believe what he was hearing. This was not putting it to 'the man', this wasn't stirring up a revolution; this was something else entirely. This was dangerous.

He was about to give his forceful answer, but the sound of movement nearby stopped him. He looked around the tree. In the distance three dark shapes were approaching. No sign of Owain this time, though.

'Come on, we need to keep moving.'

'Yeah,' Charles agreed, standing. 'Let's reach some kind of high ground, go on the offensive.'

Charles set off at a run. Lewis remained where he was for a moment. What was Charles on about? They couldn't fight abominable snowmen. They were just two boys and those things were... He swallowed. Charles was mad, and was going to get them both killed.

Lewis closed his eyes for a minute, once again seeing his brother advancing on them by the Manor, eyes glowing. He swallowed. This was wrong; both of them should have been home, safe, asleep.

'You really should go and sleep,' Lethbridge-Stewart said. He and Sally had talked a little about their intended holiday, anything to distract his mind from what was going on, but he could tell that Sally was in desperate need of sleep. She tended to cackle a lot when too tired, laughing at things which were barely pithy.

It was bad enough that his private and professional lives were colliding; he didn't wish to compound things further by bringing Sally into whatever was going on in Bledoe.

'When you sleep, so will I.'

He looked around the cramped telephone box. 'Unfortunately I don't think this thing is made for sleeping in. I will need to drive back to Redrose Cottage before I manage to get any sleep.'

'Redrose Cottage? Sounds lovely.'

'Yes, it's my...' He stopped himself. He was about to call it his home, but that wasn't right. No matter how much the cottage felt like his home, he was an intruder here. A man alone. He was the forgotten son of Bledoe, and he preferred to keep it that way. He did not belong here. But until he solved the mystery of his memory and his mother's return, he knew he was stuck here. '...It's where I've been put up for the night.'

'You work yourself too hard, Alistair, I keep telling you this.'

'Yes, you do, but I have a job to do, and I intend to do it. You knew my career comes first, you've always known that, Sally. Ever since Dougie introduced us. I never kept it a secret.'

'No, you didn't.' He could hear her shaking her head on the other end of the line. 'What is this lead?' Sally asked abruptly.

Lethbridge-Stewart smiled. She never could let something go, and in this instance it served him well. Gave him a reason to switch back to official mode.

'I'm afraid it's need-to-know, Corporal. Please advise General Hamilton of my position and tell him I shall contact him in the morning and fully brief him on developments.'

'Alistair, I...' She stopped. 'Yes, sir,' Corporal Wright said, and the phone went dead.

He remained there, the receiver in his hand, pressed against his ear. The dialling tone continued for a few moments before the voice of the operator broke in.

'Is there somewhere else I can connect you to?' she asked, tired but respectful now she knew he was a military man.

Lethbridge-Stewart wondered how much of the conversation she had listened in on. Too much probably. Tomorrow he would need to find a signal for the RT; he couldn't report to Hamilton over an open phone line.

'No, thank you,' he said and put the phone down.

He pushed open the door of the phone box, never as easy as it should have been, and stepped out into the fresh air. It was only as the air hit him that he realised that the phone box had stunk of cigarette smoke. He had never been one to smoke, and didn't much care for the smell, although he found himself getting used to it as more and more people took up the disgusting habit. Soon everywhere would be clogged up with the fug of cigarette smoke. Including any home he set up with Sally, as she was a habitual smoker herself.

What a glorious world, he considered, glad that for now at least he was in the clear air. He fully unwound the window of the Land Rover as he set off back to Redrose Cottage, enjoying the cold breeze on his face.

Lewis shivered and looked up at the greying clouds in the dark sky. The weather was about to turn. He could smell the rain coming. He'd lost track of Charles a little while ago. More of the snowmen had come at them, and without even checking, Charles had hared off, leaving Lewis with no choice but to continue on his own.

He had found his way to the gorge. It was a bit too open, but if he could cross it then he might have been able to put some distance between him and the pursuing beasts.

He looked around. If he remembered correctly… Yes, over there he saw the little rope swing that he and Owain had built a few summers ago.

Lewis walked over to it, his eyes continuously roaming the spaces between the trees. The first drop of rain fell. He glanced up. It was soon going to get worse, and he'd left his parka at home. If he didn't get out of the wood soon, he was going to get soaked. Although if the rope swing didn't hold… well, a bit of rain would be the least of his problems.

For a moment he froze, his hand barely inches from the rope. Owain. He had to find his brother, save him from whatever trouble he'd found himself in. Charles said Owain was controlling the snowmen but that was insane. His brother – behind this? No. He didn't know what was going on, but he knew his brother.

Lewis unwrapped the rope from around the tree trunk and pulled on the stick fastened at the end of the swing. It seemed strong enough.

Just then he heard the crunching of twigs. He looked back. Abominable snowmen closing in. Lewis smiled, feigning a bravery he was far from feeling.

'Bye, fellas,' he said and swung.

He hadn't even reached halfway across the gorge when one of the snowmen lifted what appeared to be some kind of gun, and fired.

Lewis wasn't quite sure what he expected to come out of the gun – from its fantastical appearance, maybe a death ray of some sort – but it certainly wasn't a type of web.

The sticky substance hit him and his fingers lost their hold.

His limbs freezing as the web wrapped itself around him, Lewis could do nothing but fall helpless into the gorge below, and in those last moments his mind went to his brother, to his parents.

He should never have said he was going to leave them.

He knew she wasn't there before he even woke. It was an odd feeling, but one he had honed after almost twenty years of marriage. George lifted himself onto his elbow and looked at the empty space left by Shirley, the sheet still creased in the shape of her. He sighed and listened to the rain hitting the bedroom window.

He had been a little drunk when he returned home, only to find his wife still sitting at the dining table, looking out to the window. Neither of the twins had returned, and he reminded her once again that they were almost eighteen and had to take care of themselves. It was time their mother stopped worrying; was she going to worry every day after they moved out? Which, for Lewis, was likely to be the next day.

What followed was an argument about how George never showed the twins enough affection, and how their family was falling apart and he didn't even care. Of course he cared, but he showed it in his own way. Shirley wasn't there when he and Owain did their weekly rounds into Liskeard, she knew nothing of their quiet pints in the beer garden, neither did she know about the long discussions he and Lewis had about life in London and the impact The Beatles had, and how both of them wanted to one day visit India and meet some of those Buddhists who Lennon talked so much about.

Instead of telling her this – after all if she didn't know how he felt by now, after the trouble they'd gone through to even have children, then there was no point explaining it to her – he had turned on the television to watch a snooker match, something that he found relaxing now that he had a colour television and could actually follow the game properly. After half a dozen frames, the argument forgotten, he had gone up the stairs to bed.

He sat up in the darkness. Something hard was

caught in his chest, a deep stabbing pain. For a moment he thought he was about to have a stroke, brought on by too many cigarettes and alcohol, but the pain passed. He looked around.

The room felt empty all of a sudden, the silence deafening. Before he knew he was going to do so, he'd slipped his feet into his slippers and crossed the landing to Lewis' room.

There he stood, looking in at the empty bed, feeling tears fall down his face.

It was unusual for the boys to be joined by the girls, but Mrs Fleming had insisted on bringing her daughters with them for the picnic along the River Fowey. Young Ali didn't mind, as it meant he was not the youngest for a change, and didn't have to feel like Raymond and James were leaving him out. While the parents continued to chat some distance away, the children went to a relatively narrow part of the river. James and Raymond decided it would be fun to impress the girls by jumping the four-foot wide gap.

James, being the tallest and the fastest, bravely volunteered to go first.

'Come on, Jim!' Raymond shouted, and pretended to fire an imaginary starting gun.

Making sure Jemima was watching, James took a short run up and comfortably reached the other side, shouting 'easy-peasy' as he landed. Raymond soon joined him. Next up it was Ali, who, at only seven, was still somewhat short and almost certainly would never make the jump. But Jemima and Joy were watching so he knew he had no choice.

'Come on, Ali! You can do it!'

Ali looked at James on the other side of the bank. The older boy urged him on, and not wanting to disappoint him, Ali took his run at the river. His short legs worked against him and he hit the edge of the bank. He flapped his outstretched arms in a circular motion, trying to keep himself upright. But he only succeeded in making matters worse when his right foot slipped on the wet mud and he collapsed head-first into the freezing water…

Lethbridge-Stewart awoke, gasping to fill his lungs with air, before his mind took over and he realised he was lying on the bed in his old bedroom. It was still dark, the cottage quiet.

He remained sitting there for a while, recalling the events of the dream. It was his first fully formed memory of the James he had heard about. He closed his eyes, picturing James' face. The eyes, the smile… It was all very familiar. But still Lethbridge-Stewart couldn't quite work out how.

He laid back down. Perhaps he would learn more if he continued to sleep? If not, then he would have some questions for Raymond in the morning.

Owain sat within the pyramid. His eyes were closed, his legs crossed with his hands resting on his knees, his thumbs and forefingers touching together gently. A meditative asana known as *the lotus*. Gordon watched him. Owain was almost ready. Gordon could no longer leave the Manor; to do so was to risk dissolution, and he could not risk that, not when he was so close. So close to being restored, to becoming that which he had once been.

He could no longer feel the trace within Albert, although he knew it was there, and neither could he feel Mary. Both were close though; he had felt that much before they had vanished from his mind.

It was fitting that it had been Owain who had awoken him once more, who had finally given him the strength needed to bring himself together. This time he would not make the same mistakes that he had made with Gordon. He had thought much about the mistakes…

Thought! What else could he do? He could whisper, urge people on, but that was all. He could no longer affect matter. He checked himself. That was true once. Not now Owain had come to the Manor.

Now Owain was ready. No more need to risk joining and damaging the entity; now he could control Owain from afar, as he had done with so many others over the centuries.

'Owain,' he said, still using the voice and form of Gordon Lethbridge-Stewart. 'Return to Bledoe, be my eyes and ears. Find Albert and Mary, bring them to me. Make us whole once more.'

Owain removed himself from the pyramid and smiled at Gordon. 'Of course I will,' he said, and turned to leave.

CHAPTER EIGHT
Looking Back

ON THE SURFACE IT LOOKED LIKE A NORMAL DAY IN Bledoe. The rain had died down shortly after sunrise, leaving dew over the village, a light refreshing fog in the chilly spring air. Parents rose early, getting themselves ready for a day of work before rousing the children and preparing them for school. The village post office opened as usual, although it was Mrs Vine who greeted the customers and not Mr Vine, an inconsistency that Mrs Vine chose not to discuss.

All across Bledoe, the villagers continued about their business, most unaware of the meeting taking place in *The Rose & Crown*.

Lethbridge-Stewart had expected more people to turn up, until Mr Barns – *Henry*, he reminded himself; after all they were friends, or at least had been many years ago – explained that Bledoe was not so large that they needed to disturb the entire village at this point. Before she left, Henry's wife, Jemima, had prepared them all tea and bacon sandwiches. She'd be back later to 'feed the troops', after she had dropped their teenage children to Liskeard Grammar School. The 'troops' in this case were Rifleman Bishop, George Vine and his son Owain, and Raymond, who sat at a nearby table nursing a hangover and drinking black coffee. The rest of them were gathered around another table, a map of Bledoe laid out before them. Lethbridge-Stewart was happily letting Henry organise the first phase of the search, since he knew the village better.

'We can easily break up the search into three main areas. If Ali and Ray take the area around Penhale Meadow and Well Lane, George and Owain can take Trethevy Close across to Diggory's Field. Bishop and I will cover west of Tremar Lane all the way down to Humphrey's Lane. That leaves the sport's field, but I can't see any reason Mrs Lethbridge-Stewart would head there. Can you, Ali?'

Lethbridge-Stewart had removed his uniform jacket and was now in his slacks and shirt; even his tie had been removed and rolled up inside his cap. Upon entering the pub an hour earlier he'd realised that he wasn't in Bledoe in an official capacity, despite what he had told Sally last night, and had removed as much of his uniform as he could, just to show the men gathered that he was one of them. As such he accepted the informality in Henry's address, although he wasn't sure he'd get used to his childhood name again.

'No reason that comes to mind, no. She's an old woman, and is probably very confused, but I can't imagine any reason she would have for visiting a sport's field.' Lethbridge-Stewart smiled sardonically. 'Mind you, I can't see why she'd be anywhere else in Bledoe, either.'

'No, and I've been thinking about the places our parents used to frequent back in the day. Ray,' Henry called, 'what about you? Your mother and Ali's were best friends; do you remember what they liked to do together?'

Ray looked up from his coffee. He looked terrible. According to Henry, Ray was not a man known for getting drunk and had, last night, drunk way more than his usual limit. It showed. Lethbridge-Stewart felt sympathy for the man – it must have been a shock to wake up feeling worse than usual and then be confronted with a man he had not seen in twenty-four years.

Ray had certainly taken a while to adjust to the presence of the two men in his house. Watching the man behave in such an awkward fashion only served to remind Lethbridge-Stewart how much of an outsider he really was; he could barely marry that with the fact that they had once been friends. He could not wait to get out of the cottage and back to the pub, a place that he always felt at home, no matter where the pub was.

It was probably a good thing that Henry had put him and Ray together, since it would give the two men a chance to talk properly.

'Nothing comes to mind,' Ray said, in answer to Henry's question. 'There wasn't much to do in the village back then, not for two young mothers especially. They'd take us over to Draynes Wood or down to Venslooe Hill, used to like visiting Higher Tremarcoombe...' He shook his head. 'Other than that, what else could they do? They had children to raise, husbands to keep.'

A memory flashed to the forefront of Lethbridge-Stewart's mind. Three boys this time: Ray, James and, he assumed, Henry. He was with them, three years younger and tagging along as always. They were out on the fields, playing around a stone structure that looked like a poor man's Stonehenge.

'Redgate Smithy?' he asked looking at Higher Tremarcoombe on the map.

Ray smiled at that. 'Yes, over at Trethevy Quoit.' He got up to join them at the table.

'It rings a vague bell,' Lethbridge-Stewart admitted. 'I have a distinct memory of you and I up there, Ray,' he continued. 'Early '40s, I think.' He shook his head. 'But before that...? I don't know.'

'Simpler times, Alistair,' Ray said.

'Always enjoyed it up there,' Henry said, joining in with a wistful smile. 'The Cadets enjoyed a good kick-about in the stone circle, until the smugglers ruined it.' He chuckled. 'Those were the days. Used to take my kids up there, too.'

For a moment the men fell into small talk, discussing the good times they had at Redgate Smithy and further afield at the Pengriffen Fogou, back when they didn't need television to distract them, back when children knew how to enjoy themselves outside. It was a skill the parents continued to try to teach their kids in Bledoe, but Henry admitted that it was a losing battle. Television was becoming too popular, especially now that it was colour, as was the fast life of London. A dark look passed between George and his son.

Ever since they had arrived at the pub Lethbridge-Stewart found himself unable to shake the feeling that he knew Owain. Of course that was not possible. The boy was no more than eighteen, had lived his entire life in Bledoe… Yet there was something very familiar about him, and every time Lethbridge-Stewart caught Owain's eyes there seemed to be a flicker of recognition in them. Like when Owain had first walked in to the pub; for the briefest moment the young man had faltered, looking like he was about to say something. Lethbridge-Stewart hadn't a chance to question this, and even now tried his best to dismiss it.

They clearly did not know each other.

He looked around the men in the pub with him. For the first time, Lethbridge-Stewart felt like he was talking with old friends, which indeed he was. Perhaps the feeling of intruding would pass too? He hoped so. These men seemed to be good people, and he'd like to call them friends again. It would make a nice change to have civilian friends, and certainly Sally would approve. She was always complaining that the only real friend he had was Dougie, and everybody else he called friends were barely acquaintances, colleagues if anything, met during his military career. He never told her that he agreed; that would be giving just too much ground.

'Okay then,' Henry said, once the reminiscences had died down. 'We'll look on foot. Won't take us more than a few hours, I expect, and if we have no luck, then we'll expand our search to include areas beyond Bledoe.' He looked at Lethbridge-Stewart, and offered a smile. 'May even get to revisit Redgate. Have a kick-about for old time's sake?'

'Under the circumstances, let's hope I don't end up there,' Lethbridge-Stewart replied. The further they expanded their search, the less likely it was that they'd find his mother. 'Besides, more of a rugger man these days.'

Henry grinned and slapped Lethbridge-Stewart on the back. 'Me too! Got the figure for it,' he added, patting his belly.

Lethbridge-Stewart couldn't help the laugh that erupted out his mouth.

Owain was puzzled. He knew things were changing – they had been since he first awoke Gordon over a week ago – but he hadn't expected to be confronted with a search for an old woman when he returned from the Manor.

'Why are we doing this?' he asked, once they had all spread out to search the agreed sections.

'Because Mrs Lethbridge-Stewart used to live here, which makes her one of us,' his dad replied. They glanced up and down the road, and crossed. 'And never mind that. Where were you last night? You had your mother beside herself.'

Owain hadn't really spoken to his mother since he'd come back. The house had been quiet, his parents still asleep, which was good as he didn't wish to be questioned. He hadn't realised how tired he was until he stripped off his soaking clothes and stood in his bedroom, cold, hungry and tired. He didn't make it back downstairs to grab a snack; instead he'd fallen onto his bed and was out cold within minutes. He was still in the same position, lying on top of his bed covers in only his underpants, when his father had looked in around 7am.

Since then both his mother and father had asked him his whereabouts, but he hadn't responded, simply put his pyjamas on and ran himself a nice hot bath while his mother prepared him breakfast. There was an atmosphere between his parents, the result of another argument. From the little he could work out it seemed Lewis hadn't returned home either, something for which his dad was being blamed.

Owain had barely managed to finish his cereal before his dad rushed him into his coat and out of the house. For a long time they walked in silence, except for a comment from his dad about why Owain was wearing Lewis' grey thin-rimmed Fedora. Owain simply said there was no real reason, but really it kept hidden the metal cap that served to keep him connected to Gordon up at the Manor.

It was only now, as they turned off Fore Street and onto the lane which led up towards Diggory's Field, that Owain realised he was the same height as his dad. Around six-foot. Unlike his dad though, Owain and Lewis both had fair hair, something they must have inherited from their mother's side of the family, but both had their dad's deep brown eyes. Owain still had a few more years of growth left, and he hoped to become taller than his dad. He took an odd moment of pleasure in that knowledge for reasons he couldn't put his finger on.

'Were you at the Manor?' his dad asked rather abruptly.

Owain forced a laugh. 'What makes you say that?'

'Ray thinks he saw you there.'

Owain shrugged. 'Maybe I was then.'

His dad raised an eyebrow and shook his head. 'Why were you up there? Wasn't the best night.'

'Doesn't matter why.'

'With the Connolly girl? What's her name? Karen?'

Owain chose not to answer that. He couldn't tell his dad why he'd been up at the Manor, so if his dad chose to believe he'd taken a girl up there... well, so much the better.

'Unless you're one of them?'

Owain glanced at his dad. 'One of what?'

'You know, *them*.'

Owain couldn't help but feel offended by the insinuation. 'No, I'm not.'

'Well, you've never had a girlfriend, and I don't think I can remember you ever even showing an interest in a girl. Lewis has had a few over the years, but not you.' His dad pulled out a packet of cigarettes. 'No boy of mine is going to be a woofter,' he said, putting a cigarette in his mouth.

'I'm not!' Owain snapped, pulling the cigarette from his dad's mouth and inserting it into his own. 'Give me a light.'

His dad sparked a match and lit the cigarette, picking out another for himself.

'Good, didn't think so. But people do start talking, so maybe you need to call in on Karen Connolly. We're passing her house soon.'

'She's probably out anyway. Hear she got a job over in Liskeard.'

His dad eyed him for a second. Owain puffed on the cigarette and ignored the lingering accusation.

'What brought Mrs Lethbridge-Stewart back?' Owain asked. 'Never heard of her before.'

'Appears to have returned here looking for her dead husband. Poor dear thinks he's waiting for her here, or something.'

'Her husband?'

'Yes, they used to own Redrose Cottage, but gave it to Ray's family shortly after Mary's husband died back in '45.'

'Mary?'

'That's her name. Mary Lethbridge-Stewart.'

Owain was a bit reticent to ask the next question, because he felt sure he knew the answer, but ask he did. 'What was her husband's name?'

'Gordon,' his dad answered. 'Wing Commander Gordon Lethbridge-Stewart of the Royal Air Force, believed to have died near the end of the last war. From what I've been told, the Phillips used to live over at…'

Owain didn't hear another word his dad said. His mind had returned to the last conversation he'd had at the Manor. About how Mary was lost to them.

No wonder Gordon wanted her to return; she used to be his wife!

Ray couldn't imagine how it must have felt for Alistair to return after so long. The two men now stood before a row of white crosses in the graveyard of Bledoe Parish Church. They had been on the way to Kilmar Way when Alistair decided he wanted to cut through the graveyard, just in case his mother had returned now the sun was up.

The cross before them read:

Gordon Conall Lethbridge-Stewart
1902-1945

It was merely a memorial, for there had been no body to bury.

On the way they had discussed why Mrs Lethbridge-Stewart would return to look for her dead husband, and Alistair had wondered if perhaps his father had returned after all these years; if perhaps he had not been killed during the final days of the war after all? Ray had a fertile imagination and had to admit that it was not unknown for such things to happen, but surely if Wing Commander Lethbridge-Stewart had returned then someone would have seen him; after all, Bledoe was not so large.

But then again so many strange things happened in Bledoe that most people were either unaware of or ignored. He wanted to tell Alistair about some of them, get his view on them, but he wasn't sure how to start the conversation. So many years he had been on his own, without anybody to discuss things, yet Alistair had been there back in the late '30s, he had seen what had happened up at Draynes Wood. If anybody would understand it surely would have been Alistair, especially after what had happened with James.

Ray glanced at Alistair. Twenty-four years was a long time, but that time had stood Alistair well. He looked healthy and strong, not even a hint of grey in his black hair and moustache. His eyes were as sharp as ever, watching and observing everything. There was a lot going on behind his impassive face.

Ray had never expected Alistair to take up military service; he always remembered as a boy Alistair was never enamoured by the stories his father told him of life in the RAF, and after his death... If anything Alistair had turned against the military even more. Of course Alistair had not remained in Bledoe for much longer after his father's death, and other than a few letters at the start Ray had never heard from him again. Who was to say what had happened to Alistair in the last twenty-four years?

Not Ray, that was certain.

As witnessed by the many white crosses, a lot of good men had never returned to Bledoe after the last war. The country had been financially crippled after putting so much into the war effort, and for what? World peace? There was no such thing. Ray imagined there never would be.

He could never blame young Alistair for being so angry with the military and the war, and now he couldn't imagine what must have changed for him to end up as a colonel in the British Army.

Without another word, Alistair moved away from his father's memorial and Ray followed.

Lethbridge-Stewart looked down at his shoes as they squelched in the mud underfoot. He would definitely need to see about getting some fatigues after this initial search was complete. The weather, although it was no longer raining, didn't look like it was going to improve much past cloudy and damp. And there were plenty of fields and meadows about. Shoes were no good; he needed his heavy boots.

He was thankful to Henry for the loan of the coat he now wore; it was a little weather beaten, but serviceable.

He and Ray were now walking through the fields behind Penhale Meadow. So many places his mother could be hiding. They had already knocked on a few houses, but no one had witnessed a strange old woman about. He and Ray had searched the gardens of those who were not at home, and still nothing.

They were nearing Redrose Cottage. Another search of that house was probably needed, Lethbridge-Stewart decided.

'So, what is it you do now, erm, Ray?' he asked, feeling oddly uncomfortable with the familiarity.

'I'm an author, at least I was. Haven't written anything in a while.'

'I see. Do you use a pen-name?'

Ray shook his head. 'Well, no, but I doubt you would have read my books, can't imagine ghost stories are your thing after what happened at the gorge.'

'It was a long time ago,' Lethbridge-Stewart said.

Whatever had happened at the gorge was not a memory he had access to. Of course he wanted to know more, but right now was not the time.

Ray looked at him for a moment, clearly trying to work something out. For the life of him Lethbridge-Stewart didn't know what. He found it very hard to read Ray. The man was, to use the obvious pun, a closed book. He kept himself guarded, casting Lethbridge-Stewart the odd furtive look when he thought he wasn't being watched. Something was definitely on his mind.

'What is it, man?' Lethbridge-Stewart snapped, stopping in his tracks. He couldn't stand the scrutiny, especially when he didn't understand the cause. 'You obviously have something you wish to talk about.'

'Well,' Ray began, then stopped. He looked around the field, awkward. 'You're here, now, after all this time and I...' He shook his head. 'I have to confess that I am at a loss to explain why you never returned. A couple of letters and that was it. We promised to keep in touch, remember, that we'd remain friends. We owed it to...'

Ray looked away, clearly distressed about something.

Lethbridge-Stewart wasn't sure what to say.

'What reason would I have to return?'

'We were friends, Al. What we went through... One would think that would be enough of a reason.'

Ray carried on walking, leaving Lethbridge-Stewart to watch his departing back.

How could he explain to Ray that he didn't remember whatever it was they 'went through'? He had vague recollections of a childhood life in Bledoe, but mostly it involved him watching the older boys play, never quite being a part of it. He shook his head and caught up with Ray.

'I'm sorry, but my memory of Bledoe is quite vague. As you said, it was all a long time ago.'

Ray glanced at him and sighed. 'No, it is I who should

apologise. I suppose it is harder for me to forget everything since I never left here. Thirty-one years I've lived with the constant reminders of what happened up at the Manor.'

'The Manor?'

'You really do not remember? The accident at the gorge?'

Lethbridge-Stewart searched himself. 'I recall a picnic in the woods, playing by the river, but an accident? I'm afraid not. I also recall someone called James, but I see he didn't remain here, unlike you and Henry.'

'You recall *someone* called James?' A dark cloud passed over Ray's face. 'How can you forget…? But you have, haven't you? You've forgotten him.'

'I'm afraid so,' Lethbridge-Stewart said, not much caring for the look of disbelief on Ray's face. James was clearly important to their past, but other than that dream last night, Lethbridge-Stewart could recall nothing about him. 'Where did James go?'

'He never left Bledoe,' Ray said softly.

Lethbridge-Stewart cleared his throat. He wasn't entirely sure he wished to have this conversation any more. He couldn't explain it, but he felt as though to do so would open up a door to a very dark place. One he did not wish to enter. Ray knew what was in that place; he had clearly seen and lived with it for a long time. But for whatever reasons, Lethbridge-Stewart had forgotten it.

Perhaps it was best forgotten.

'Tell me about these ghost stories of yours,' he said, abruptly changing the topic.

For a moment Ray said nothing.

'Very well. They're mostly based on what we experienced back in the late '30s. You must remember, up in Draynes Wood there's a Manor house, and as kids we decided to visit there…'

*

Shirley Vine was finding it hard to keep herself occupied. George had insisted she take care of the post office while he helped to search for the missing old woman, taking Owain with him, but distracting her mind was not so easy as that.

First there was Owain, coming in at God knows what time, and barely an explanation given. Then there was Lewis, who went out to look for Owain with Charles and had still not returned. How was she supposed to focus on the usual pointless conversations the locals had to offer when one of her children was still missing?

Never mind some old woman; George should be out looking for Lewis! Especially as it was his fault that Lewis had failed to come home. Of course her husband had given the boys hidings before, but not since they were children; the twins had grown out of that, and there was no excuse for George punching Lewis like he had. That was unforgiveable.

The bell rang as the door of the post office opened. She looked up from the tins she was re-arranging and saw Mr Watts entering. He looked a lot like Charles: rough features, a face not used to smiling.

'Is my boy with your son still?'

Shirley was caught off guard by the abruptness of his question. Not even a polite hello!

'I imagine so, but don't ask me where. They left here late last night and no one has seen them since.' She stood up. 'I'd hoped Lewis was at your house.'

'No, he's not. That bloody boy. Never does anything he's told. Well, this will learn him.' Mr Watts reached into his jacket and pulled out a slip of paper. 'This is a ticket for the train back to London, and here,' he pulled out some coins from his trouser pocket and handed them over to her. 'Should be enough for a taxi back to Liskeard. Tell him I don't have time to wait for him. I've a job to return to.'

With that Mr Watts turned and left the post office.

For a moment Shirley stood there looking at the ticket and coins in her hands. She shook her head. Lewis was supposed to be with Charles, safe at his gran's house, not…

She rushed out of the post office and up to the Watts' Morris Minor. It was obvious that Mr Watts was not impressed by her banging on the door window. He wound it down.

'What now?'

'Can you pop by *The Rose & Crown* on the way out of the village? George is there, tell him that Charles hasn't returned.'

Mr Watts checked his wristwatch. 'I really don't have time for that. Why don't you?'

Shirley was about to open her mouth, not that she really had an answer, when Mrs Watts leaned over and patted her husband's arm.

'It'll only take a few minutes, Richard.'

Mr Watts wasn't convinced. He cleared his throat loudly, gave Shirley the dirtiest look she had ever seen and shook his head.

'Okay then!' he snapped. 'We'll do that, after all it's not like I haven't got better things to do than run around after that no good skinny little git of mine.'

Thinking – hoping – that Mary may have returned of her own accord, they decided to double-check Redrose. As Ray opened the door to the cottage, Lethbridge-Stewart reflected on the tale his old friend had told him. He had heard some strange stories in his time, but his recent experiences in London had left him wondering how much truth was in them. They were troubling prospects, and he could now add to his worries Ray's story about their visit to the Manor in 1937.

Remington Manor existed just beyond Draynes Wood

and the three boys were exploring, playing kick the can, while Ray's parents were elsewhere in the woods walking the family dog. It was one of those rare occasions where the young Alistair was a part of the small gang; just the three of them, Alistair, Ray and James. There was no Henry around to push Alistair away; a revelation that Lethbridge-Stewart found interesting. Boys will be boys, and all that. He wasn't going to hold it against Henry; after all, why would he want a seven-year-old tagging along and spoiling their fun? Three years was a big difference in age when you're a child, Lethbridge-Stewart knew.

Ray's tale took an odd turn when a man appeared to them only a few feet from the Manor. They had never seen him before, or anyone in such clothes. Old fashioned, dressed like someone from the nineteenth century. As Ray told it the man looked cold, his skin almost deathly white, hair as dark as night beneath a top hat. It was like looking at Death itself. The man did not speak, but he looked at the three boys, his eyes finally resting upon James.

At this point Ray's story became a bit muddled, and he admitted that he often confused himself with the real events and the fictitious version he had created for his first novel. But the upshot of it was that the man, the Hollow Man as Ray continued to call him, had touched James. Simply reached out a hand and rested it on his head. Neither Ray nor Alistair had been able to move, only watch as the Hollow Man seemed to fall apart, like ash from burning paper.

Even now, hearing Ray tell the story, Lethbridge-Stewart could understand why it had been so easily dismissed. But there was a truth in Ray's voice, a sense of fear that came from a place of honesty.

Ray went on to say how James had never been the same since then: always whispering to himself, never quite the upbeat outgoing kid Ray had known all his life.

'Where is James now?' Lethbridge-Stewart asked, following Ray into the cottage.

Ray glanced back. 'I still don't understand how you could have forgotten him. Of all people to forget... Henry I could understand, even me, but not James.'

'But why? What is so important about him?'

Ray never got a chance to answer. The sound of movement in the kitchen alerted both to another presence in the cottage. They looked at each other, and Lethbridge-Stewart motioned for Ray to be quiet.

He passed Ray, and called out. 'Hello?'

'Gordon, what time do you call this?' an old and familiar woman's voice responded.

Lethbridge-Stewart stopped at the kitchen door. There was his mother. Her clothes were dirty and still damp from a night out in the rain. Her curls had been flattened by the weather, and her cardigan hung loosely about her. She looked over at him from her position by the stove, where she appeared to be preparing food. Lethbridge-Stewart felt Ray stop behind him, letting out a breath of surprise.

Mary Lethbridge-Stewart smiled. 'I knew you'd be home soon, dear, and I came back as quick as I could. Oh, and it wasn't easy. But I'm back home now, and so are you.'

Lethbridge-Stewart frowned. 'Mother, I...'

'Mother? Good grief, Gordon, we'll have none of your...' She stopped, her lined face crumbling into a state of confusion. 'You're not Gordon, but you look like him. Who are you?'

'It's me, Mother, it's Alistair.' He stepped slowly into the kitchen, an arm reaching out.

'Alistair? But you're too old, you're...' Mary blinked tears at him. She fondled the crucifix on her necklace and gave him a sad smile. 'Oh, Alistair, you look so much like your father. Especially with that moustache. He had one just like it before he... Before he... But no, he called to me. Told me to come home.' She looked around. 'Where is he?'

Lethbridge-Stewart was at a loss. He hadn't seen his mother in years, and she'd seemed perfectly healthy and of sound mind back then. But now?

He opened his mouth to speak, to try and answer her question, but before the words could come out, his mother collapsed. He rushed forward and managed to grab hold of her before she hit the lino. He looked down at her face. She was out cold, but at least, for now, she looked peaceful.

'What is going on here?' Ray asked, and Lethbridge-Stewart wished he could explain. But, like Ray, he had no idea.

None at all.

They all met back at Redrose. Alistair was upstairs making his mother comfortable, while Ray provided them all with hot drinks. Coal was on the fire, and the men sat around it, warming themselves back up.

'Well, now Mrs Lethbridge-Stewart has been found, gentlemen, I need your help,' George said.

The Watts' had passed him and Owain on the street and told them that they were going back to London. How Charles had not returned home, and when he did, he'd find his ticket and fair waiting with Shirley.

George had never much cared for the Watts' family; old Mrs Watts, Charles' grandmother, was a battleaxe of the worst kind. Always shouting at children when they played in the streets, always complaining about being short changed when she came to the shop. Her son, it seemed, had inherited all of her manners.

George felt sorry for Charles' mother, but she seemed quite willing to stand by her husband, and George left his sympathy there. He had no time for rude people.

He explained to Henry and Ray about Lewis and how

he and Charles had gone looking for Owain the previous night. 'Owain returned eventually, although he still won't tell me why he was up at the Manor, and...'

'The Manor?' Ray stared daggers at George. 'You all laughed at me last night, but I told you, didn't I? I told you Owain was up there.' He turned to Owain, who sat on the windowsill with a bottle of Corona Orangeade in his hand. 'Why were you up there? He got to you, didn't he? The Hollow Man.'

George stood up. 'Don't start all that again, Ray. Bloody Hollow Man indeed! We've all heard the ghost stories, but that's all they are. Stupid stories your parents used to tell you.'

'They're not stories,' Ray whispered.

'He's right.'

The men turned to Alistair as he re-entered the living room from upstairs. He looked around them.

'I don't know what is going on here, but something is very wrong. And I have a distinct feeling it has something to do with Ray's story.'

George laughed. He'd heard the story many times in the last twenty years, but he never once believed it, not that he was above recounting it, with embellishments, on occasion. 'Oh come on, Colonel, you're a smarter man than that.'

Alistair raised an eyebrow. 'Smart enough to listen.' He turned to Ray and Henry. 'I want to know more about this James, and just why I don't remember him.'

Henry looked at Ray. 'He doesn't remember James?'

Ray shrugged. 'I don't understand it, either, but I believe him.'

Henry shook his head in disbelief. 'How can you not remember your own brother, Alistair?'

Alistair looked like he'd been slapped, but recovered quickly. 'Because I don't have a brother.'

'But you do,' Ray said, stepping forward. 'And you

were there, with me and Henry when it happened.'

'When what happened?'

'At the gorge, when James died.'

Alistair just stood there, looking from one man to the other. George couldn't even begin to understand what was going on in Alistair's mind at that moment. Slowly Ray's old friend shook his head and spoke, his words deliberate and determined.

'I do not have a brother.'

Some way down Fore Street, a Morris Minor was approaching the village limits. Inside Mr and Mrs Watts continued to argue about their son and Mr Watts' usual disregard. So engaged were they that they failed to notice the creature that stepped out of the hedge and onto the road before them.

The Yeti let out a roar.

Mr Watts looked away from his wife, but it was too late. The small car crashed into the Yeti, and the savage beast swung one of its great arms. The car, carried by its momentum, was battered sideways off the road, smashing into the nearest lamppost.

If the Watts' had bothered to use their seatbelts they might have been saved, but as it was, both crashed through the windscreen.

The Yeti, impassive, paid no attention to the carnage. Instead it remained standing in the middle of the road. Its mouth opened and a strange sound emitted from it. It was hard to make out, a vibration that moved up and down like a chant without words.

All around the edge of Bledoe the same chant reverberated, linking the Yeti that surrounded the village. In unison they raised their guns.

CHAPTER NINE
The Art of Denial

IT WAS ALL SO ABSURD. LETHBRIDGE-STEWART MAY HAVE experienced some bizarre things in the past month, and he was the first to admit that he could not explain the gaps in his memory, but the idea that James was his brother… Last night, in the dream, was the first time he could even recall seeing James.

It *was* absurd. Impossible!

How could he possibly have forgotten something so important? A brother who was, apparently, dead. He shook his head, looking at the men gathered in the room.

They were all watching him, even Rifleman Bishop and young Mister Vine. No, he would not accept that. He had no brother; he knew this, and nothing anybody could say would convince him otherwise. He didn't know what was going on in Bledoe, but he knew that much at least.

'Okay, gentlemen, this joke is running tired now, but clearly something is not right about this village. And I feel certain it's connected to Ray's books.'

Ray shook his head. 'Books?' he said, frustrated. 'They are more than books, dammit! It all happened.'

Henry tutted wearily. 'Ray, enough. We all know the story of the Manor, we all know about the Whisperer, but this nonsense about the Hollow Man is just that – nonsense.'

'It is not nonsense, Henry! And you know it.'

Lethbridge-Stewart watched the two men. It was clear

that this was an old argument, and he had no time for such things. For now his mother was comfortable, resting, but he knew when she woke up she'd still be expecting to find her dead husband waiting for her.

He glanced through the window which overlooked the small driveway of the cottage. Arnold was out there somewhere, maybe even in the village, and whatever had drawn him there was almost certainly the same thing that had drawn his mother.

It had to be connected to Ray's story – he checked himself, Ray's *account* – of the Hollow Man that had appeared before them in 1937. It was another memory Lethbridge-Stewart did not recall, but that didn't make it untrue. Just another thing forgotten.

He stepped further into the room, and directed his question at Ray. 'Why does he know it's not nonsense?' He looked at Henry. 'You were friends with Ray and James, so you were around when all these strange things happened. What did you see?'

'I didn't see a damn thing,' Henry said, lowering his eyes.

Lethbridge-Stewart didn't believe him. 'You used to visit Draynes Wood with us, Henry, I know this. It's one of the few things that have returned to me since I came back here. Did you see the Hollow Man, too?'

'No, I did not.'

'You're lying,' George piped up. 'I recognise that look, Henry.'

Lethbridge-Stewart smiled. He liked these men, liked the way they all knew each other, had history together. And he liked how George had clearly caught Henry out. Henry was less pleased.

'Okay, so I saw it!' Henry snapped. 'I was there in Draynes Wood, up there with my dad. I took a stroll and heard the rest of you. Went to look and I saw it. Saw the man appear, saw him fall apart like the embers of a fire.'

He looked up at Ray, accusing him of something. 'James told us to never talk about it. But no, you couldn't just leave it there, could you? Let it be a story?'

Too many departments and too little communication between them. Bureaucracy, one of the worst parts of the British Armed Forces, and the sole reason General Hamilton had only just received the news.

He perused the report once again, waiting for the phone call to be picked up on the other end. There was only one man he could talk to about this, the only officer of staff rank in a position to do something about it. And the man had failed to report in that morning – despite calling Corporal Wright the previous night.

Finally the phone was picked up.

'Corporal Wright, has the colonel reported in yet?'

'No, sir,' came the quick reply. 'Not since last night.'

'I see. So we can assume he is still in the area of Liskeard?' Hamilton considered that for the moment.

The trail of Staff Sergeant Arnold had dried up in Liskeard, and now Lethbridge-Stewart was in the area following a lead that he had failed to reveal. It was clearly connected, and almost certainly related to the report before him. The report was from the Vault, somewhere in Northumberland. Apparently the storemen had received telephoned orders from the Vault quartermaster, Captain Sam Hawkins, to transport the Yeti and other ephemera from the London Event to a place called Remington Manor, just a mile from Draynes Wood in Cornwall. *Near* Liskeard. The curious thing was that Hawkins insisted that he had given no such order.

Steps needed to be taken, and quickly. They could not afford another incursion like the recent one in London.

'Wright, put Major Douglas on the line. It would appear Lethbridge-Stewart was right; the Great Intelligence is still out there, and it's mobilising.'

*

George wasn't liking this at all. All this time he'd believed it to be just a story. He'd never read any of Ray's books, didn't care for such novels, but he knew the story. And now it was real.

'My son is up there,' he said, his voice shaking more than he would have liked.

'Your son is here.' Alistair turned to Owain.

'Not Owain, Lewis. He went there to look for Owain, I know it.'

'Why would he do that?'

George looked at Owain, but his son had his head lowered. 'Because Owain hasn't been himself all week. Neither of my boys have been.'

Henry spoke up. 'It's just boys turning to men, George.'

'No it isn't,' Ray said. 'You told us in the pub that Owain had been up at the Manor last weekend.' He stabbed a finger at George. 'I warned you all, but you just wouldn't listen. Just think I'm the madman, the author and his crazy stories.' He looked down at Henry sadly. 'You knew I was telling the truth. Do you think I had forgotten that? Think I'd forgotten what happened at Alistair's birthday party? But I left you be, let you live with your denial. But now you all know different.'

George didn't want to admit it, but Ray was right. Something had been wrong all week, ever since his boys had gone to the Manor. If this Hollow Man was real, then what else was real about the stories he'd heard? And Henry had known all this time. George wasn't sure what angered him more; that he hadn't listened to Ray, or that Henry had been keeping it all a secret for the last twenty years.

'Gentlemen, secrets are all very well, and we all have reasons for keeping them,' Alistair said. 'But now is not the time. Mr Vine.' He turned to Owain. 'What happened up at the Manor? What did you see?'

Owain looked up, and George recognised the contempt in his eyes. He wasn't going to tell Alistair a thing. Owain never had been the type to confide in people he didn't know, especially when put on the spot.

'Did you see those beasts?' Ray asked. 'Big hairy things.'

'You really saw them?' Henry cut in, turning to his friend. 'Those grizzly bears?'

Ray swallowed, coming out in a sweat. 'Yes. I went up there yesterday. I had to go and find Owain... I'd failed to keep people away, but I couldn't get too close. I...' He swallowed again, his voice sounding raw. 'They were no bears. I don't know what they were, but they weren't bears.'

'No,' Alistair said, his eyes now steel. 'They were Yeti.'

For the first time all morning Owain felt Gordon with him. He wasn't sure how Gordon was feeling, but he was watching the whole conversation unfold.

How does he know?

Owain waited for an answer, while Lethbridge-Stewart quizzed Ray on what he had seen.

I know Colonel Lethbridge-Stewart of old, Gordon said.

Owain had worked that out. Gordon was Lethbridge-Stewart's father, or at least the ghost of him. But it wasn't Gordon who had answered, it was the pure consciousness. It had encountered Lethbridge-Stewart before. Somehow it had touched the soldier.

'I saw them, too,' Owain said before he even realised he was going to. He looked around the room, and shrugged. 'How could I tell you?' he asked his dad. 'You would have just laughed at me.'

'I'm not laughing now.'

Owain wasn't sure if his dad looked disappointed or relieved. Possibly a mixture of the two.

*

'Did you feel this Hollow Man?' Lethbridge-Stewart asked. 'Any of you?'

The men looked around, each keeping their own counsel.

'What about you, Mr Vine?'

Owain Vine shrugged again. 'I don't know. Maybe. There was something there. I felt it, a week ago.'

He went on to describe his previous visit to the Manor with Lewis and Charles. Lethbridge-Stewart listened. Suddenly it was all making perfect sense to him, and he couldn't believe he had not considered the possibility.

He had been warned by the Doctor that the Great Intelligence was still 'out there'. Only it wasn't so much 'out there' as 'here', all this time. What else could have resurrected a corpse? The last thing the Great Intelligence had succeeded in doing was possessing Arnold, and now it was using him again.

But how did his mother fit into it all? Lethbridge-Stewart had been certain the two events were connected, but now? He couldn't for the life of him think how. If Ray was to be believed, the Hollow Man, whatever it was, was connected to the Great Intelligence, and it had been in the Manor for over thirty years.

Lethbridge-Stewart was missing something still, he was sure. The final connection.

'So you believe Lewis went to the Manor to find Owain?' he asked George, once Owain had finished his story.

George nodded. 'Where else would he go? He hasn't returned all night.'

Lethbridge-Stewart let this fit into the puzzle. Still there were pieces missing.

'Very well. What I am about to tell you, gentlemen, can never leave this room. Indeed, I will be breaking the Official Secrets Act by telling you. But I believe the events happening here are directly connected to recent occurrences in London.'

He looked around the room, and his eyes came to rest on Rifleman Bishop. If Hamilton discovered this conversation, Lethbridge-Stewart knew there would be hell to pay. But he had little other choice.

'As you know, last month London was evacuated. The official story is a major gas leak and bears escaping from London Zoo, but the truth is London was under siege by an alien intelligence...'

Gerald Sherwin hated walking the dog. He didn't trust dog-walkers. It always seemed to be them who found dead bodies or unexploded bombs. He'd seen it on the news so many times and found it hard not to be suspicious. His mother was a dog-walker, the one who usually walked their little Red Setter, Pat, but she wasn't feeling too well today and so this morning it was down to him. Pat: a stupid name for a dog if ever there was one. He resented having to shout it after the creature.

His plan was to go as far out as he could, maybe even let Pat go. He never liked the dog anyway. Stupid thing was far too needy; like all dogs. If anything, Gerald decided, he was a cat man.

It was a cold morning and Gerald was wrapped up warm, but it didn't stop him shivering when he spotted a blanket of snow in the near distance. He stopped, surprised to see that the snow appeared to be moving. Stretching out like some kind of fence, covering the hedges. Only...

He peered closer. It wasn't snow at all, more like some kind of thick web. But it seemed to be alive, pulsating hypnotically.

He shook his head and looked around. At some point he had released hold of the lead and Pat had ran off. He didn't remember letting go, yet as he looked around the field he could see no sign of the Red Setter.

His mother was going to go spare.

He turned around to retrace his steps, but thoughts of his dog and his mother were forgotten as, as if from nowhere, a large claw swept down towards his head.

There was no time to question, no time even to be surprised – just enough time for one final thought: *Sometimes it isn't the dog-walkers that* find *the dead bodies...*

'And there you have it, gentlemen, the level of threat Bledoe appears to be under,' Alistair concluded.

'So we now have a ghost in the Manor and a dead soldier somewhere near our village?' Henry said, his limit of incredulity long past.

George offered a lopsided smile. Henry was glad he was not the only one taking this all with a pinch of salt, not that he was best pleased with George for putting him on the spot earlier. There were some things best forgotten, and what he had seen in 1937 was one of them. He did not appreciate being called on it.

'That's the long and short of it, Henry, yes. What I suggest then is a quick recce of this Manor. If it was indeed a Yeti you saw, Ray, then you can be sure the Intelligence will have others. Although how it got them here is beyond me.' Alistair rubbed his chin. 'I think I shall have to get onto General Hamilton, let him know the situation here, once I know the strength of the Intelligence's forces.'

Alistair was deadly serious, more so than Ray, which said a lot. Ray was sitting down now, his head in his hands. Henry couldn't blame him. He had lived with this for years, believing it all, but never being believed. Henry supposed he should feel guilty for not supporting Ray, but Henry had a family to worry about, Ray had only himself. Henry couldn't afford to indulge in the things that would drive a man insane.

'Don't forget the aliens,' George said.

'Of course. And not grizzly bears, but robotic Yeti.' Henry shook his head and stood up. This was all quite insane. He was a publican, and a good one at that. This was all too much for him.

'Sir,' Bishop said. 'When we were looking for your mother, Mr Barns and I questioned a woman who told us that some fruit had been stolen from her house during the night.'

'Stolen fruit, too,' Henry said, no longer able to contain his mirth. 'Whatever next.'

Alistair raised an eyebrow at him. 'Mr Barns... Henry, I can understand how this must all seem to you, but you yourself witnessed this Hollow Man, and I assure you I did not break my oath to tell you a pack of lies.' He turned back to Bishop. 'However, I fail to see how stolen fruit could be important.'

'Because the woman also told us she found muddy prints in her kitchen. Boot prints, sir.'

'Combat boots?'

'That would be my guess, sir. After all, Staff Sergeant Arnold must need food at some point, surely?'

Henry really didn't like where this was going.

'Henry, I want you and Bishop to talk to this woman again, see if she saw anything else.'

'Sure, why not?' Henry slumped his shoulders and walked out of the cottage, not waiting to see if Bishop was following. He needed fresh air, and Alistair had given him the excuse he needed to get it.

Owain looked up from the magazine he was reading to see his dad entering the kitchen. The big meeting must have finished.

'We're going up to the Manor.'

'We are?'

'Not you. We need someone to remain here and keep

an eye on Mrs Lethbridge-Stewart.'

Owain shook his head and let out a grunt. 'Guilty, then, is that it?'

His dad's face creased in a frown. 'Excuse me?'

'It's your fault, you know, if Lewis is in trouble. If you hadn't punched him, he would have come back by now.'

Owain could see he had hit a sore point. He knew his dad, not one for expressing his feelings at the best of times. Sure, the two of them had enjoyed some good times over the last year, going for a sneaky and illegal pint in Liskeard when his mother wasn't around, but it didn't make up for half of the stuff Owain had witnessed over the years.

'If it's anybody's fault, then it's yours, son. If you hadn't disappeared yesterday, then Lewis would never have had to go out looking for you.'

Owain let out a snort of laughter. 'I'm not surprised he wants to leave Bledoe.'

His dad stepped forward and grabbed Owain by the shirt. 'Listen to me, Owain, I've had enough of Lewis' lip, and if you don't want the same as he...'

Owain pushed his dad aside with ease. Joining with Gordon had changed him, in more ways than one. He didn't need anybody any more. Just Gordon.

He looked back at his dad. The old man looked weak, every one of his forty-eight years showing. With a smile, Owain carried on out of the kitchen.

Only Lethbridge-Stewart was in the room now.

'Your mother will be safe here,' Owain said. 'I'll make sure of it.'

Yes, Gordon agreed. *Quite safe.*

Ray opened the top drawer and removed the sepia-toned photograph. He had lived with the pain for so long, he didn't need more reminders of what had happened, and had removed all pictures of his best friend from the living room some years ago. But this one he kept, safe in the top drawer in his bedroom.

It showed three boys sitting outside Redrose Cottage. The youngest of the three, Ali, stood slightly away from the elder two, dressed like the older boys, in grey shorts and a tanktop over his neat shirt. All three wore smiles, excited about going back to school. If nobody knew any better they would have assumed the boys were brothers, and that's how it had felt back then.

Ray smiled at the picture. 'Soon,' he said, 'soon we'll understand it all.'

He was still confused as to why Alistair did not remember James, but Ray knew that determined look on Alistair's face. Things were coming together. Years of pain, of not understanding, were about to come to an end. Up at the Manor were all the answers, and with Alistair by his side Ray knew they'd find them.

Finally he would be vindicated, no longer considered the madman of the village.

CHAPTER TEN
Face of the Enemy

THE WEB WAS BLOCKING THEIR WAY. STAFF SERGEANT Arnold lifted an arm to deflect it as it moved in the breeze that swept through the Underground tunnel. He had seen what the Web could do. Already it covered much of the Underground and a fair amount of London above; many had died in it, and he didn't plan on being one of them. Standing behind him was Driver Evans, a less than exemplary sapper from the Royal Engineers, while Corporal Lane knelt next to him, a much more dependable non-commissioned officer from the regular infantry. They all crowded around a small trolley that sat on the rail tracks.

Arnold gestured down the tunnel. 'The colonel will be through there at Covent Garden in a few minutes, right?' he said rhetorically. He knew Colonel Lethbridge-Stewart and his men were above ground, trying to find another way to Covent Garden. He thought of the fury of the Yeti's onslaught; hopefully they'd avoided the worst of it.

'Do you think they'll be able to load the police box on here, Staff?' Evans asked, the trace of cowardice evident in his strong Welsh voice.

Arnold didn't see why not. He still didn't understand why the colonel needed a police box, or indeed why there was one in the Underground anyway. But orders were orders, and Arnold was a soldier who didn't question them when given.

'Well, if we can get this thing through the fungus stuff,' he pointed out.

He peered through the Web, which was now pulsing. He

could just about make out the rest of the tunnel beyond.

'There's not much of a gradient in this section of the tunnel. Right.' Arnold stood up. 'I want one volunteer.'

'Volunteer?' asked Evans, looking at Arnold in a way that could only be called insubordinate. He glanced sideways at Lane. 'That's a dirty word, that is. Not me!'

Arnold was not surprised. Evans had proven his cowardice several times already. If they got out of this, Arnold intended to have a word with Evans' regimental staff sergeant. There was no way he would have put up with such backchat in 21 Regiment. Arnold turned to the corporal.

'Lane?'

'What for, Staff?' Lane was weary, and Arnold couldn't blame him, but at least he was willing.

Arnold pointed at the trolley and explained. 'Well, if this thing wants some help going through to Covent Garden, I'm going through with it...'

'Into that stuff?'

'Have we got those respirators?'

'Well yeah, here.' Lane placed his rifle on the trolley and reached for the packs that held the respirator masks. He handed one to Arnold.

'I reckon we should be all right in these.' Arnold removed his beret and hung the pack around his neck. He opened it and retrieved the mask inside. He handed the other pack to Lane. The corporal didn't take it. 'Oh, all right, Lane lad. I'll go by meself.'

'No, 'ang on a sec, Staff.' Lane removed his own beret and took the pack off Arnold. 'That trolley's heavy,' he said, offering a smile. 'It'll take two of us to shift it.'

Evans was watching them, looking from one to other as if they were both mad. 'You're potty, the pair of you!'

Arnold had just about had it with the sapper. 'Shut up, will you! Do as you're told. Play that rope out as we go; any sign of trouble whip us out sharpish. Right?'

'Well, it's your neck.'

And so it was. Arnold and Lane placed their masks on and

turned to face the Web. They signalled they were ready with a thumbs-up and braced themselves. They paused for a moment, looking at each other.

Once again Arnold knew he was not the master of his own actions. He had fought so hard, but this was it. Finally the end had come. No one had survived in the Web before.

He awoke sharply, looking around. He was no longer in the Underground but some kind of barn, lying behind bundles of hay. Arnold stood up slowly, trying to remember where he was. It took a few moments, but then he remembered. Everything since waking up in the hospital mortuary. Only now there was more; the dream that wasn't a dream.

It had all happened. For the first time in what seemed like weeks he knew exactly who he was. Staff Sergeant Albert Arnold of the Royal Engineers, 21 Regiment. He closed his eyes, reaching for his head, expecting his hands to brush against the cold surface of that device the Yeti had put there. But all he felt was his thin hair.

Corporal Lane hadn't made it, but then neither had Arnold. Killed by a shot from Lieutenant Max Dawlish, in front of that woman, Elizabeth Shaw. He hadn't been dead for long, but long enough for the Great Intelligence to get inside his head and use him.

He screwed his eyes shut, pressed his palms to his face. He could see it all. He thought he was in control, but he wasn't, not really.

From the moment he woke up in that Underground tunnel he'd been a slave to the Intelligence, like sleep walking his way through a nightmare. He could see it all, feel it all, every word exchanged between him and Corporal Blake as they found the explosives covered in Web, removing the little Yeti models and placing one in the explosives store, making sure the Army's weapons would be of no use. He'd been responsible for the deaths of so many; even Craftsman Weams. Poor lad, cocky as they came, but a good man. He'd tried to warn them, to fight against the Intelligence's control...

'Any luck?' Colonel Lethbridge-Stewart asked, as Captain Knight and his patrol joined them in the tunnel.

'Afraid not, sir. The fungus beat us to it. A hundred yards this side of Holborn.'

'Just as if it knew what we were up to, sir,' Arnold said quickly, and as he said it he could feel the Intelligence inside him. It wasn't happy, and it began to tighten its hold. It wasn't much, but for a brief moment Arnold had been free.

It was his last true moment of freedom. From that point the Intelligence didn't let up, guiding him through the motions of life, ensuring the Army always remained one step behind while the Intelligence continued to bait the trap for that Doctor fella. But he'd continued to fight, all the way until he was underneath Covent Garden with Lane and Evans.

And for a while he slept, the Intelligence giving him a reprieve while it spoke through Professor Travers. But that didn't last; once the suspicion was thrown off him, the Intelligence reanimated Arnold again.

But something had gone wrong, only he couldn't remember what. Whatever it was, it had killed him.

He inspected his hands. They still showed signs of severe burning. It didn't hurt, but when he had awoken his entire body had been as black as charcoal.

He needed air.

Once he was outside the barn he looked around. In the distance, due east he could see the roofs of small houses. A village of some sort. He blinked, seeing in his mind a signpost that said, *Bledoe 1 Mile*. Yes, he remembered: he had passed through that village.

Something caught his eye. He rushed over to the nearest hedge and peered through. Between him and the village were several shaggy forms. They looked different, leaner, taller, but he knew them well.

Yeti!

Arnold crouched down, keeping himself as hidden by the hedge as possible. It was like the Underground all over again. Well, they wouldn't get Albert Arnold this time. This time he'd fight them to his last breath, make the Intelligence pay for all the good men it had made him kill.

He looked over at the barn. He needed weapons.

Rifleman William Bishop wasn't sure what to make of the colonel's briefing. He had to believe him, of course; after all, no one made colonel in the Scots Guards without integrity of character. Bishop was a Royal Green Jacket, part of the 5th Battalion, and so he had not been stationed in London, but he knew men in the 4th Battalion and hadn't heard much from them in the last month. Now, at least, he understood why the 4th Battalion was so quiet. According to the colonel hundreds of soldiers had been killed; how many of them were known to Bishop? How many were his friends? He was was from London; what about his family?

He now stood in the kitchen of Mrs Hardy, a kindly old woman of about sixty who lived on her own. She had been most happy when he and Mr Barns had returned to ask her more questions about her late night visitor. She didn't mind that someone had helped themselves to her fruit; after all, if it didn't get eaten it would only go rotten, and she always bought more than she needed. She usually gave some to the children who played on the street of Windsor View.

'I remember when fruit was a luxury,' she had told them. 'Thirty years ago we didn't see such things.'

Bishop was too young to remember the war properly, he was born as it ended, but he remembered growing up in a world where rationing still happened. It took the UK a long time to find some kind of economic balance, and although he enjoyed reasonable affluence now, he'd experienced enough of rationing as a kid to respect what Mrs Hardy said.

But other than anecdotes about life in Bledoe during the war, she had nothing more to tell them. The first she knew about her visitor was when she found the muddy boot prints. They had dried and took a while to clean, which meant the intrusion had happened a few hours before she woke at 7am.

Bishop checked his watch. It was almost eleven o'clock now. He was about to thank Mrs Hardy for her time when something caught his eye through the window. He looked closer, moving the net out of the way. 'Mr Barns.'

'Henry, please, Mr Barns was my dad.' The older man joined Bishop by the kitchen window. 'What is it?'

Bishop pointed at a shape in the far distance. 'What do you think that is?'

It was hard to make out with the sun in the sky. Henry narrowed his eyes. 'A scarecrow?'

'There's no scarecrows in the fields out by Puckator Farm,' Mrs Hardy pointed out.

The shape moved. It was indistinct, as if its limbs were covered in fur. Bishop let the net fall back into place. He smiled at Mrs Hardy.

'Thank you for your time, Mrs Hardy.'

The old woman smiled. 'My pleasure. Not often I get such a handsome young man visiting me,' she said. 'Not since my Christopher passed on.'

Bishop was about to ask if that was her husband or son, but thought better of it. He wanted to take the Land Rover down Fore Street and see what that shape in the field was. They hadn't got as far as the farm when looking for the colonel's mother. He now wished they had. They may not have found her there, but they would have found something all right.

So much for the books he read as a kid. Life was getting much stranger than any fiction.

Owain sat on a small chair beside the bed on which Mary lay, the felt Fedora in his hands. The bedroom was smaller than his own, very Spartan and seldom used. On the chest of drawers, neatly folded, was the colonel's uniform jacket, his black cap resting upside down on top of it, a tie folded inside.

Mary Lethbridge-Stewart still slept, her eyes moving rapidly underneath their lids. Gordon spoke to him.

Place the control-millin on her head.

Owain went to move the metal hat from his head, but stopped. If he removed it he would not be able to hear Gordon's thoughts, and Gordon would not be able to see through his eyes.

Do not worry, Owain. My Yeti are spreading the Web. It is a part of me and it extends my will on the village. I can still sense you. But I need to reach the pure consciousness that is trapped in Mary. You do not need to feel me, Owain. We are one, with or without the control-millin.

Owain wasn't sure he agreed, but he trusted Gordon, so he removed the control-millin and placed it gently on Mary's grey hair.

He sat back and watched, feeling with a chill his sudden isolation.

The black Humber Sixteen Saloon continued its way up another unnamed road in Cornwall, still at the start of the six-hour journey to Lancashire. The driver, Thomas Davies, focused on the road ahead, mindful of the narrowness and the possibility of oncoming traffic. In the passenger seat his nephew, Ali, was leaning with his head hanging out of the window, enjoying the wind as it blew through his black hair. He ducked in for a second to check on the woman in the back of the car, smiled and put his head back out of the window.

Although the woman smiled back, inside she was sad. She was leaving everything she had loved. But there was too much pain in Bledoe for her now.

In the distance ahead of her she could see the houses that made up Resurgum Row, Higher Tremarcoombe. She had always considered them a long way to go, but she knew where she was going was a long way further. A long way from Cornwall, in fact. Would she ever return? Mary honestly didn't know.

Her son didn't seem too affected, probably looking forward to spending time with his Uncle Tommy and Aunty Isobel. They would be good for him. She couldn't tell any of them her real plans. They thought she was moving to Lancashire to be with her family, to find the support she needed to get through her loss. But Mary had no intention of staying there.

Once she knew Ali was settled she was going. She didn't know where, but she knew she had to get away from him. Before he paid the price, too.

First her parents and then James, and just when she thought she was coming to terms with that, she received the letter from the Air Force. Her husband, dead. She couldn't let Ali go the same way.

She looked out of the car window and saw a little boy. She kept seeing him in the shadows, watching her but never able to talk. But she saw the accusation in his eyes. The warning. He told her to leave, to never come back. And she wouldn't.

Thomas turned the car left, taking it out of Bledoe once and for all.

Mary felt a brief tug of pain in her heart. She looked back at the boy, but he was no longer there. She sniffed back a tear.

She had lost too much. Her parents and her husband. Mary leaned forward and ruffled Ali's already messy hair. She couldn't lose her only child, too.

The three of them had passed the sports field and taken

a small one-way lane due west. Lethbridge-Stewart was glad that Ray and George knew their way to Draynes Wood since he was beginning to lose his bearings a little. On either side of them were hedges that afforded little view of the surrounding countryside, and to him it seemed that one lane was much like another.

To think he was once a country boy himself. He had spent far too much time in cities and small towns in recent years, and had clearly lost his countryside instincts. Ray and George hadn't stopped talking since they'd left Redrose, but Lethbridge-Stewart wasn't inclined to join in. It was mostly small talk anyway, and he had too much on his mind to let such talk distract him.

His mind kept returning to the absurd notion that James had been his brother. He remembered the dream which he'd had the previous night, no doubt inspired by his stay in his old bedroom, and the feeling he remembered when James had been urging him to jump across the small river. In the memory Lethbridge-Stewart had only been a boy, and at first he'd simply chalked up the feeling to being egged on by older boys. The need to impress. But now he was thinking it might have been more than that.

'I should apologise for earlier, Colonel,' George said. 'All that business with Henry. He's not usually so stubborn, but I think all this has thrown him somewhat.' He laughed mirthlessly. 'Thrown us all, I should think.'

'No doubt. But you've both had military training,' Lethbridge-Stewart pointed out, smiling at the look of surprise on George's face.

Ray chuckled. 'He's got you there, George.'

'Yes, well, I only made private. As did Henry, although some years after me.'

'National Service.' Lethbridge-Stewart nodded sharply. 'As I thought. Well, I know it's been a while, but both of you will need to pull yourselves together since

I'll need all the troops I can get. Especially if I am right about the Intelligence being at the heart of this.'

'We'll do our best, sir,' George said, offering his best salute.

'That's all I ask.'

They continued on in silence for a while before George piped up again. 'I still can't believe Henry knew about all this and never mentioned it.' He looked at Ray. 'I feel like I owe you an apology.'

'If anybody owes Ray an apology, it's Henry.'

'Thank you, Al.' Ray shook his head. 'It hasn't been easy, trying to keep the children safe and away from the Manor. After James I was certain it was over. But still I kept returning to Draynes Wood, like somehow I knew it wasn't…'

Lethbridge-Stewart had seen many a haunted man in his time in the Army, haunted by the things they'd done and seen. The reality of war. In his way Ray was no different; he had lived with this weight for too long on his own. At this Lethbridge-Stewart felt a brief stab of guilt.

He had promised to keep in touch with Ray, and in that he had failed. If he had been true to his word then maybe most of this could have been prevented. Ray's isolation… Lethbridge-Stewart was as much to blame as Henry.

They stopped next to a gate onto an open field. Ray waved ahead.

'We can cut through here,' he said, 'just watch out for the cows.'

As Ray opened the steel gate, which creaked from lack of use, Lethbridge-Stewart looked over at the field, watching for cows walking in circles. No such odd behaviour here. Lethbridge-Stewart wasn't sure if he was glad about that or not. Circling cows would have at least suggested Arnold was near.

The three men set off across the field. They had only crossed half way when, on the horizon, Ray spotted three very familiarly shaped figures. They looked different from how Lethbridge-Stewart remembered them, but then he had been told that those he'd encountered in London had looked different from the one Travers had brought back from Tibet. Mark two, as the Doctor had called them. He guessed that made these Yeti mark three.

They may have looked slightly more advanced, but the guns they held were exactly the same as those he'd seen used in London.

The men pressed against the hedge that lined the field.

'Grizzly bears, eh, George?'

George shrugged at Ray's question. 'It wasn't me who said that. But, no, definitely not.' He looked at Lethbridge-Stewart. 'These the Yeti you were expecting?'

'Yes.' He glanced around. Beyond the Yeti was something else familiar to him: the strange pulsating Web the Intelligence had used to block off London. 'We need to move around them somehow, that is, if there is a gap in the Web. Hopefully it hasn't spread too far yet. If we can get to this Manor, I may know a way to stop the Yeti before they attack the village.'

'Attack?'

'I'm afraid so, Ray. Almost certainly.' Lethbridge-Stewart lifted his head up, trying to get a better lay of the land. 'In London the Intelligence used these little model Yeti to guide the real things, like pieces on a chess board. If we can destroy those...' His voice tailed off as he looked back to George and Ray. The two men were staring ahead, their eyes vacant. 'Ray? George?' He waved his hands in their faces. There was no response.

This was all he needed.

As Owain sat watching Mary sleep, Lethbridge-Stewart was on his mind. Or rather, the events in London as the colonel had explained them.

Owain was confused. He knew from joining Gordon that he was part of this Great Intelligence that had been the cause of the evacuation of London, but he also knew from Gordon that the boy meant no harm. He just wanted Mary and that Albert person to make them both whole, to bring them to the pure consciousness that was the end result for all men. Gordon wanted to bring peace, not kill people.

But Lethbridge-Stewart had been right about the Yeti. They did attack people. Now that the control-millin was removed and Gordon was silent, Owain remembered.

He remembered the Yeti racing off after Lewis and Charles. He shook his head. How had he forgotten that?

He hoped his dad found Lewis.

No, this made no sense. Gordon was Lethbridge-Stewart's dad returned. Why would a man once responsible for protecting England be connected to the entity that was responsible for so many deaths in London?

Owain stood up.

The colonel had to be lying. Owain knew Gordon, there was no way he'd be connected to something so evil.

Without Gordon nothing was making sense. He needed to talk to Gordon, to understand again.

'What the hell happened?'

George held his head in his hands. 'I don't know. I just went... blank. I could see you, hear you, but nothing was going through my mind.' He looked up at Lethbridge-Stewart. 'I don't think I've ever felt anything so peaceful.'

He had pulled both men back to the lane, first George and then Ray. The two of them were now sitting on the concrete dirt path, while Lethbridge-Stewart peered around the hedge at the Yeti through the gate. They weren't moving, still on the horizon, static. Watching or waiting? Probably both.

The last time he encountered the Yeti it had cost him many good men. All over London soldiers had been slaughtered, while of those under his direct command only a handful had survived. If they attacked Bledoe...

Lethbridge-Stewart didn't even want to finish that thought. At best he had three privates at his disposal, and only one of them on active duty; the other two hadn't seen service in at least fifteen years.

He turned back to Ray and George. Both men looked peaceful, although confused. Whatever had happened was related to the presence of the Yeti; Lethbridge-Stewart didn't know how, but he'd bet his Army pension on it. The Intelligence had shown an ability to possess people, he'd seen it twice. First with Professor Travers and then with Arnold. Was this the first sign?

'Are you both okay?'

Ray frowned. 'I think so.'

'Me too.'

'No voices in your head?' Lethbridge-Stewart asked. The men shook their heads. 'Good. At the first sign of a voice, even a whisper, you let me know.'

'Yes, sir,' George said, and Ray nodded his agreement.

'This Intelligence thing, is it the Whisperer?' Ray asked.

'It could be.'

'I always thought the Whisperer and the Hollow Man were the same thing, but now...' Ray looked down at his sweating hands.

'We need to find out,' Lethbridge-Stewart said. 'Ray, you need to tell me...'

The rumbling of a vehicle sounded along the path. Lethbridge-Stewart looked away from them and smiled. It was his Land Rover. It slowed and stopped by them.

Rifleman Bishop stepped out of the vehicle and saluted.

'Sir, we've just scouted the outer limits of the village and there's no way out. The Yeti have surrounded us, sir. They've blocked every road and guard the fields and meadows. And they appear to be spreading a kind of fungus stuff from some sort of gun.'

'Web, Bishop, not fungus. The Intelligence used it in London, too. Which means we're likely cut off. Pass me the binoculars.'

Bishop reached in to the Land Rover and pulled out a pair of binoculars. He chucked them to Lethbridge-Stewart, who opened the passenger door and used the inside of the front cab as a step to lift himself up for a better look. He put the binoculars to his eyes and surveyed the area around them. It was true. At strategic positions, as far as the eyes could see, Yeti ringed the area surrounding the village. He couldn't see very far east of them, but he suspected there were more Yeti that side too. Even with the binoculars the full extent of the Web was hard to make out, fading as it did under the glare of the sun. But he would lay money on it blocking the entire village, and if not yet, then it would soon.

It was decided. Lethbridge-Stewart ushered Ray and George into the back of the Land Rover and ordered Bishop to take them all back to Redrose.

The men gathered in the living room, each taking a seat. Lethbridge-Stewart stood before them, his swagger stick held in his hands. He had found it on the dashboard of the Land Rover, and gratefully picked it up. He probably looked an odd sight, only in partial uniform and a weather-beaten old coat, brandishing the swagger stick like a weapon. But he never quite felt right giving orders without his stick to wave around.

'We seem to have a problem, gentlemen, and we need to find a solution. But before that, I think we all need to gather our stories, find all the pieces. We know now that the Intelligence is connected to this Hollow Man of the Manor, although how we've yet to work out.' He turned to George. 'Can you go and get your son? He knows something, he must do. He spent the night up by the Manor.'

'If he said he doesn't know anything then...'

Ray snapped, talking over George. 'You know that's not true. You said yourself he's been acting odd since he visited the Manor last week. He knows something,' he added with a whisper.

George looked furious, but swallowed his anger and nodded at Lethbridge-Stewart. 'Very well, Colonel. But I still don't think...'

'Snap to it, Private!'

Without another word George stood and left the room. It was the old story; once a soldier, always a soldier. Which reminded Lethbridge-Stewart of another point he needed to clear up.

'Henry, how are you holding up?'

The pub landlord glanced around the room, and received a nod of encouragement from Bishop.

'Sorry about earlier, Ali. I did my National Service, of course, but I returned for my family. And all this...' He shook his head. 'They are my priority.'

'Which regiment?'

'I was with the 1st Battalion of the Gloucestershire Regiment at the Battle of the Imjin River,' Henry said. 'I served my two years then returned home. I was never called up again.'

Lethbridge-Stewart nodded. 'I was in Korea too,' he said. 'And I've seen a lot more death since, Henry, but nothing compared to the events of London. I need you at your best if you wish to help me protect this village. And your family.'

Henry nodded solemnly. 'You can count on me, Colonel.'

'Glad to hear it,' Lethbridge-Stewart said, the same time as Ray mumbled, 'About time.'

Henry turned to Ray. 'What was that?'

Lethbridge-Stewart hefted his stick, ready to bring it crashing down on the table before an argument could begin, but he reconsidered. Neither man would be any use to him, or each other, if they did not get their house in order.

'I said about time,' Ray said, this time louder. 'Have you any idea how it's been for me? To be mocked at every turn? Even when people were patting me on the back for the books I'd written I could see their sly looks. They believed I was making up stories, embellishing the local *myth*. And you could have done something about it!'

Henry shook his head. 'Perhaps, but what good would speaking up do? What good did it do you, Raymond? No, I'm sorry, but I did the right thing.'

Ray clearly couldn't believe his ears, for he sat down like a man defeated. For his own part Lethbridge-Stewart was not surprised by Henry's reaction. Even now the man looked at Ray like he was barmy. Too many years had passed by for this issue to be resolved. And they had no more to waste on reconciliations right now. They had to move before the Web completely sealed them in, if it hadn't already.

He turned to Bishop. 'You say all the roads out of Bledoe are blocked by Yeti? Very well. I want you and Henry to take the Land Rover across the fields and see if there's a gap in their perimeter. We still need to recce the Manor, but if that's not possible we can at least get some figures for when I contact General Hamilton.'

Ray looked up. 'You're bringing the Army here?'

'It's either that, or we take care of the Intelligence on our own.'

Ray didn't like the sound of that idea. Once Bishop and Henry had gone and Lethbridge-Stewart returned his attention to Ray, he noticed his old friend fingering a photograph.

'What's that?'

'This is all connected to your brother, I'm certain of it,' Ray said.

'Not that again. Listen to me, I do not have a...'

Ray handed the photograph to Lethbridge-Stewart. 'Yes, you do. Look, this a photograph of you, me and James, taken in the autumn of 1937. Look at James, tell me he's not your brother.'

Lethbridge-Stewart looked down at the picture. The three boys all looked familiar: dark hair, similar clothes. But two of them especially looked alike. There were a few years between them, but Lethbridge-Stewart could not deny the evidence of his eyes. There before him was his brother, the brother he had forgotten.

What kind of man forgot his own brother?

'It's all connected,' he said, looking up. 'My memory loss, my mother returning here to find my father, Arnold... Somehow it's all connected to the Intelligence being here now.' He handed the photograph back to Ray. 'You need to tell me everything that happened in 1937, everything that led to James' death. The answer is in the past, it has to be.'

Colonel Lethbridge-Stewart listened as Ray told his story, and as the words continued so too did the fuzziness of his memory. Upstairs, Mary Lethbridge-Stewart continued to dream of the events that caused her breakdown.

And all the while the Great Intelligence's Web continued to spread.

CHAPTER ELEVEN
The Forgotten Son

IT WAS THE LAST DAY OF THE SUMMER HOLIDAY IN 1937, and the Lethbridge-Stewarts had decided on a day break to Pentire Head before the children returned to school and Gordon to military service. It wouldn't be long before life went back to normal, the fun of summer forgotten, and Mary would resume her part-time voluntary work with the Salvation Army once again. It had been a while since she'd been sent anywhere interesting, now that England seemed to be coming out of the depression it had sunk into over the past decade. No more visits to London or being sent up North to help out with the soup kitchens, just the odd bit of charity work here and there, arranging fêtes and helping out at festivals. She was sure her sons were at least grateful for that. Her weeks away meant they often stayed with the Phillips. Not that either James or Ali minded being put up by the Phillips' when the need arose, but they obviously preferred it when their mother was around. Especially Ali, who was definitely a mummy's boy.

She watched from the blanket on which she and Gordon sat, while her boys played out on the field, not too far from the bluff. Raymond had been allowed to join them, and James was clearly glad of that. The two boys were always inseparable, especially during summer holidays, and she knew that had Raymond remained in Bledoe, James would have sulked the entire day. He was almost twelve now, they both were, and tomorrow they would be moving up to Liskeard Grammar School; where such sulking would not be looked kindly upon. She had tried to warn him of this, but James hadn't listened. Even Gordon had tried to have a word, but their eldest son was almost twelve and was starting to think he knew better.

Well, he would soon learn. The chances were that he and Raymond would not even be in the same class, not like they had been throughout infants and juniors. It would be quite a shock for him, and only the first of many. Almost twelve, then he'd be a teenager... How would she cope raising a teenage son?

And then there was Ali. Every lesson she learned from James she would apply to her youngest. There may have been over three years between them, but that was a huge gap in development. In some ways, despite eleven years of experience, she still felt like she was new to all this. That she had so far to go. She wondered if her own mother had ever felt like that. Life now was so different to how it had been back when she was James' age.

Ali was chasing Raymond now, the boys' game of piggy-in-the-middle having turned into an unfair version of It. James was egging Ali on, as he often seemed to be doing these days, and calling for Raymond to throw the ball over the younger boy and to him. Poor Ali, he didn't have very long legs and the older boys ran rings around him. Still, the sight made both Mary and her husband laugh.

'Fit as a fiddle,' Gordon said around his pipe. 'Mark my words, Mary, Alistair will end up in the Army.'

Gordon always liked to say such things, but Mary wasn't so sure she agreed. Ali hated everything about the military, though he was careful not to tell his father that. Mary had taught him well. She suspected, as Ali got older and his understanding grew, that his views would change, but for now he blamed the military for taking his father away so often. It didn't matter to Ali if his daddy was a hero; he just wanted his dad to attend school sports days and the like.

One day he would understand that the Lethbridge-Stewarts had a proud military history, going back well over four hundred years to when they were the Stewarts up in Lanark and the Lethbridges in Devon, before the two families had become one through marriage. Mary couldn't recall who the first Lethbridge-Stewart had been, although she knew Gordon had told her several times. She wasn't one for family history; even her own held little interest to her. She could barely remember what Grandpa Gore did for a living when she was a little girl.

'Let's not talk about your job now,' she said to Gordon. 'This is the last day we have as a family for a while. Let's make the most of it, shall we?'

Gordon looked at her, his deep brown eyes dragging her towards him. He pecked her on the lips with a smile and tapped her on the shoulder.

'You're It!' he said, and scrambled to his feet.

Mary gathered up the low hem of her skirt and stood up as primly as she could, giggling like a schoolgirl ready to play kiss-chase.

She wished they could have more days like these, but life always found a way to intrude. But not today, she decided, chasing her husband to whistles of encouragement from the boys.

Mary laughed, quite giddy with happiness.

It was several weekends later that the boys decided to visit the Manor. Ali wanted to come with them but James told him no. That didn't stop Ali. He followed them anyway. James tried to send him back, but Ali promised to tell their mum, and James knew he was beaten. After all he wasn't allowed up to Draynes Wood on his own – and being with Raymond probably wouldn't count in their parent's eyes.

They had barely made it to the Manor when they encountered the strange apparition that would one day be known as the Hollow Man. After their encounter, puzzled by the odd event, Raymond and Ali had no choice but to follow James back home.

'What happened?' Ray asked again, as they crossed the sports field, his mind still unable to grasp what he'd seen. 'That man... He... What happened to him?'

James looked back at him, his brown eyes darker than usual. Ray swallowed. Words weren't necessary.

Both James and Ali had been very quiet on the walk back from Draynes Wood; Ali in a sulk because his brother was ignoring him, but James...

He turned away from Ray, just in time to notice Henry running across the field towards them. He was out of breath, his excitement bubbling over.

'What was that?' he asked as soon as he reached them.

James didn't stop walking. He just kept on going forward, ignoring Henry completely. Henry turned to Raymond.

'I saw it all – up by the Manor! That man! You have to tell me what happened!'

Ali pulled on James' sleeve. 'James, we have to tell someone!'

James shook Ali off, the suddenness of the action causing Ali to fall onto his rump in the muddy grass. Both Raymond and Henry stopped, looking from James to Ali in shock. They had never seen James look so angry.

'We keep our gobs shut, do you hear me, Ali-stare?' he snapped. 'We never talk about this again!'

'But what *did* happen? Where did the man go?' Raymond asked.

'What man? There was no man!' James walked up to Raymond and jabbed him in the stomach with his finger. 'We didn't see anything because there was nothing to see.

Got it?'

Raymond didn't know what to say.

'And that goes for you, too, Henry. I don't know what you think you saw, but you're wrong. Now go home!'

With that, James stormed off, leaving his brother behind.

Raymond was at a loss. He had seen James upset before, but never so bossy and angry. If anything he was the least angry boy in the Bledoe Cadets. Every day at the gang hut was funny when James was around. No playtime at school was ever boring with James. But this… Raymond had never seen anything like it.

'We need to meet with the rest of the gang,' Henry said, helping Ali to his feet.

Ali's face beamed, his hazel eyes lighting up despite the tears that had been welling there. 'Can I come?'

Raymond didn't like this. 'James said we can't talk about it.'

'James isn't the Cadets' leader,' Henry pointed out. He looked down at Ali, who was now pulling at his sleeve. 'No,' Henry said, 'you can't come. Only boys over ten can be a Cadet.'

Ali's face scrunched. Then, a moment later, he smiled again. 'But what about Jemima? She's not a boy, and she's only nine!'

'Jemima's different.'

Ali was not to be beaten, and so began a series of questions, growing more and more indignant as Henry's answers proved less and less sufficient.

Raymond knew why Jemima was allowed; because Henry fancied her, even though she was always talking to James and barely ever spoke to Henry. But James didn't fancy her, he just saw her as a girl who he could play his jokes on. Jemima never seemed to mind; indeed, the more cruel the joke, the more she seemed to fancy him. And so, ealier in the year after she had helped the

Cadets with the smugglers, Henry and James had let her in officially.

Raymond would never understand girls, he was sure. Just like he didn't understand the sudden change in James. But he did know it had something to do with that man in the woods. Something had happened when the man touched James. Something very bad indeed.

Mary looked out the window, and was dismayed to see James sitting on his own while Raymond and Henry continued to play in the garden. They were even letting Ali join in, which was most unlike them, and her youngest kept looking over at his brother, his face torn between concern at James' apparent solitude, and joy at finally being part of the gang.

Apparent solitude only because, even though James sat alone, he appeared to be talking to someone. It wasn't a very heated conversation, at least not this time, but it was keeping his attention completely. He barely even noticed his friends in the garden with him.

Mary turned away and let out a deep breath of air.

'Still worried?' Eileen asked, peering out the window beside Mary.

'It's not normal, is it?'

Eileen turned her back on the window and resumed pouring out the hot water from the kettle, a small cloth covering the handle so she didn't burn herself. Mary idly wondered when Eileen was going to start using an electric kettle, instead of risking burns over the hot stove. They weren't that cheap, but they were surely quicker than fussing with matches and gas.

Mary smiled at herself; how easily her mind distracted itself from the worry she felt about her eldest boy. It was always the same; when worried it always found small things to focus on. Her way of coping, she supposed.

It was their weekly bridge game, but this week the game was being held at the Phillips', since Harold Phillips was at *The Rose & Crown* with Jonathan Barns after a little row with his wife. Eileen didn't look like she was in dispute with her husband, but then she never did. She didn't even explain what the row was about, simply told Mary and Maureen to bring the kids over and they'd play bridge at hers.

But Mary could guess: once again Eileen had expressed an interest in returning to work, not that she had lasted very long in it before she and Harold had married and the marriage bar had come into effect. For her own part Mary had no problem with the marriage bar – after all, to her mind, if a woman chose to marry and have children then she had to accept the consequences. And that meant no joining the work force.

Raising children and running a house was a full-time job in itself, who had time for another? Women earned so little working anyway. Now if it had been charity work, like she did now and then with the Salvation Army, then that was a whole different thing. Of course, Eileen would never agree. Which is why she'd not told Mary or Maureen the subject of the row; they'd only try and talk her around again.

Things may have changed a lot for women during the previous twenty years, and Mary was happy to take advantage of most of those changes, but the freedom to work was not one of them.

'What isn't normal?' Maureen asked, joining them in the kitchen, having popped upstairs to check on the girls.

'James,' she said, taking the offered cup. 'It's been weeks now.'

'Nothing wrong with an imaginary friend,' Maureen said, taking her own cup and walking back into the living room where their game was waiting.

Usually Bridget joined them to make up the two pairs,

but today she wasn't feeling very well, and so the women had to make do with an uneven game. Naturally Maureen became the solo player, as she always considered herself best. As such she resumed her seat in the armchair while Eileen and Mary sat side by side on the sofa.

'Didn't you have an imaginary friend?' Eileen asked.

'I think so, but times were different twenty years ago. Besides, he's a boy, and he has plenty of friends. Why would he need an imaginary one?'

'Perhaps he's feeling isolated at school?'

Maureen nodded her agreement as she struck a match and lit her cigarette. Ever the modern woman!

'Eileen could be right, Mary dear. All these years James and Raymond have been together in Juniors, and now they're not. I could have a word with the headmaster? Maybe he'll let James join Henry's and Raymond's class?'

Mary didn't think it was that simple. 'He's twelve in a few months, it's too old for imaginary friends, and besides it's not just that.'

'Then what is it?' Eileen asked, wafting Maureen's smoke away. At this Maureen smiled and offered the cigarette.

'You really ought to try it, my dear. It's quite relaxing. It's not just for men, you know.'

Eileen lifted an eyebrow at this, knowing full well that Maureen was baiting her to talk about the row. Instead she simply looked back at Mary.

'I don't know what it is,' Mary said, lowering her head at this. 'There's a look in his eyes... Oh, I know it's silly, but sometimes when he looks at me, it's like a stranger is watching me.'

Eileen patted Mary's knee. 'It is silly, you're right. He's just going through a phase. It's what boys do – and I doubt they ever grow out of it. Look at Harold. He's constantly going through phases.'

Maureen laughed. 'Oh, darling, do tell us more. Just what has Harry done this time?'

Eileen relented and told them, but Mary was no longer listening. Her mind was still on her son.

Was Eileen right? Was it simply a phase? James was growing up, and boys changed as much as girls through puberty. Some earlier than others. She wanted to believe it was that simple, but deep down she just knew there was something more going on.

Christmas was over and soon it was time for school again. Usually that was cause for celebration, as the Cadets compared notes on what presents they had received and traded their least favourites with each other. It was all part of the fun of returning to school and boasting to their classmates about how they all got exactly what they wanted. This year, though, it was different. And, as with the last few months, it was all because of James.

He could hardly blame James for being in a different class, but Henry was happy to fault him for putting a downer on the traditional present exchange among the Cadets. Raymond thought Henry was being unfair. He hadn't half got bossy since the *happening* in Draynes Wood in September, happily appointing himself as leader of the gang, something which would never have happened had James been his old self.

The gang was gathered in the disused barn at Puckator Farm, which they had claimed as their own a couple of years before. But the usual excitement was missing; this year there was a dark atmosphere lingering around them. They all knew why, but no one was saying anything, although several glances were made towards the entrance of the barn and the field beyond, where they all knew James was standing, looking out as if he was seeing something that nobody else could.

At least James had stopped talking to himself.

Henry was showing the Cadets his new Daisy BB rifle, which had been bought for him by an uncle who had visited America. Henry was not interested in guns, and wanted to trade it for something a bit more useful for school boasting purposes. He was a bit of a class swot, and he needed something that fitted in with that image. Raymond wished he brought with him that rubbish chess set his grandad had bought him; that was much more Henry's thing, and Raymond could have traded the BB gun with James. Not that James was participating, of course.

Raymond looked away from the group again. He really missed his best friend. So much that he had allowed Ali to join them for the annual present exchange, although not before making sure Ali promised to keep it a secret from his parents. Parents were not allowed to know; as far as they were concerned presents were simply loaned out or lost.

Ali had left the group already, to join his brother outside. Not really feeling the festive spirit, Raymond also removed himself from the group, and stepped out into the surprisingly mild air. The cows were out in the field, used to the lower temperatures as they were, and James and Ali stood with their arms resting on the fence, looking out at them. Raymond couldn't see what was so interesting – cows were hardly an unusual sight in Puckator Farm – but then he noticed what had drawn his friends' attention.

The cows were walking around the field in circles, four of five in a row, weaving in and out of each other like carriages on some strange train journey.

As he neared them, he heard Ali and James talking.

'What's sign language?' Ali was asking.

'It's like when people who can't talk speak to each other with their hands. Like when we wave goodbye to people.'

Raymond smiled. That sounded like the old James, the chatty one who was always sharing information with his little brother.

'But the cows aren't waving.'

'No, but the way they're walking is like writing symbols in the air. Like letters... They're just symbols, same with other languages.'

'But who are they talking to?'

'No one. I think they're just confused, listening to the wrong voice and trying to translate it.'

'What voice? I can't hear anybody.'

'Is your new friend talking to them?' Raymond asked, joining them. He rested his own arms on the fence and watched the cows intersect and separate.

James looked at him and blinked slowly. 'My new friend?'

'Yeah, that invisible one you keep talking to.'

'I don't know what you mean.'

'I'm not stupid!' Raymond snapped, feeling angry quite suddenly. 'We've all seen you talking to someone, ever since that *man* touched you in the woods.'

For a moment James didn't respond, he just looked at Raymond in a way that made Raymond shiver. James shook his head.

'You won't understand. No one will. No one can.'

'We can if you explain it,' Ali said. 'Like you did about sign language.'

'No. I can't explain it. Not to you, Ali, not to you, Ray... I'm sorry, but I can't.'

Raymond watched as James walked off, once again leaving him behind with Ali. The younger boy looked up at Raymond.

'Why can't he?'

Raymond wished he had an answer. James never kept things from him, not ever. With a sigh he looked down to Ali. 'Guess I'll just take you home then,' he said, feeling more disheartened than ever he had before.

Mary stood by the kitchen door and watched her husband silently. He had been very quiet the last few days. Shortly before he had returned home he had been promoted to wing commander, and as his Christmas leave neared its end, and the thought of returning to take on his new duties loomed, his jovial mood had diminished with increasing speed. She knew he loved his job; indeed he saw his career in the Royal Air Force as much more than a job, considering it his personal mission to protect not only his country but his children's future. For that she loved him dearly. But he had warned her that things were turning grim out there. Soon, he predicted, Britain would be pulled into a war it couldn't really afford. It had barely recovered from the last one, and despite the best intentions of the Peace Pledge Union, he knew it was only a matter of time before the British government committed itself to defending those countries threatened by Germany.

As much as all this troubled her – not that Mary had much of a head for politics – her first concern was her children, in particular James.

It had been a good Christmas, full of the usual joy and fun, all the local families joining forces to make it one for the kids to remember. Nativities at the community centre, the kids helping out the older people of the village... Families visiting each other, sharing what they had. Things may be better now than they had been in ten years, but the people of Bledoe remembered when times had been hard, when the community had been tested, and the spirit of support that had been born of those times remained. Mary doubted it would ever really go, especially if Gordon's fear about war was proven true.

But in all that Christmas joy, one thing continued to

bring Mary down, and that was James and his imaginary friend, who James had, in the last week, taken to calling Maha.

What kind of name is that? Mary thought, feeling even more uneasy than ever. It was alien, foreign... She just couldn't understand it.

She supposed it was a good thing that James was finally talking about Maha, that the invisible person had been given a name with which he – *it*, she reminded herself – could be referred, but for her it didn't make things any easier. She had already been called to the school on more than one occasion by concerned teachers. James had never really been a boy with a fanciful imagination, so his insistence that Maha was real was proving to be a bone of contention; not to mention a source of derision from some of the other children.

She had tried to talk to Gordon about it, but her husband didn't want to be burdened with such concerns. His time home was limited and he had bigger things to concern himself with than the increased imagination of their eldest child.

Mary entered the living room and sat on the armchair in the corner, looking at Gordon until he finally relented and put the newspaper onto the seat next to him.

'Did you ever have an imaginary friend?' she asked.

Gordon sighed and reached out for his pipe. 'I'm not sure. I suspect I did. But, you know, it was a very different time before the last war, children had a greater imagination back then because we *had* to. We didn't have half of the things kids have today.'

'How old were you?'

Gordon thought about this. 'Probably younger than James,' he admitted, and for the first time Mary saw the concern on his handsome face.

He may not have wanted to express it, but it was there. This, at least, gave Mary a sense of comfort, that she was not the only one bothered by James' behaviour.

'But boys always go through phases; I'm sure I was no different,' Gordon continued. 'One phase following another. Isn't that simply part of growing up? Besides, children are much younger in themselves nowadays. They don't need to grow up as quickly as we did.'

Mary knew Gordon was speaking sense. As times changed, so did the development of children. But... It was no good, she had no choice. She steeled herself.

'I think we should get some medical advice, contact a psychiatrist of some sort.'

Gordon nearly spat out his pipe. 'Good Lord, Mary, don't you think you're being a bit of an alarmist there? A psychiatrist? What an absurd idea!'

'I don't mean take him to see one, but we can surely talk to someone. We must know someone who has some connection to a psychiatrist? Get some kind of advice.'

'But why? What has James done that is so strange?'

'The other day I was talking to Eileen, and she told me about something Raymond had seen. Well, not seen so much as overheard.'

Gordon replaced the pipe in his mouth and leaned forward. 'Go on.'

'Last week Raymond overheard James telling Ali about sign language, because they saw the cows down at Puckator Farm acting all strange. It didn't make much sense to Eileen, so she couldn't explain exactly what Raymond had seen, but then a couple of days later Raymond found James down at their gang hut. He was talking to Maha. Raymond tried to explain to Eileen, but I think she must have got bored, as she couldn't recall much of it to tell me. But it seemed to involve how Maha and James were never supposed to meet, that somehow James and Maha were like brothers... only much more.'

Gordon chuckled at this. 'I think we would know if we had another son.'

Mary smiled, glad for the humour in his voice. 'Apparently James and Maha argued about this for a while, with James telling Maha that he couldn't leave now. That they had to be together always.'

'Together?' Gordon sat back and frowned. 'What does that mean? No one stays together forever, except for a wife and husband. Even siblings drift apart over the years – like you and Isobel, me and Matthew.' He shook his head. 'Can't say I much care for the idea that James thinks he should be together forever with another boy, even if it is an imaginary one.'

'Maybe you need to talk to him before you leave?'

'Yes, I think I should. He's obviously becoming confused, and we can't have a son of ours becoming confused about this kind of thing.'

Mary felt settled by this. Perhaps they would not need to seek professional help after all. Gordon and James had always been close, and she felt sure James would listen to his dad. And then everything would return to normal.

How wrong she was.

That year 22nd February fell on a Tuesday, but they couldn't really have a party on a school night, and so it had been decided that the Sunday before would do. It didn't seem to matter to Ali, who decided he'd simply have to have twice as many presents. Mary didn't have the heart to tell him that this was unlikely, but she did promise herself to bake him a second cake for Tuesday, so he could at least make a wish *on* his birthday. She knew what the wish would be, too – for his father to arrive and wish him happy birthday, but Mary knew that wouldn't be happening. There would be no sign of Gordon now until at least the end of March.

Pastor Ronald Stone at the parish church had excused them from the evening service, so long as Ali promised to help out next Sunday. It was an easy promise to make, since Mary knew Ali was especially looking forward to this birthday; this, definitively, was to be *his* day and not James'.

Mary was worried about the jealousy developing in Ali towards his brother, but she knew she could not blame him. Things had not eased up since the New Year, and James' issues with the ever-increasingly real Maha were taking up more and more of her attention. The last week alone Ali had to be picked up from school by Eileen three times because Mary had been called in to talk to the headmaster about James' behaviour.

She was hoping for a day without incidents, but she knew it was to be a vain hope.

The party was in full swing, presents given and received, dirty children now running around the garden, laughing and playing without a mind to the cold. Two of the adults stood either end of the garden, each holding an end of a large piece of rope, which was used for skipping. Almost all the children wanted to get involved – girls in their petticoats and carefully applied pony-tails, and the boys in their shorts and long socks. Some of the boys took a run into the skipping throng, trying to jump the rope without actually looking soft by skipping like the girls. Those not wanting to take part were sitting in a small group playing Film Stars, a simple enough game as Mary understood. Going through the alphabet, the children had to think of a film star, and the other children had to guess who, and when guessed right the next person went on to the next letter. Going to the picture house in Liskeard was not a regular thing for most of the children, and so they had never actually seen the 'stars' in action, but thanks to the tabs found in packs of sweet cigarettes they were at least familiar with the names.

It felt like all of Bledoe was in her garden. She wondered what Pastor Stone would have thought had Ali's party emptied out the church entirely.

She looked out for James, and found him, as expected, sitting on his own next to the fish pond. She really wished he'd get more involved again.

Raymond and Henry, not to mention a few others of their little gang, had been allowed to Ali's party simply so they'd bring James into the throng. But it wasn't working. All of James' friends seemed to be intentionally giving him his space. Things had soured greatly between James and the Bledoe Cadets in the last few months.

Mary sighed. This all had to end soon.

Her mood perked up a short while later. She was sitting, chatting to Eileen about the latest scandal between Nicholas and Tabitha Hardy up at Windsor View, when she noticed a couple of the children moving over to James. One of them was Henry, although she didn't know the names of the other two – they were the Moynihans' children, that much she did know. Eileen offered Mary a smile.

'There we go. Soon have him joining in.'

Eileen was too hopeful.

The women watched. It started off well enough, Henry and the Moynihan boys talking to James about the *Dick Tracy* cards they had collected. James liked to collect the cards, a newer more fun version of the tab cards found in the cigarette packets, and exchange them with his friends. James though didn't seem especially responsive, and all of a sudden Henry was shouting.

Mary couldn't hear the words exchanged but she saw the change in mood sweeping across the garden as both children and adults stopped what they were doing to watch. She jumped to her feet and rushed across the garden. It was about time this was all nipped in the bud.

'You spoil everything!' cried Ali, joining the boys in their row.

'Look, you're upsetting your brother now. What you going to do about it?' Henry asked, pushing James.

James stood up, barely having been moved by Henry's shove. He squared up to Henry, a look of rage in his eyes. The Moynihan boys pulled back, no longer wanting to get involved. Ali, not usually one for conflict, pushed his way between Henry and James. Where James was quite tall for his age, Ali had a long way to go; it was like David and Goliath, Mary thought as she ran towards them. She called out, but they paid her no attention. Still everybody else watched in surprise.

'What have you done to my brother?'

James looked down at Ali. 'What? Nothing has happened to me.'

'Yes it has. You're no fun no more. And I wasn't talking to you, anyway, I was talking to Maha!'

James was confused. He looked around. 'You can see him?'

'Of course not. He's still invisible!'

Mary was stunned by this – Ali accepting that Maha was real. Bad enough that James wouldn't be persuaded otherwise, but to have Ali believe it too! She finally reached them.

James was smiling with pride. 'See, Maha is real,' he said, victory in his tone.

'It's not even a real name!' Ali shouted.

James' face fell and he turned on his brother. 'What did you say?'

'You made it up. Maha! You're losing your marbles, you are!'

Mary shook her head, and looked down at Ali, disappointed at the way he was goading his brother.

'This has gone on long enough,' she said, stepping between her boys. 'Look at the scene you're all making.'

'It's James' fault. Him and Maha spoil everything!'

Mary wished she could argue with that, but Ali was right. Ever since Maha entered their lives it had been one disruption after another.

'You're just jealous,' James said, stepping forward. 'All of you are,' he added, looking around the garden. His eyes lingered on Henry and Raymond. 'Especially you two! Because I have a *real* friend now, one who won't leave. Because I was chosen for something special.'

Mary looked closer at her son. There was a horrible hard look on his face. Contempt, she would have said if she had to name it. 'Something special? Chosen? What do you mean?'

'He thinks he's going to live forever.' Ali's lip was beginning to tremble, his eyes darting around. He was very upset, but Mary wasn't entirely sure why. She knelt down to look him in the eyes and calm him down.

'Don't be silly, nobody lives forever. And you know Maha isn't real, don't you?' she asked, keeping her tone as even as possible.

'He's going mad. Thinks Maha is going to show him space... Thinks Maha is a spaceman!'

That was all Mary needed. Bad enough that James had an imaginary friend, but now he believed Maha was from space. What was the world coming to?

Ali was close to crying, not that it seemed to matter to James, who merely looked at his brother like he'd betrayed some secret.

'Okay, that's enough. Come on, James,' Mary said, pulling him by the arm, 'you can go to your room and tell me all about this Maha. *All* of it.'

James resisted, but Mary wasn't to be stopped this time. Months of this nonsense... and it was time to put an end to it finally.

So taken up by James was she, that Mary didn't even notice as Ali broke down in tears, his birthday ruined.

Raymond looked on, shaking his head.

A month passed them by, and in that time James' mother seemed to let James get away with much more than usual.

It was like she now believed in Maha, too. Raymond wasn't stupid, he knew that Maha wasn't imaginary, and he also knew Maha was that man who had appeared to them back in September. The things Maha and James seemed to talk about made little sense to Raymond; but then, nothing about his old best friend made any sense these days.

Raymond and Ali stalked through the woods seeking out James, who had left the picnic almost half an hour earlier. It was his birthday next week and his mum had taken the chance to surprise him: as a special birthday treat, his dad was to return for the day. Raymond would have thought the news would make James happy, but on being told, James had sulked off with a 'no, I don't want to see him'.

Raymond had wanted to follow straight away, but Mrs Lethbridge-Stewart told him to let James have his head.

'You okay?' Raymond asked Ali.

The younger boy didn't answer; he just set his jaw firmly and continued to plod on.

No, Ali wasn't okay. Raymond couldn't blame him. They had both lost James in one way or another.

They carried on in silence, eventually breaking through into the clearing at Golitha Falls. It was there that they found James. He was standing at the edge of the Falls, looking down at the water crashing into the stream below. Raymond and Ali stopped, both shocked at the look on James' face.

He was facing them, his expression crumbling as he fought back tears.

'It was meant to be you,' he said, his voice shaking. Neither Raymond nor Ali knew who he was addressing. 'Maha came for you, but he found me. I'm where he began.' He looked around, his eyes seeming to notice the long drop beside him for the first time. 'He tells me I can't be happy. Defeat comes in all shapes is what Maha says.'

Raymond stepped towards his old friend. 'What...' He swallowed, scared suddenly. 'What do you mean?'

For the first time it seemed like James was really seeing Raymond. 'I'm sorry,' he said. 'I should never have listened to him.'

'No,' Ali whispered beside Raymond. 'Don't go.'

What was Ali talking about? But before Raymond could truly question him, James jumped.

Ray paused in his narration, his eyes lingering on the shaking of his hands. 'I haven't thought so hard about those events in years,' he continued, not daring to look up at Alistair's face. 'It was the worst day of my life, yours too, I imagine. If only you could remember it.' He lifted his eyes slowly. 'Do you?'

Alistair was resting on the sideboard, his arms folded defensively. He was looking out towards the garden, only Ray suspected he was not seeing the garden at all.

'Alistair?'

The man blinked. 'No,' he said, his voice so low that Ray had to struggle to hear it. 'Only... It's like a daydream from years ago, something that doesn't seem real, yet somehow I know it is.' He swallowed and looked directly at Ray. 'What happened next?'

'At the time it seemed like everything happened so slowly, but I think it all happened so fast that I barely had time to really comprehend.

'I was twelve, you were eight, how could we hope to understand what had happened? But we were there, both of us, just looking at the edge of the gorge, as if James hadn't moved at all. Even now, when I close my eyes I can see it. James standing on the edge, clearly fighting his feelings, arguing even then with the voice in his head. The Manor in the distance like a spectre. He was so scared, Alistair. He knew he was being sacrificed to cause you pain.

'Defeat comes in all shapes. For years I wondered what he meant, wanted to discuss it with you, but I think we both had to forget things, find a way to move on. We never discussed it again. But I understand now. Whatever the Hollow Man was, he was out to hurt you, Ali. And used James to do so.'

'He didn't do a good job of it,' Alistair said, his tone bitter. 'I can't even remember James properly. What kind of defeat is that?'

Ray shrugged. 'I don't know.'

'What happened after James jumped?'

Ray took a deep breath. 'I rushed to the edge of the gorge, trying to see where James had gone. Stupid really, where else could he have gone? But I couldn't see him. The water had claimed him.

'I remember turning to you. I think I wanted to hold you and tell you that it was okay, to protect you. I think, at that moment, I knew I had to try and become the big brother you needed. Like James, I'd actively kept you away from the Bledoe Cadets, never really let you in. I was a kid, and kids can be spiteful, but right then I think I knew I had been wrong. That we had both lost the best friend we both had. James was, in some ways, as much my brother as yours.

'So, when I turned to you I found you had already gone. You were running down the side of the gorge. I called after you, but you didn't listen, or didn't hear. I'm not sure which. For a moment I stalled, part of me knowing I should run and find our parents, tell them what had happened. We needed them more then than ever before, but instead I ran after you.

'By the time I reached you, you were down by the stream where it joined the River Fowey. The water was wild there, moving fast, and it had dredged James' body up, got it caught on some broken branches. You were there, kneeling by the edge, trying for all your worth to reach and grab your brother. But your arms were too short.

'All I could do was stand there, watching. I'm not sure how but our parents found us. They said they heard me shout out. The worst sound they had ever heard. I don't remember shouting.'

Ray had run out of things to say. For a few moments the men sat in silence, the tale sinking in.

Ray wanted to understand how Alistair was feeling, but he couldn't. He had lived with it his whole life, but for Alistair this was all new. However true it was, it was still new. How did one deal with that kind of news?

'Alistair, I just want you to know that...'

Ray was interrupted by the sound of movement upstairs. Something falling. Alistair's head snapped up.

'Mum!' he almost hissed, and darted towards the staircase.

CHAPTER TWELVE
Village Under Siege

LETHBRIDGE-STEWART LEFT RAY TO ATTEND GEORGE, while he gave chase. Even as he darted out of the kitchen door and scanned the fields beyond, his mind raced. He should have realised the Intelligence would have control of someone in Bledoe. It always had control of someone. In Tibet it was some lama, in London it had been both Travers and Arnold. Why should Bledoe be any different?

Owain Vine was the obvious candidate, considering his long stay at the Manor. There was little doubt in Lethbridge-Stewart's mind that the Yeti had come from the Manor, too.

There!

Despite the cold his mother was in the same damp clothes, no coat to protect her against the air. The sun may have been shining, but that didn't stop the wind from biting icily at Lethbridge-Stewart's skin. He could only imagine how his mother must be feeling. She was walking almost casually, her arm linked in Owain's, as if the two of them were off for a normal stroll in the countryside. They even appeared to be chatting.

Lethbridge-Stewart set off after them, shouting Owain's name.

The young man looked back and smiled. But he didn't quicken his pace.

Damn fool. At this rate Lethbridge-Stewart would be on them in minutes.

Then he realised the reason for Owain's casual gait. On

the horizon a Yeti appeared. Neither Owain nor Mary paid the shaggy creature any mind, they simply walked past it.

Well, it would take more than a Yeti to stop Lethbridge-Stewart. He reached down for his revolver.

His hand rested on an empty belt.

He slowed to a halt. The Yeti continued to advance on him. It raised its web gun.

'Let me get a damp cloth,' Ray said as he followed George down the stair. The man looked back up at him with a mix of anger and embarrassment.

'I'll be fine,' he snapped. 'I'm done with that little...'

Ray stopped listening, his mind a jumble. He'd barely managed to process all that was going on. Going so deeply into his past wasn't easy. Even when he wrote his books he had forgotten a lot of what he had told Alistair, but talking about it... And then, before he'd even been able to let those feelings settle Owain had kidnapped Mrs Lethbridge-Stewart. Not only that, but he had attacked his own father.

Things were making less and less sense. None of this fitted with the Owain he had seen grow into a young man. What could have possessed him?

Ray swallowed, remembering the look in James' eyes moments before he jumped into the gorge.

Possessed.

The Hollow Man; this Great Intelligence of Alistair's, it had got to Owain after all. Just like it had done with James.

Who was the Intelligence pretending to be this time, Ray wondered, that Owain would listen to it so?

George was pacing the living room when Ray returned from the kitchen. Ray handed him the wet cloth, but George batted his hand away.

'I told you I'm fine! What the hell has got into that boy? Kidnapping old women! I did not raise my sons to be like this.'

Ray frowned. 'No one is blaming you, George.'

'Maybe they should,' George responded quietly.

The back door opened and both men turned to see Alistair return. He was breathing heavily.

'Damn him,' he said, glaring at George. 'The Yeti has cut off Owain's retreat with Web. There's no way to follow him.'

Ray looked from Alistair to George. The two men were still regarding each other coldly. Ray couldn't have them fighting in his house. They had enough trouble.

'What happened?' he asked. 'Owain would never act like that, not unless he was possessed.'

George turned on Ray. 'What the hell are you on about now? Possessed? Good God, man, that's my son you're talking about there.'

Alistair took a deep breath to calm himself down.

'He's right, George. Your son has been taken over by the Great Intelligence.'

'The...? You mean this Hollow Man that Ray's been writing about all these years?' He shook his head. 'This is absurd. Completely ridiculous.'

'Pull yourself together, man!' Alistair barked. 'You've seen the Yeti, the Web, and I've told you all about recent events in London. Put the pieces together, use the brain God gave you.'

George stepped forward but Ray placed a hand on his chest. For a moment George stood there, pushing himself forward. But, slowly, he relaxed and nodded his head.

'You're right, sorry. It's just that... It's my son, Colonel. How can this happen to him? Lewis is missing, Owain is...'

'We'll do what we can to get your boys back, George, I promise you. But first we need to work out a strategy of our own. All this distraction with my... brother.' Alistair glanced at Ray. 'We've spent more than enough time on that. All the while the Yeti have surrounded Bledoe. We need to defend this village. Go on the offensive.'

Ray wasn't too happy with calling the death of James a

distraction, but he had to concede that Alistair was right. The village was now under siege. A woman had been kidnapped. He asked the only question that mattered.

'How?'

They tried as far east as possible. It made sense to Bishop; after all, from what he could gather the Yeti were coming from Remington Manor, to the west of the village, so their best bet of a gap in the perimeter was as far from the staging ground as possible.

He was mistaken.

He stalled the Land Rover and turned to Henry. 'What do you think?'

'We could try ramming it.'

'Most likely won't work. This stuff managed to block all access to London.'

It seemed like the Web was everywhere. The Yeti certainly worked fast to be able to cover such a wide area in so short a time. Of course that depended on when they started. Sometime after he and the colonel had returned to Redrose the previous night, or they would have spotted them surely.

'We should keep trying,' Henry said. 'There must be a gap somewhere.'

Bishop wasn't sure he agreed, but he tried to remain hopeful. He changed gear and released the brake.

The Land Rover bumped its way along the field, while they searched for a gate into the next one. They continued on like this for a short while, going from one field to another, but when they reached their fifth field Bishop slammed the brakes.

Several Yeti stood at the far end of the field spraying Web from their guns. But the Web didn't just stay where it landed; instead it continued to move, spreading out on the breeze, catching on every branch in the hedge lining the field. Even then it continued on, stopping only when it came into contact with Web from another gun. It pulsed, seemingly alive.

Could it be? Bishop would need to ask the colonel. He knew more about this stuff than any of them.

It wasn't just the Web that caught his eye, though. A group of five people stood about ten feet from the Yeti, ignored. None of the group moved, they just stood there, their faces vacant, their bodies limp, as if they were puppets waiting for their strings to be pulled.

'Just like Ray and George?' Henry asked.

From the colonel's descriptions of what had happened, Bishop nodded.

'We need to get them away from here.'

'How? If we move too close to the Yeti...'

'I know. Same thing might happen to us. But the colonel was okay, so maybe we will be, too. We have to risk it. We can't leave them there.'

It looked like Henry wanted to protest again, but he simply nodded.

'Okay, as soon as we're near enough, jump out and get them into the back,' Bishop said.

'Me? Why me?'

'Because I need to be ready to pull out as soon as the Yeti move towards us.'

Henry swallowed hard. Putting the Land Rover into first, Bishop inched forward, closer and closer to the group, his eyes darting to the Yeti and back again. So far the Yeti were ignoring them.

'Now, Henry, and look sharp!' he ordered.

Hesitating for a moment, Henry unlatched the door and jumped out of the Land Rover. Bishop looked back and forth from the Yeti to Henry. At first Henry moved fine – one, two, three people safely in the Land Rover – but on the fourth he started to become sluggish, blinking rapidly. Bishop leaned out of the window and called out to him.

For a moment Henry didn't notice, then with great effort

he looked at Bishop.

'Get in, before we lose you too.'

Henry didn't seem to understand. It was as if he was losing his free will. Bishop knew it was a risk, but he had no choice. He jumped out of the Land Rover and grabbed hold of Henry.

The Yeti turned in unison.

Moving as fast as he could, Bishop herded Henry into the back of the Land Rover with the other three people, and rushed around to the driver's seat. He released the brake and rammed his foot onto the accelerator. The Land Rover skidded in protest, but the tread on the tyres finally caught and the vehicle reversed through the field.

The Yeti stopped and turned to the two people left behind.

Once Bishop had returned and reported, the response was decisive. Lethbridge-Stewart refused to let his home village fall to the Great Intelligence.

Proximity to the Yeti was like a switch in the minds of people, turning them off, giving the Intelligence some kind of control of them. The only thing to do was to gather all the villagers in the centre of Bledoe, as far from the Yeti as possible. No doubt they'd advance at some point, but in the meantime the villagers could at least find a way to protect themselves.

To that end Lethbridge-Stewart had called a meeting in the village hall, and sent out the men to round up everybody they could. At first it proved to be difficult, most simply refusing to believe, until Henry spoke to the local vicar, a Reverend Edwin Stone, an open-minded chap for a man of the cloth and, unsurprisingly, also another old Bledoe Cadet.

With his help they were soon able to round up most of the villagers who remained in Bledoe, except those who lived near the Web perimeter. They had to be left alone for now, already enraptured by the mind-cleansing ability of the Yeti.

The meeting itself was a difficult affair, taking the testimony of trusted men like Henry and George to convince the villagers of the danger. Most laughed and appeared uncomfortable at the idea that Ray's Hollow Man was real, but Reverend Stone used a parable of faith to assuage their doubts.

The discussion soon turned to weapons. There were some in the back of the Land Rover, but they would need more than a few handguns and rifles. Lethbridge-Stewart was surprised, although probably shouldn't have been, to learn that quite a few villagers owned their own rifles and shotguns, and not all legally. Beyond that there were plenty of hand-to-hand weapons that could be used, everything from spades and rakes to meat cleavers, but from experience he knew such weapons would have little effect on the robotic Yeti; besides how many of the villagers would get close enough to use the weapons? What they needed were firearms that could be used from a distance.

'Firebombs,' someone from the back of the hall suggested.

A few mutters and grumbles followed, including one loud voice claiming he always knew Billy was an arsonist. Lethbridge-Stewart hardly wanted to encourage criminal behaviour, but needs must and all that.

Billy was a fifteen-year-old boy who seemed to know an awful lot about Molotov cocktails. In other circumstances Lethbridge-Stewart might have been troubled by that, but as things were they had to make use of every advantage on hand.

He sent George with Billy to supervise a small group and make whatever explosive weapons they could. True, explosives had not served them very well in London, but any small deterrent would help.

Meanwhile he tasked Bishop and Henry to come up

with a way to breach the perimeter. He had to get a message to Hamilton, and not only was there still no signal on the RT, but it seemed all the phone lines were down. Just like in London.

Whatever happened, reinforcements would be needed.

Lethbridge-Stewart still wanted to find a way to the Manor, not only to find out what the Intelligence was up to, but to rescue his mother. First though it was necessary to secure the village. Besides, it didn't look like his mother was in any immediate danger, if the casual way she had walked away with Owain was anything to go by. The Intelligence needed his mother for something.

He wondered if Arnold had reached the Manor yet. For surely that was his intention.

Arnold had a plan, but without matches or some way of creating a fire it was a plan that he could not put into operation.

The barn he had woken up in was one of three; the two larger barns either side were full of bales of hay. If he could entice a Yeti or two to the barn and ignite the hay… He remembered them fighting the Yeti in London, and although the Yeti were indefatigable, and seemingly immune to guns and other artillery, the Army had never thought to use fire on the Yeti; after all, flamethrowers had no effect on the Web that surrounded London. The way he saw it, the Yeti were only robots protected by thick fur. Fur burned. How strong would they be once exposed, their bodies no longer protected?

There were plenty of rakes and spades that he could use as weapons once the gears and wires that propelled the Yeti were exposed. But first he needed a way to start a fire.

He had never been a boy scout, and so wasn't up on surviving in the wilderness with nothing but dry sticks and the sun. Not that there were many dry sticks around anyway. The sun may have been out, but it had been a cold night and the air and ground was still damp.

What he needed was a box of matches. He patted his pockets again, just in case.

He wished he could remember what had happened to him, how he'd come to be in the barn. Even as he'd searched the haysheds he had racked his brain, trying to remember beyond going into the web with Corporal Lane, but he couldn't remember a blasted thing. How had he got from London to here… wherever here actually was!

He was once again huddled by the hedge, looking out at the Yeti. They hadn't moved much, other than to spread the Web. He had to assume the worst, that London had fallen and Colonel Lethbridge-Stewart's plan had failed. Perhaps they were all dead now? God knows enough men died before he had.

Arnold shook his head. No, he couldn't berate himself over that any more. He had to focus. Take back a little of what the Intelligence had taken from him.

His head whipped around at the sound of movement.

'Ere, who the hell are you?'

A young man, in his early twenties at the most, stood nearby, looking a little worse for wear. His clothes were dirty, his coat torn. His hair was short, almost military in its closeness. He looked at Arnold like a wild thing.

'Well, speak up, lad. Who are you?'

'Charles… Charles Watts. Who the hell are you?'

'Staff Sergeant Arnold, Royal Engineers 21 Regiment,' Arnold replied automatically. He shook his head. 'Never mind me, lad. What's happened to you? You look like you've been pulled through a hedge backwards.'

Watts blinked, and his lips curved into a slight smile. 'Something like that. I've been running all night, hiding, trying to keep away from those things.'

Arnold considered. From what he could see the village was surrounded, and he knew from experience that attempting to break through the Web was futile, which meant...

'Running from where?'

'The Manor,' Watts said. 'It's up there, the Whisperer, controlling those abominable snowmen. I think they must have got Lewis... I haven't seen him in hours.' He looked around. 'I need to get back to the village, but there's no way in. That Web. It's everywhere.'

The Whisperer. Arnold vaguely recalled a voice whispering to him. Could it be the Intelligence? Arnold couldn't see what else it would be, especially if it was controlling the Yeti.

He looked back through the hedge. He wouldn't be able to get back into the village, and without matches he... No, never mind the matches. He had a better plan.

'You need to show me to this Manor.'

'You're out of your head. I ain't going up there again.'

Arnold didn't have time for this, but he could tell Watts was scared, so he said, as calmly as he could, 'Listen, lad, those *things*, as you call 'em, have already taken London, and if they're here a lot more than one city has fallen. If I can get to the Manor I may be able to put a stop to this. Those Yeti have killed hundreds already, but they're just weapons. If I can stop the Intelligence...' He frowned, trying to remember. What was it McCrimmon had said in London? 'A pyramid. Did you see a pyramid in the Manor? If we destroy that, we can stop the Yeti.'

A dark cloud passed over Watts' face. 'What do you mean, taken London? But that's my home. How...' He shook his head. 'What the hell is going on?'

'The rout of civilisation, I should think. Now, we need to get to that Manor, and you need to show me the way.'

He wanted to be out there, but Lethbridge-Stewart was the Officer in Command for the duration of the siege. There was nobody else in the village who could take his place, with his experience, and besides which, he was the only person in the village with any official lawful authority. No police were stationed in Bledoe to take charge or help, although as a result of the meeting earlier he had learned that there were several ex-military men living in the village. These he had put to work immediately, sending them out to keep an eye on the activities of the Yeti, armed with their own firearms; short range rifles and shotguns primarily. If the Yeti were advancing, Lethbridge-Stewart wanted to know before it was too late.

He didn't like commanding civilians, but he had little choice in the matter. Still, in some ways, this village was his home as much as theirs and they all deserved the right to protect it.

He had commandeered the pub as his centre of operations; although the village hall was bigger, it was too close to the church and thus the graves of several brave men who had given their lives for their country. If there was to be final battle, then Lethbridge-Stewart wanted to make sure it was as far away from the graveyard as possible.

The pub door opened and Mark Cawley, the local vet, entered.

'Colonel, there seems to be something very strange going on.'

Lethbridge-Stewart looked up from the map on the table before him and raised a laconic eyebrow. 'You don't say. Specifically?'

'Getting reports of a... vibration.'

'A vibration? Machinery?'

'Not so we can see, sir.' Cawley shrugged. 'It's not a physical vibration, more something in the air. Sets your teeth on edge, according to Ross.'

Lethbridge-Stewart wasn't sure who Ross was, no doubt one of the runners who conveyed messages from the watch-points to the command centre. He nodded slowly, not sure exactly what such a vibration could mean. Another weapon of some sort, no doubt. Perhaps connected to the

Yeti's new mind-clearing ability.

'Any more debilitating bouts of peacefulness, Mr Cawley?'

'Not at the moment. But I suppose if the Yeti advance that will change.'

Lethbridge-Stewart checked his wristwatch. 'Bishop and Mr Vine should be in position by now.'

Cawley glanced up at the clock above the bar. 'Do you reckon they'll get through?'

'Let's hope so, Mr Cawley, or you may end up working on humans instead of animals. If we don't get reinforcements, Dr Starling may well be in need of your help.'

They had chosen Fore Street. It was narrow, and thus easily controlled, plus it had a ready-made weapon.

George couldn't believe how easily he accepted that, how little it troubled him. But he had spent over half his life in Bledoe, raised his children there; as far as he was concerned, it was home, and he had to do whatever was necessary to protect it. He looked through the binoculars at the crashed car, feeling a very brief moment of sadness.

He could see the two bodies draped half across the bonnet, tangled up in the smashed windscreen. He was relieved to see no other bodies; no sign of either Charles or, thankfully, Lewis. He still had no idea where his son was, but at least he could hold on to the hope that he was alive out there.

George hadn't known the Watts' well, and what he did know he didn't much care for, but he didn't think they deserved such an end. He tried to think of what they were about to do as igniting a funeral pyre and sending them on their way.

A Yeti stood in the middle of the lane, only a few feet from the crashed car. Close enough for their purposes.

George moved the binoculars and watched the two

people sneaking along the verge, almost pressing themselves into the hedge as they neared the car.

Young Billy Moynihan was your classic ne'er do well, a bad influence on everybody he knew. Fifteen and already out of school, expelled for his trouble-making ways almost two years previously. The only kid George had ever forbade his children from bothering with. That Billy had such a knowledge of explosives came as no surprise. Even now, through the binoculars, he could see the excitement written all over the boy's rough little face. The man with Billy, Adrian Shosty, looked more cautious, fearful almost – as he should. They were risking their lives after all.

He glanced back at the Land Rover parked behind him. Bishop and Henry sat inside, waiting patiently. It was decided that Henry should go with Bishop, an extra voice should one be needed, and back-up in case the close proximity of the Yeti should affect either of them. George smiled grimly and returned his attention to Billy and Mr Shosty.

Still undetected, they approached the car. In one hand Billy held a milk bottle with a rag emerging from its long neck. A home-made petrol bomb all ready to ignite should the Yeti spot them. Shosty held another rag in his hand. They reached the car and Billy kept his eyes on the Yeti, his hands itching to ignite the bomb, while Shosty opened the petrol cap at the rear of the car. Into this he stuffed the rag and retrieved a box of matches from his pocket.

George frowned. The zealous look on Billy's face was fading, replaced by a docile limp look. Already the Yeti was affecting him. Shosty was thus far his normal self, fortunately, and he flicked a match off the box. It took a few attempts to light in the cold breeze, but it did and he cupped his hand around the flame, bringing it into contact with the rag.

George shuddered, feeling a tooth-jarring vibration run through his body. He closed his eyes, trying to ignore it. It was more than a vibration. Now he had his eyes closed he could feel it more clearly.

A harmonic resonance, more like a tune than a simple vibration. Like chanting. Just like he'd felt in the cow field earlier, before the presence of the Yeti had affected him and Ray.

He opened his eyes and focused, fighting the fugue in his mind.

Shosty was pulling Billy away from the car, trying not to attract the attention of the Yeti. The furry beast turned to the car, most likely alerted by the smell of the burning rag. It lumbered towards them. Shosty noticed it and, no longer needing stealth, ran as fast as he could, dragging Billy after him.

The Yeti had barely reached the vehicle when the flame disappeared into the petrol tank and the car exploded in a ball of fire and black smoke.

George dropped the binoculars, caught off guard by the noise of the explosion. He took a deep breath and retrieved them. The sight that greeted him brought a smile to his face. The flames from the car licked at the Web, burning a hole right through. The Yeti staggered around, consumed in fire.

George looked back at the Land Rover and gave the thumbs-up. Bishop returned the signal and the Land Rover rolled forwards.

Picking up speed, the vehicle careered through the gap in the Web, knocking the stumbling Yeti aside as it did. George grinned. It was a small victory, but hopefully one of many. His elation was short-lived, however.

As he continued to watch, the Web overcame the fire and sealed the gap, once more cutting them off from the rest of Cornwall.

George ran down the lane towards Billy and Shosty. The teenager was back to his old self again, jumping and jeering at the Yeti, which continued to stagger around, the fire slowly lessening as it ran out of fur to burn. George had barely reached them before he felt it again; that harmonic chant.

He called out to Billy, to warn him away from the Yeti, but the words hardly escaped his mouth when a metal claw emerged from the flames and gripped Billy by the neck.

Shosty went to move forward, but George pulled him back. They watched, horrified, as the flames died down and the Yeti was revealed in its full robotic glory. George wasn't sure what to make of it.

Bits of fur hung off it in clumps, the silver surface was scorched by the flames but otherwise it looked undamaged. Although standing a good six-foot, the bulky machine looked squat and dangerous. A pneumatic hiss accompanied every movement of its powerful metal arms and legs, hydraulic muscles pumping. At the centre of its chest was a gaping hole, the size of a softball. George had never seen anything like it before; even on TV, with the wonders of modern film making, nothing quite rivalled the robot that even now choked the life out of Billy.

There was no doubt that the boy had lost. But he clearly did not agree. Struggling, choking as the metal claw tightened its grip, he pulled out a lighter and ignited the rag sticking out of the petrol bomb to which he still clung fiercely.

'No!' George yelled. 'It's no good!'

For as long as he lived George knew he'd never forget the look in Billy's eyes.

The boy knew that the petrol bomb would not harm the Yeti now that its fur had been burned off, but he didn't care. He simply wanted to feel the bomb explode around him. Feel the fire consume him.

George turned away at the sound of the petrol bomb going off, sickened that someone so young could have such a disregard for his own life.

Lethbridge-Stewart rubbed his eyes and took the tea that Ray offered him. He sat on the table, turning his back to the map. He wondered if Bishop had succeeded in breaching the Web; he hoped so. They had failed to in London, but things had been different then. The way the Web was acting, the strange chanting from the Yeti... It was almost as if both were being controlled by a different Intelligence.

'There's something that still puzzles me,' he said.

Ray looked around the busy pub, and smiled wanly. 'Just one thing?'

'James. I don't understand why the Intelligence would go after him. Or, rather, me.'

Ray nodded. 'Yes, that puzzles me, too. What would an alien want with you? *Defeat comes in all shapes*, James said. Why would it wish to defeat you?'

'Exactly. I had never even heard of the Intelligence a month ago. Indeed, the whole idea of aliens...' Lethbridge-Stewart sipped the tea. 'Well, it was quite absurd. Not even a month ago... Yet it wanted to defeat me thirty years ago.'

'Maybe we're reading this all wrong. Maybe the Hollow Man wasn't the Intelligence after all? As you say, it never came to Earth until a month ago.'

'No, that was when I first confronted it. It first came to Earth, as far as I know, in 1935, in Tibet. Which, at least, explains the Yeti.'

'Two years before James...' Ray bit his lip. 'Still not sure this makes any sense to me.'

'But it must have been the Intelligence,' Lethbridge-Stewart said, remembering the engraving he'd seen on the windowsill in James' old room. 'James scratched "GI" into the sill of his bedroom. At first I thought it stood for Gordon, my father, and someone else. But... Well, it obviously stands for Great Intelligence.'

Ray frowned, and then smiled grimly. 'That's still there? I never knew. I remember when James did that; that had to be at least 1934. *Before* we met the Hollow Man. Before Tibet, too.'

'But...'

'I think it must have worn over time. The "I" isn't an "I" at all. It's a "J".'

'Ah. Gordon and James. My father and brother, of course.'

Yes, that made sense to Lethbridge-Stewart. From the story Ray had told, it did seem like his father and brother had been close. Only the look on Ray's face now suggested something else.

'What is it?'

Ray put his cup down. 'I think I need to show you something, and everything will make sense.'

Lethbridge-Stewart finished his own tea and followed Ray out of the pub, rather looking forward to getting some answers finally.

Mary was growing tired. She was too old for so much walking. But she liked her company. The young man, Owain, had been sent to her by Gordon and he was now taking her to her husband's ghost.

She needed to rest.

Gently Owain helped her to sit on a fallen tree trunk, and together they looked out over the gorge. She remembered this area of Golitha Falls, but she wasn't sure how. She closed her eyes, wanting to sleep.

The boy stood on the opposite side of the gorge and beckoned her across.

That was it. This was the place she'd seen in her dream. She looked up at Owain.

'What does he look like now?' she asked.

Owain smiled. 'Like a boy, about twelve years old. He's wearing an old school uniform, like they used to wear at Liskeard Grammar about thirty years ago. I've seen it in photographs. Dark hair, very brown eyes.' He looked at her. 'Eyes like mine, actually.'

Mary looked him in the eye, and he was right. It was like looking at her…

No. That was wrong. The description was of the boy in her dream, the ghost of her husband, except…

Now she was looking into Owain's eyes she got the sense that she was missing something. Something very important.

'It's not my Gordon,' she said. 'I know it's not. Why would he be dressed in a thirty-year-old uniform?' She shook her head. 'He was a grown man thirty years ago.'

Owain shrugged. 'I don't know, but he is Gordon. Believe me, I know everything about him, and he *is* Gordon.'

Mary swallowed hard. 'But he's not my Gordon,' she said sadly, knowing for certain that she was right.

Lethbridge-Stewart stood before the gravestone, the sun reflecting off its polished surface while the cold air continued to bite at his skin. Ray had been right. It didn't explain everything, but it certainly explained *some* things.

His mother wasn't looking for his father after all, but rather the only person in his family who had been touched by the Intelligence.

'We all called him James,' Ray said, 'but that wasn't his given name. Like you, he was named after one of your grandfathers… *and* your father.'

Lethbridge-Stewart read out the name on the headstone, as things started to fall into place.

'Gordon James Lethbridge-Stewart.'

CHAPTER THIRTEEN
Waiting it Out

GEORGE WOULDN'T MEET HIS GAZE, BUT LETHBRIDGE-STEWART recognised the look in the man's eyes as he explained about Billy Moynihan's death. Naturally Lethbridge-Stewart took the responsibility on his own shoulders; he was, after all, the commander here and every action and consequence in their campaign against the Great Intelligence fell at his feet. Of course, everybody in the village deserved to do what they could to protect Bledoe, and Lethbridge-Stewart would not deny any of them their moment, but he could have stopped Billy if he had wished. But he had allowed the boy to go. Lethbridge-Stewart could feel bad about it all later, right now he had a village to protect.

'And you say Bishop got through?'

George nodded silently.

That was good news at least. In London fire had no discernible effect on the Web, but here... Another difference. Once again Lethbridge-Stewart was at a loss to explain why things were so different from the incursion in London, but he was not one to look a gift horse in the mouth.

'Take a few minutes to gather your strength, George. Ray,' Lethbridge-Stewart said, calling over his old friend. 'A shot of Henry's finest whisky for George here. Man looks like he could do with a bit of fortifying.'

Ray nodded and made his way behind the bar.

'Aren't you going to ask?' George said.

'Ask what?'

'About Billy's parents.'

Lethbridge-Stewart could see the challenge on George's face.

'Now is not the time, Private,' he said, keeping his tone firm. 'There will be plenty of time to take stock and lick our wounds once Bledoe is safe again.'

George shook his head. 'Our wounds? A boy died, Alistair.'

'Yes, I am well aware, thank you. Many more could die before this day is out, and every death lies squarely on my shoulders.'

Ray arrived with the whisky and offered it to George.

George looked at the glass. 'You think this will make everything okay? Billy's father is in prison, you know.'

Lethbridge-Stewart raised an eyebrow. 'Is he indeed.' He turned to Ray. 'Take Mr Vine into the back. I have work to do here.'

Ray swallowed but did as he asked. George protested, but a sharp look from Lethbridge-Stewart quietened his protests and he followed Ray out of the bar.

Once they were gone, Lethbridge-Stewart turned back to the map and glanced at his watch.

How long would it take for Bishop to contact Hamilton? And, more importantly, could he really hold the village long enough with only ex-servicemen and civilians as his troops?

Bishop waited until they were a couple of miles out of Bledoe before he pulled the Land Rover onto the verge of the A38. He took out the large Army issue walky-talky and turned it on, looking around as he rested momentarily against the vehicle. He wasn't too far from the railway bridge, the same bypass where the pile-up had occurred only yesterday.

The RT crackled and he tuned it into the frequency Lethbridge-Stewart had shown him. Within moments he was being put through to General Hamilton. He launched into his report, beginning with the pertinent facts, but Hamilton cut him off: Major Douglas was already en route to Liskeard with a regiment of troops and special equipment for dealing with Yeti. Bishop was ordered to give a full report to Douglas once he arrived at Liskeard.

Bishop turned the RT off and looked at Henry. 'Well, that's a turn up.'

'Bloody good news, if you ask me. But how did they know?'

Bishop shrugged and climbed back into the Land Rover. 'Beats me. Guess I'll find out when I report to Major Douglas.'

'The colonel will be pleased.' Henry glanced back in the general direction of Bledoe. 'Do you think they'll be okay in the meantime?'

'Let's hope so. Colonel Lethbridge-Stewart knows what he's doing. He'll keep your home safe,' Bishop said with absolute certainty.

'You're quite taken by him, aren't you?'

'Of course,' Bishop admitted. 'He's one of the Jock Guards; you can't touch them with impunity.'

Henry nodded at that. 'Yes, you're probably right. Knew men like him in Korea, all good men, always looking out for their units.'

'Do you miss it?'

'My National Service?' Henry laughed briefly. 'If you'd asked me that a few days ago, I'd have said no, but now... I'm not sure. I was raised by a publican, spent most of my life behind a bar, but protecting what you love...' He smiled, and Bishop recognised the look of fire in his eyes. It was the same reason he'd joined the Army. 'It kind of grows on you.'

As they raced up the A38 towards Liskeard, Bishop

found himself smiling. He was warming to Henry's company more and more, enjoyed watching the man open up. In some ways Henry reminded Bishop of his father. Just like Bishop Senior, Henry had spent way too much of his life hiding from the world, but once exposed to the importance of fighting for what matters...

Bishop didn't see Henry remaining a publican for much longer.

'Lewis is dead, you know.'

Ray looked over at George, who was sitting on the armchair in Henry's living room. Ray had been flicking through Henry's LPs to see if he could find some relaxing music. Since returning to the back of the pub, the Barns' home, George had not said a lot, simply sat there nursing the shot of whisky in his hands.

'What? Why would you think such a thing?'

George looked up from the whisky, red rings around his eyes. 'He went to find Owain last night, never returned. He's dead, he must be.'

'Don't be so daft, man, there's no reason to think that. He's probably just on the other side of the Web, trying to find a way home. Or maybe going for help.' Now he said it, Ray wondered if he believed it.

Up until now he'd been the one convinced by the evil up at the Manor, scared for Owain and the influence of the Hollow Man, but he'd not really considered Lewis. Forgot the other twin was missing.

'No. I felt it. Last night.' A visible shiver ran through George. 'I didn't want to admit it but seeing what happened to Billy...' He finally sipped on the whisky. 'You know why old Brân Moynihan is inside, don't you?'

Ray didn't want to talk about that. The whole village knew, that's why Billy and his antics surprised none of them. He was a product of his dad's actions. Though he'd be damned for thinking it, Ray considered the village better off without the male Moynihans in it. Perhaps Susan Moynihan could get some peace at last. Although Ray doubted it; the damage had already been done.

'I don't want to end up like that,' George whispered.

At first Ray wasn't sure what George meant, but then it sunk in. He supposed he'd always known, deep down, but the twins were always so well behaved, as for Shirley... Okay, so she was a bit timid, but... Ray needed a shot of whisky himself.

'Listen to me, George, the way I see it, it's simple. If you see a problem you do something to fix it. Not mope about.'

For a moment Ray thought George was going to stand up and punch him, but the anger on his face subsided and was replaced by the crestfallen look of defeat. He took a deep breath and downed the rest of the whisky. He stood and handed the empty glass to Ray.

'You're right. Enough of this nonsense. The colonel needs my help, and I need his. I have to find my boys.'

Ray looked down at the empty glass as George left the living room. Whatever happened after today, one way or another he knew that life in Bledoe would never be the same again.

Not for any of them.

They finally reached the old house. Mary didn't like the look of it, she never had. There was a time when the family living there were well regarded in the village, almost revered. An American family, as she recalled, but they had all left the Manor in the late '30s, quite abruptly. Around the time the rumours about the ghost had started.

And now her Gordon was waiting for her there. She knew that was no coincidence, and wondered if perhaps it was her husband's ghost that was the source of all those stories.

Only the memory of the boy, and the way Owain

described Gordon...

Owain squeezed her hand gently and led her into the house, past the Yeti that guarded the large door. They entered the grand hall, and there in the middle of the hall, standing next to some kind of plastic and metal pyramid was the boy she had seen in her dreams.

'I know you,' she said, her breath almost catching in her throat.

'Of course you do,' Owain said, walking over to the boy. 'It's your husband. And he's been waiting for you.'

The boy looked up at Owain and smiled, shaking his head. 'Is that what you thought?'

'Well yes.' Now Owain looked puzzled. 'You said you were waiting for her, and I know that you're the colonel's father, Gordon, so...'

'That's not my Gordon,' Mary said.

She didn't understand it, but she knew without doubt that it was not her dead husband as a child. She had seen pictures of him from when he was a boy, and although the child before her bore similar features, he was definitely not the same person.

'But I do know you.'

'Well, of course you do, Mother.'

It hit her like a lead weight in her chest. *Mother*. The boy had called her *Mother*, but she only had one son and he was now grown. He was in the village, in fact. But...

Mary felt herself going faint, her head spinning.

'James?' she asked, and the boy nodded.

It was her son. Gordon James.

The world went black around her.

'It's like a small army,' Henry said.

'After what happened in London, can't say I'm surprised,' Bishop said, as he pulled the Land Rover to the side of the road to join the convoy of military vehicles. He pulled the brake and went to step out of the Land

Rover. 'You can stay here, if you like,' he said, looking back at Henry.

'No, I'll come. Be nice to stretch my legs. Besides, you might need me to support your report.'

The two men stepped out of the Land Rover and walked the length of the convoy, passing several jeeps and Land Rovers full of troops, all armed to the teeth. As they neared the truck at the front, the passenger door of the cabin opened and two people emerged. One was the major, and the other was an elfin-faced woman in her late twenties with dark hair and sparkling eyes.

Bishop saluted. 'Sir, Rifleman Bishop, Green Jackets 5th Battalion, reporting as ordered.'

Major Douglas returned the salute and looked at Henry. 'And you are?'

Henry gave his best salute. 'Private Henry Barns, 1st Battalion, Gloucestershire Regiment.'

Douglas raised an eyebrow. '1st Battalion?'

'Retired, sir,' Henry said.

'Ah, I see.' Douglas turned to the woman standing beside him, regarding the men with some amusement. 'This is Miss Anne Travers, our resident science advisor.'

Miss Travers reached out and shook hands with both Henry and Bishop. 'Pleased to meet you both. Perhaps you'd like to see my new toy?'

Bishop looked at Douglas in question.

'That can wait a moment, Miss Travers. First of all, let's hear your report, Rifleman. I assume Colonel Lethbridge-Stewart is in good health?'

'Yes, sir, he is. He sent me, in fact.'

'Thought so. Very well, fill me in.'

Bishop explained everything he'd been witness to in Bledoe and the state of affairs as they stood when he left. Douglas didn't look like he entirely believed the report, but he nonetheless listened to it all without challenge, looking at Miss Travers at certain points, in particular when Bishop explained about the Yeti's ability to clear the minds of those in close proximity.

'What do you make of that?' Douglas asked her once Bishop had finished.

'It's a new one on me. The Yeti never exhibited such behaviour in London, and my father never mentioned anything like that from Tibet.' She shrugged. 'Not to worry, I'm sure we'll be able to take care of them from a distance.'

'I'm glad you think so. I have to admit I'm still not entirely convinced by all this.' Douglas waved Miss Travers on. 'Very well, let's show these chaps what we have on our side.'

'My pleasure,' she said, and led the three men to the rear of the Army truck.

In the back, under the watchful eye of three armed soldiers, was a device the likes of which Bishop had never seen before. It was huge, a box of switches with some kind of antenna sitting on top. A silver sphere poked out of the side of the box, cables connecting it to the antenna.

Bishop looked to the major, but it was clear that Douglas was no wiser to it than Bishop.

Miss Travers folded her arms and looked at the machine proudly.

'My father and I built that, based it on a smaller device me and... a friend devised in London. When activated it will send a signal through here,' she pointed to the sphere, 'and transmit it to the spheres that control the Yeti. We can turn them on each other.'

'I thought the Great Intelligence controlled them?'

Miss Travers nodded. 'You're right, Rifleman, but it does so by transmitting some kind of signal on the astral plane apparently. The control spheres that sit in the Yeti chests receive the signal. This machine will interrupt that signal, and allow us to control them instead.'

'Bit of a boffin, our Miss Travers,' Major Douglas said,

clearly impressed.

'A bit?' Miss Travers looked affronted by this. 'I didn't spend all those years in Cambridge, and other places, to become a *bit* of anything. And I'll thank you to remember that, Major Douglas.'

Henry knelt near the machine for a closer look. He glanced back at Miss Travers. 'You built this?'

'With help from my father, yes. Is that so hard to believe, Mister Barns?'

Henry whistled in appreciation. 'She's right, Major, she is more than a *bit* of a boffin.' He shook his head and stood up again. 'So, this will take care of the Yeti, but what about the Web? Have you invented something to defeat that, too? This machine won't be much use to us if we're stuck outside the village.'

Bishop could only grin at the broad smile on Miss Travers' face. He was never one for short hair on women, but he had to admit she wore hers well, and it certainly added an element of beauty to her face.

'Well, of course I do,' Miss Travers said. 'Let me show you.' She moved deeper into the truck and the men followed. 'I've been studying the Web since London, and have come to the conclusion that it is basically a copy of a human brain, only much larger, of course.' She glanced back and grinned at the stupefied expressions on Henry and Douglas.

Bishop shared her smile. He liked his sci-fi, and read a fair few science journals. It wasn't too hard to follow Miss Travers.

'But why a human brain?' he asked. 'I thought it was alien.'

'Very good point... Er, what's your first name?'

'William,' he said, almost blushing at the request of informality.

'Okay. Very good point, Bill. It's something I still haven't worked out. But, like I was saying, it is a copy of a human brain, and much like a real brain it's a mix of chemicals and electrical impulses. I intend to disrupt the brain activity by means of a specially aimed electromagnetic pulse set to a frequency of...'

The three men listened intently, and luckily Major Douglas was so focused he didn't even notice the rapidly expanding smile on Bishop's face.

Miss Travers was amazing!

Owain stepped back from the pyramid and looked from Mary to Gordon.

He'd thought he knew all about the Great Intelligence, what it was, where it came from, but now he wasn't sure. He had been certain that the form it took was Gordon Lethbridge-Stewart, the war hero father of the colonel, the one who had died protecting his country. The Intelligence knew he thought this, so why did it lie to him? What else had it lied about?

Before agreeing to bring Mary to the Manor he had insisted on being told everything. To learn how much truth there was to the colonel's story about recent events in London. Gordon, or James, or the Intelligence – Owain wasn't even sure what to call him now – had explained that what was recent for Earth was a long time ago for the Intelligence. That it came from a long way in the future...

'Owain, you must attach the wires,' the boy said.

'Why?' Owain looked around at the Yeti that remained in the hall. 'You still haven't told me why you need her.'

Gordon titled his head, like a dog hearing a strange sound. 'I am weak, spread too thin, trying to control the Yeti and the Web... too much for me. There is a trace of me left in Mary. She was touched by me. I didn't realise how weak I was then, and clearing her mind of James took more from me than I expected. But joining with you has restored some of my strength. Drawing from the source. But it's still not enough.'

'Clearing her... You mean you made her forget about her own son? Why?'

'Too many questions.' Gordon walked towards him and reached out a hand. 'You must trust me, Owain. You know why.'

The boy's hand rested on Owain's chest and Owain felt the peace fill him once more.

Yes, Gordon was right. He did know why he could trust Gordon. They were the same. The beginning and the end.

'I can feel him,' Owain said.

Gordon closed his eyes. 'Yes,' he whispered. 'Albert is drawing close.' He looked over at Mary, who sat in the pyramid, her eyes staring like she was in a trance. 'Soon I will be whole once again. At last.'

Lethbridge-Stewart didn't understand it. He'd received several reports now and they all said the same; the Yeti weren't advancing at all.

If he were the Great Intelligence he'd be pressing home the advantage. As they'd proved, whatever weapons they had were, by and large, ineffective against the Yeti. They were surrounded, their defensive position as close to hopeless as was possible. And yet, still the Great Intelligence kept its soldiers in place. Not allowing anybody in or out of the village, but not attacking.

He surveyed the map and considered the placing of the Yeti in relation to the village. He had used a red pen to trace a line around the village, representing the Web. Bledoe was smack bang in the middle.

If the Yeti moved in at the same time then the cleansing field they were generating would subdue the entire village in less than an hour. The villagers would be herded into the area immediately surrounding the pub. They wouldn't stand a chance.

'What can we do?' Cawley asked.

Several men were in the pub, sitting at the bar while Ray served them a bit of scotch to bolster their reserves.

'Wait it out until the Army get here,' Lethbridge-Stewart replied. 'We can't get near the Yeti without the majority of us succumbing to the chant, and as young Mister Moynihan has proved firebombs are not terribly effective.'

He tried to catch George's eye, but the man didn't return his look. Instead he stared down at the scotch in his glass. Lethbridge-Stewart, though, didn't look away; he knew one thing he could do while the rest of them waited it out.

'I'm going to try and find a way to the Manor. Confront the Intelligence head on.'

Now George did look up, meeting Lethbridge-Stewart's gaze and holding it while the rest of the men in the bar voiced their concerns. Lethbridge-Stewart raised a hand to silence them.

'Yes, I know, it's not likely I'll get there, but we need a distraction to make sure the Yeti keep their distance.'

'They are keeping their distance,' Fred Murray said, to murmurs of agreement.

'He's right, Alistair,' Ray pointed out. 'Why risk upsetting the apple cart?'

'Because his mother is up there.'

Lethbridge-Stewart nodded at George. 'One of the reasons, yes. Whatever the Intelligence wants my mother for, it's a safe bet that it's not going to be good for her or anybody else.'

George downed his scotch and stood. 'Good. I need to get my boys back, too. I'm going with you.'

Lethbridge-Stewart expected no less. 'And you, Ray?'

For a moment Ray didn't answer. He knew what Lethbridge-Stewart was offering him. A chance to be there at the end, to finally chase off the ghost that had haunted him for so long. Ray swallowed and looked around the bar.

'I'll… I'll stay here, keep an eye on everything for you. Sorry.'

'I quite understand.' It was too big a request, but Lethbridge-Stewart had to ask. Ray needed to be offered the opportunity.

'Just you and me, then,' he said, turning back to George.

Arnold and Watts crouched in the brush, looking out at the Manor. The grounds were empty, which pleased Arnold. He had expected a couple of Yeti to be standing on guard. That made things easier. He looked across at Watts. The young man was sweating in the cold air.

'Come on, lad, we need to do this.'

'Do we? Why? We're just two people. And you're not even armed.'

It was a point the young man had raised a few times on the way through Draynes Wood. Arnold had to admit he would have felt better with a gun in his hand, instead of the rake he'd borrowed from the hayshed. But he hefted the rake and stood up.

'Come on.'

He set off, his eyes continuously darting about just in case the Great Intelligence had any surprises in store.

He froze at the sound behind him. A sort of choked gurgle. He raised the rake and turned around, ready to defend himself.

A Yeti stood at the edge of the woods, a claw wrapped around Watts' throat. How the hell had that thing been able to sneak up on them?

'Damn it!' Arnold hissed and charged forward.

He barely got two steps before he stopped and the rake fell from his limp hands.

*

'Finally.'

Owain turned from the pyramid as the door of the hall opened and a uniformed man entered. This had to be Albert. The final piece of the Intelligence's puzzle.

Gordon walked over to him. 'I can feel it,' he said, walking around Albert, eyes closed. 'Inside him, part of me trapped, torn from the whole by the feedback when the Yeti attacked my pyramid in London.' He opened his eyes and smiled. 'Centuries in my past, and yet only a few small weeks ago on this wretched world. If only I had known what was to come.'

Owain didn't like the sound of that. The words, the tone, the relish in his voice. This was not the sound of someone who wanted to bring peace to all men. But he had to trust Gordon, he had no choice.

'And just in time,' Gordon said.

'What do you mean?'

'Lethbridge-Stewart has brought reinforcements to Bledoe. I can see them through the eyes of my Yeti.' Gordon grinned, like a child with a secret. He turned to the many silver spheres that sat discarded on the wooden floor. 'Aren't they in for a surprise.'

The small convoy of Army vehicles stopped on Fore Street, the Web before them. Major Douglas jumped out of the truck and banged on the back. 'Let's see what your toy can do, Miss Travers,' he said, as she climbed out.

The guards clambered out of the back, the remote control machine carried between them. Miss Travers walked over and guided them in placing it gently on the road's surface. She stepped behind the machine and started pressing switches.

Douglas was still finding it a little hard to accept, but he could not deny the Web before them, nor the robotic form on the other side. He assumed that was a Yeti, or at least what it looked like without fur. Lethbridge-Stewart's report, which Douglas had received from Hamilton, had explained that the Yeti were robotic. Presumably its new look was down to Bishop's escape. He glanced back as a low hum emitted from the machine.

The antenna on top of the machine began to turn. Miss Travers looked up from it with a smile.

'Now, let's make magic.'

Douglas waited, but the robot didn't move. It remained where it was, impassively looking at them through the Web.

'Is something supposed to be happening?'

'Well, yes.' Miss Travers checked the machine. 'I don't understand. It's transmitting, so why isn't...' She stopped suddenly and rushed over to Major Douglas. Her hand went to her mouth. 'Oh no.'

'What is it?'

She pointed at the robotic creature. 'Look, in its chest.'

Douglas looked, but he saw nothing. Just a gaping hole.

'Exactly,' Miss Travers said. 'It's not controlled by a sphere. My machine is useless.'

CHAPTER FOURTEEN
Final Approach

OWAIN STOOD OUTSIDE THE MANOR HOUSE, HIS EYES closed, feeling the cold air on his face. The Intelligence was occupied, and so he'd taken the opportunity to get a little space. Be alone for a short while.

Being connected to the Intelligence – he refused to think of it as Gordon any more – opened up so much to him. If he focused he could see everything the Intelligence could see through the eyes of the many Yeti surrounding the village.

There, on the other side of the Web he could see two men. His dad and the colonel, crossing the sports field, walking towards him. Owain smiled.

The Web was an extension of the Intelligence. If the Intelligence could control it, then so could Owain. After all, they both came from the same place.

Neither man needed to talk. They had their mission and too many thoughts to share.

Lethbridge-Stewart was wondering about the Web, which was barely fifty yards away. He held one of the Molotov cocktails in his hand, hoping that the heat would be enough to open a gap big enough for them to pass through. He supposed a couple of grenades might have worked, had there been any in the back of the Land Rover, but the explosive potential of the Molotov cocktail should prove sufficient; if it did, Lethbridge-Stewart decided he may need to re-christen it from the *poor man's grenade* to the *desperate man's grenade*.

George, however, was more focused on his sons. He should have listened to Ray and stopped their visits to the Manor at the start. Maybe done something sooner. Been a better father, a better husband. If he had been, perhaps the Watts' boy would not have so easily led Lewis astray, and Owain would not have been such an easy target for the Hollow Man. But such what-ifs were of little use, George knew that, since they changed nothing. All he could do now was rescue his boys and make sure he fixed things with them. And he would. This he promised himself.

Lethbridge-Stewart raised the bottle in his hand and turned to George. The other man nodded and retrieved the lighter from his trouser pocket, hefting his own bottle.

'Do you honestly think this will work?'

'The exploding car was enough to create a hole big enough for a Land Rover to pass through. The hole we need is much smaller. Two of these should work fine.'

George nodded. He trusted the colonel; after all, he was the man with the experience. George was the postmaster, the useless father. What did he know about fighting aliens?

'Although…' Lethbridge-Stewart indicated the Web. A gap was forming. Just large enough for the two of them. 'Looks like we were expected,' he said, his eyes narrow.

'That can't be good.'

'No. Well, Private Vine, keep your senses sharp. This is almost certainly a trap, but needs must when the devil drives.'

George followed Lethbridge-Stewart through the gap. 'What is it the spider said to the fly?'

'Quite. Into the parlour we go.'

*

'Now what do you suggest?' Mr Barns asked, having joined them by the edge of the Web.

Major Douglas was wondering the same thing. He turned to Miss Travers.

'Let's hope the web disruptor is more effective than your transmitter thing.'

Miss Travers folded her arms. 'Well, it's not my fault that the Yeti no longer seems to be controlled by the spheres.'

Douglas knew it wasn't, but he couldn't help the remark.

'Sir,' Bishop said, saluting. 'If I may make a suggestion?'

'Go ahead.'

'Can I suggest we save Doctor Travers' disruptor for a more strategic moment? The colonel said these Yeti are connected to the Great Intelligence, so it wouldn't do to give away all our advantages straight away.'

Bishop had a good point.

'Perhaps so, son, but we still need to get through the Web or we're no use to anybody. Do you have a better idea?'

'I do, sir. Use my Land Rover as a weapon. Same way we did to escape the village, sir.'

Douglas would hardly have called it *Bishop's* Land Rover, but it was a good idea. Although a costly one. Still, if the Intelligence was watching them through the Yeti, then it made sense to save revealing the disruptor until a better moment.

'Very well, Rifleman. Let's get to it, then.'

It didn't take too long to prepare the Land Rover. Bishop brought it to the front of the convoy, driving on the verge of the road, brushing against the hedge. They'd fashioned a way to keep the accelerator down, and stuffed some rags down into the petrol tank.

'Everybody back in the truck,' Douglas ordered.

Once there was only him and Bishop left, he lit the match in his hand and brought it to the rag. The flame connected and he nodded at Bishop. The rifleman leaned into the Land Rover and released the brake. The two men stepped back and watched as the Land Rover accelerated towards the Web.

'We should probably get some cover, sir.'

Douglas smiled grimly. 'Good idea!'

They climbed into the truck cabin and watched as the Land Rover rammed into the Web. The fungus-like substance held, causing the tyres to squeal and smoke against the road. Then the flame reached the petrol in the tank and the Land Rover exploded. The three men in the truck cabin covered their eyes with their arms.

They looked again to find the Web around the flaming Land Rover burning away.

'Now!' ordered Douglas. 'Evans, let's go.'

Driver Evans just watched the flame, singing softly to himself.

'Evans! Snap out of it, man.'

Evans blinked. 'Bloody hell. Here we go again.'

'Put your foot down, man, before the Web repairs itself.'

Eyes wide in terror, the driver did as ordered and the truck surged forward. Behind them the rest of the convoy began to move, too. Soldiers in the open-aired jeeps prepared their rifles, ready to shoot.

Even as the convoy rushed towards the Web, Douglas could see it had started to grow back. He glanced at Evans. The Welshman's brow was furrowed in concentration. The truck swerved ever so slightly and clipped the side of the flaming Land Rover, buffeting it further into the Web, causing the substance to shrink back, giving the convoy enough space to pass through.

'Well done, Evans,' Douglas said.

'Not good for nothing after all, see,' Evans said,

grinning like a madman.

Lethbridge-Stewart could see the gorge ahead of them, and remembered Ray's tale. He was at the place his brother had died. Even now he could not recall the event, even the memory of the dream was fading no matter how hard he tried to hold on to it. It seemed he was forever destined to never remember James.

The question remained; why? He suspected the answer lay in the Manor with the Great Intelligence.

'What the hell is that?'

Lethbridge-Stewart looked at where George was pointing, and pulled out his gun. Whatever the thing was, it was covered in web.

A strange look crossed George's face and he scrambled forward, jumping over a small fallen trunk and skidding to a stop beside the stream. Lethbridge-Stewart looked around, checking for Yeti. If there was web, then the Yeti couldn't be too far away.

By the time he'd joined George, the other man was on his knees, his body shaking. Lethbridge-Stewart wished he could blame the cold air for the convulsions, but it was the shape that George held in his arms that was responsible. The Web hid the contours of the body within, but George had managed to pull away some of the substance to reveal a lifeless face inside.

At first Lethbridge-Stewart thought it was Owain, but then he noticed the much shorter hair.

It was George's other son, Lewis.

'I knew it,' George said, his voice so calm it unnerved Lethbridge-Stewart. 'Last night, I woke up and I just knew it. It was like a part of me was just cut off.'

Lethbridge-Stewart didn't know what to say. He had dealt with death so much since joining the Army, buried people he had known well, people close to him. But he had never faced the death of a loved one before. Except…

He looked away, his eyes roaming to the top of the gorge a short distance away.

He didn't remember it, but he had witnessed his own brother's death. A boy even younger than Lewis. Two lives cut short by the presence of the Great Intelligence.

How many more needed to die before it was stopped?

Bishop had guided them directly to the pub, the command centre of the siege. There Douglas found an older man in glasses looking over a map on a table. He introduced himself as Raymond Phillips, and quickly filled Douglas in on the current state of play in Bledoe.

Once briefed, Douglas turned to Miss Travers.

'Remind me, you said your machine cuts off the transmission from the... what did you call it? The astro plane?'

'*Astral* plane. The aether, if you like. Why, what do you...?' Miss Travers stopped and a broad smile covered her face. 'Oh, I like the way your mind works, Major. You think it can cut off the link between Owain and the Intelligence?'

'Well, wouldn't it? If I read the report correctly, isn't that how the Intelligence possesses people? Like it did with your father.'

'The same way it controls the spheres.' She nodded. 'That would make sense, yes.'

'Excellent. Can you show Bishop how to operate it?'

'I could,' Miss Travers said slowly, suspicion in her tone.

Douglas looked down at the map. 'Very well. This is what we're going to do. We shall split into teams, each one taking the fight to the Yeti. Keep them distracted, while a smaller team heads to this Manor and assists the colonel. Bishop,' he said, looking over at the younger soldier, who was in the corner chatting to Mr Phillips. 'I want you to lead the team. You will use Miss Travers' machine to free the young man who's currently under the Intelligence's influence, and then render whatever support Lethbridge-Stewart needs.'

Bishop saluted, but before he could say anything Miss Travers stepped forward.

'Now, excuse me, Major Douglas, but I'm not staying here. I'm going to the Manor, and I will work my machine myself.'

Douglas shook his head. 'Out of the question. Your expertise is of vital importance to the British Army, and General Hamilton expressed, quite strongly, that I am to ensure we keep...'

'I survived London, I can survive this. Besides,' she added with a grin, looking over at Bishop, 'I will have my little soldier hero here to protect me.'

'It'll be my pleasure, ma'am,' Bishop said, trying his best to keep from grinning. He was not doing so very well.

Major Douglas looked from one to the other, then at Mr Phillips. 'Never get involved with strong women, Mr Phillips.'

'Confirmed bachelor,' Phillips said.

'Don't blame you.' Douglas cleared his throat. 'Very well then, Miss Travers. You will go with Bishop's team. Private, make sure you keep her safe or Hamilton will have my head. And then I will have yours.'

'Yes, sir.'

'If I may,' Mr Phillips said. 'I'd like to go, too.'

'Appreciate the offer, Mr Phillips, but I can't risk civilians, too.' Douglas pointed at the map. 'Besides, the route to the Manor seems straight forward enough.'

Phillips joined him at the table and considered the map carefully. 'Yes, it does, but there are almost certainly Yeti along that road. Whereas I can show them a path that isn't on this map, and one less likely to be guarded by Yeti. Just the Web.'

Douglas wasn't sure how he felt about this, but Phillips had a point. He knew the area better than any of them.

'Okay then, seems I'm out-voted again. The plan *now* is that you will lead a team to the Manor, Bishop, which will include Miss Travers *and* Mr Phillips. In the meantime we will keep the Yeti occupied and as far from the village itself as possible.'

The colonel led the way and George followed, his mind a maelstrom of thoughts. He had been too late in realising how bad things had got in his house. It took the death of the broken Billy Moynihan to make him realise. And now it was too late. Now he had lost one of his boys and maybe the other, too, and it was too late to fix anything.

He wasn't even sure why he was following Lethbridge-Stewart any more. The man seemed to know where he was going, he didn't need George's help.

'Another one,' Lethbridge-Stewart said.

George dragged himself out of his slump and caught up with the colonel. They were now at the edge of the woods, the Manor some yards before them. Lethbridge-Stewart knelt down and rolled the body over. It was Charles Watts.

George felt a coldness fill him. He didn't care for the Watts family in general, especially not the influence Charles had on Lewis, but now both boys were dead…

'This has to end,' he said.

Lethbridge-Stewart nodded. 'It will. Today. Come on.'

The two men set off towards the Manor.

CHAPTER FIFTEEN
The Last Shot

LETHBRIDGE-STEWART WAS MINDFUL THAT HE WAS walking into a trap, but nonetheless he entered by the main entrance. There were no Yeti in the grounds of the Manor, which meant they were almost certainly inside the house. George had picked up the rake they'd found at the edge of the woods, but Lethbridge-Stewart knew that such a weapon was of little use. His own pistol would likely do no good. The Intelligence had no form, and he couldn't believe he'd shoot Owain, not with George beside him at any rate. The man had lost one son, and Lethbridge-Stewart intended to save the other one.

The doors creaked open and the two men entered the dank and dusty hall. A large staircase stood before them, doors either side, but they held no interest for either man. What mattered most was the scene before them.

To one side lay several silver spheres. Two Yeti stood by the main door, but they didn't make a move towards the men. Near the staircase sat a pyramid; Lethbridge-Stewart was certain it was the same one he'd seen in Piccadilly Circus Station, although it had been enhanced somewhat since then. At least that explained where the Yeti had come from; like the pyramid, they had been brought from wherever it was they had been stored after being cleared from London. He wondered how that had happened, but when his eyes alighted on Staff Sergeant Arnold he had a good idea. The staff sergeant stood next to the pyramid, wearing a metal cap similar to that which he had worn in Piccadilly when he had been controlled by the Intelligence. Wires connected him to the pyramid, in which sat another person Lethbridge-Stewart knew.

His mother, also wearing a metal cap wired up to the pyramid. Both she and Arnold were looking into nothing, their eyes staring and vacant. A trance-like, meditative state.

He raised his gun and pointed it at the pyramid.

'I wouldn't advise that. Remember what happened to Arnold the last time someone interfered with the transfer?'

The voice was strong, cultured. And icy cold.

A boy emerged from behind the staircase, followed by Owain. Although he had no memory of the boy, Lethbridge-Stewart recognised him from the photograph Ray had shown him. It was his brother, Gordon James. Despite this child-like appearance, though, the voice that spoke was a man's.

Lethbridge-Stewart didn't change his aim.

'Sometimes dead is better,' he said firmly. He wasn't sure he would be able to sacrifice his mother should it come down to it, but he couldn't let the Intelligence know that.

'How very philosophical of you, Brigadier.'

'I'm sorry?'

The boy shook his head with a smile. 'My mistake. You're still only a colonel, of course. Sometimes being me is confusing.'

'Owain, come away from him,' George said.

The younger Vine didn't move. Instead he continued to watch the apparition of James. 'He's promised to bring peace to all of us,' Owain said. 'Make us all part of the pure consciousness.'

'What are you talking about?' George asked. 'You can't listen to this thing. It's not a boy.'

'I know. It's the Great Intelligence, the ultimate evolution of the enlightened soul.'

'Is that what it's told you?' Lethbridge-Stewart asked. 'It's no enlightened soul. It's an alien parasite, responsible for the deaths of hundreds.' He narrowed his eyes and looked directly at the Intelligence. 'And it is not my brother, just a poor copy of him.'

Without warning he twisted his body around and shot one of the Yeti directly between the eyes. It dropped like a lead weight. The other Yeti reacted instantly, grabbing George by the throat.

'You see? Is this the reaction of an enlightened being?'

Owain frowned. 'But it told me… It's changed since you last met.'

'It killed Lewis,' George growled, his voice raw from emotion and pain.

Owain reacted like he had been slapped. He staggered backwards, collapsing into the banister of the staircase. He looked around, shaking his head.

'What? But you…' He pulled himself to his feet. 'I knew. Somehow I knew. You lied to me.'

The Intelligence shook his head. 'Not entirely. Everything I have told you is true. I just haven't told you everything.'

'But you showed me. I saw into your mind.'

'You saw only what I wished to share. I am the Great Intelligence, how can a mind such as yours hope to understand me?'

The boy that had been James Lethbridge-Stewart fell apart, like burning embers in a fire, and was replaced by the figure of a man. He was tall, a few inches shorter than Lethbridge-Stewart, his face stern and cold, lank black hair under a top hat, his clothes a hundred years out of time. He must have noticed the look on Lethbridge-Stewart's face, because he laughed.

'Don't fool yourself into thinking you're seeing the real me. I haven't had form for centuries, but this avatar, Walter

Simeon, I have something of an affinity with.'

'What do you want?' Lethbridge-Stewart asked, walking towards the spheres, drawing the Intelligence's attention away from the pyramid, to which Owain was edging closer. 'Last time we met you wanted to add another mind to yours.'

'Did I? Oh, that was so long ago. My goals have changed since then. Right now I want only what every living thing wants. To survive.'

'So you brought my mother here? Reanimated Arnold. To help you survive.'

The Intelligence smiled. 'Yes, although I do not expect you to...'

Understand!

It is alone, lost. For centuries it has lived without form, seeking to add more minds to its own. But now it is lost, falling through time, weak. It cannot even remember its name. If it ever had one. It falls to Earth, like snow in winter. On Earth the year is 1842 and there it meets a boy, Walter Simeon.

For fifty years it survives on Earth, connected to Walter Simeon as the boy becomes a man. It grows stronger, but not strong enough. Its memory, covering centuries, is full of gaps, but it remembers a name given to it in Tibet – Great Intelligence.

Although still weak it survives, outlives the man, but retains his form. For over a hundred years it lingers on Earth, searching to find other minds to bring into its own. Technology advances on Earth and soon humans discover new ways to store information, in a cloud of knowledge contained in something they call the World Wide Web.

Hiding in this repository of information amuses the Intelligence, using this web. It doesn't understand why, until it learns to break through firewalls and access secret information hidden by governments and military organisations. It learns and remembers.

Tibet, London... So many times humans have encountered it, and it seems one man is always there to defeat it. The same man who defeated it in the nineteenth century. The Intelligence grows hungry for revenge, and plots. It learns everything it can about the man, the Doctor, and while it learns it rediscovers the extent of its own influence on the corporeal plane.

The plan is simple. It will travel through the timeline of the Doctor, undo every victory, and kill his enemy hundreds of times over. But it doesn't account for that irritating porcelain girl, Clara. She also travels down the timeline, stopping it at every turn. With each defeat it becomes weaker, until it finds itself in London again. Only now it is the past.

But even here Clara has prepared and time runs as it is intended. Jamie McCrimmon blunders in and uses a Yeti to smash the pyramid, causing feedback that cuts off its younger self from the corporeal plane. The Intelligence watches, unable to do anything. Whatever it does, wherever it goes, Clara Oswald will be there.

So it goes somewhere she cannot go. It jumps timelines. No longer following that of the Doctor. Instead it travels down the timeline of the man who is destined to become the greatest ally of the Doctor, Alistair Lethbridge-Stewart.

It emerges in 1937. At first it is disorientated, much weaker than it expects to be. But it has arrived in the right place, for there before it is the boy that will become the soldier. It will kill him, defeat the Doctor vicariously. But wait, there is another presence there. Another boy, and there inside the boy...

It is a soul that the Intelligence knows so well. Its own soul at the beginning.

Young, new, and still contained in human form.

Unable to resist the pull of itself, the Intelligence merges with its young soul, ready to rebuild itself from the beginning. Prepare for the arrival of the Doctor in Tibet, and to end the battle before it really begins. But something goes wrong.

Disastrously wrong.

The two souls are not supposed to exist together – one impossibly young, the other ancient. It is too much for the young soul. Both are dying. But the Intelligence cannot remove itself. It is trapped!

It tries to communicate, explain things to the young soul. Calls itself Maha, a name plucked from its ancient memory. Mahasamatman; the name of its last human form before it transcended to pure consciousness. The young soul, Gordon, cannot understand. It only sees things in human terms, its mind is too underdeveloped.

The Intelligence needs to escape, but it also needs revenge. It knows that Gordon should die in 1949 so that the soul can be reborn in 1951, the first of thousands of rebirths as it evolves to the point where it no longer needs form. But still vengeance can be had.

It will kill Gordon, rob him of ten years. This will cause Alistair much pain. It is not much of a defeat, but it is something. And so it forces Gordon to kill himself, his death freeing the Intelligence once more. But it is now weaker than ever, and it retreats into the walls of the nearest building. There, in Remington Manor, it becomes the house, but is unable to reach any of the inhabitants. At best it can whisper in their ears, taunt them, drive them mad. Eventually the family can take no more and flee the house.

It tries to reach Mary, the mother of Gordon. If it can drive her mad too, that will be another defeat. But it is not strong enough. Mary leaves, takes Alistair with her. But as she moves out of its reach, the Intelligence yanks at her memory, tears out everything that was Gordon. It affects Alistair, too. The Intelligence is content for a while. It is a kind of victory – stealing from them their son and brother.

But it leaves a trace; just enough for its back-up plan.

It doesn't know how many years pass, but it remains trapped. An echo. A whisper.

And then it feels its young soul once more. But this time it will not merge with the soul, this time neither extremes of the immortal soul will be damaged. It will guide the soul, influence it, and draw strength from it.

From the mind of Owain it learns of the year, of the events in London. It reaches out to Albert Arnold, the mind that still contains a trace of itself, the younger version that was defeated in London. It has to pass through the minds of so many – animals and humans – to reach Albert. Causes much confusion, and the humans and animals try to call for help, but the only way they can do so is to create the symbols of the ancients. No one can understand, no one can help. But it doesn't matter, it has reached Arnold, and Arnold is on the way.

Just one more trace is needed, the echo it left in Mary when it wrenched from her the memory of her son. It calls to her, using the voice of Gordon...

Understand!

Lethbridge-Stewart blinked. Barely a moment passed, and he knew everything about the Intelligence. He understood its plan. He smiled.

'Defeat comes in all shapes,' he said, and turned to aim his gun at Staff Sergeant Arnold.

The Intelligence looked around in panic. 'How did you...?'

Lethbridge-Stewart raised his eyebrow. 'Young Mr Vine, who is, as I understand it, the person you once were. Centuries ago.'

Owain Vine stood next to the pyramid, his hands resting on a shoulder of both Albert Arnold and Mary Lethbridge-Stewart. He was muttering, intoning words, his eyes looking into the distance.

The Intelligence rushed over, his arm outstretched. 'No, you fool! I have seen too much. Too much for any one mind to contain.'

Lethbridge-Stewart tightened his finger on the trigger...

Before him he saw everything. His entire life, every moment open to him like a canvas. His wives, his children, his grandchildren. And there was that strange little man he'd met in the London Underground, shabby frock coat and chequered trousers, his black hair looking like something out of The Monkees. And there were many others too – so many faces, but all one man, his greatest friend; the Doctor. From rank to rank, to being knighted, Lethbridge-Stewart saw it all. A graveyard, a man in a dark suit, grey hair, eyebrows that glared more than his eyes, and finally, at the last, a salute. Lethbridge-Stewart saw his future.

…and the gun fired. The bullet shot through the air, impacting on Arnold's forehead, crashing through his skull and obliterating his brain. All trace of the Intelligence was destroyed and the once-again dead body of Arnold dropped to the floor.

Lethbridge-Stewart looked over at the Intelligence. It stood there, immobile, then it slowly began to fall apart like a piece of paper over a naked flame. The sound of explosions nearby. The spheres. One by one they exploded.

'Retreat!' Lethbridge-Stewart shouted.

Owain blinked, looked around, and was rushed out of the house by his father, now free of the Yeti, which was shaking violently. Lethbridge-Stewart stored his gun and picked up his mother in his arms.

As he darted outside, the house screamed. The Great Intelligence was dying.

The house exploded.

The battle raged around Bledoe, as the Army threw everything it had at the Yeti. Some Yeti fell, those unfortunate enough to get a bullet between the eyes, but most remained unstoppable. Until Lethbridge-Stewart's last shot found its home.

One by one, like a concussion blast, the Yeti exploded. Erupting in great balls of fire, tiny bits of them flying everywhere. The Army troops, most of whom had already faced the Yeti in London, lets out whoops of joy at the final end of the Great Intelligence. All their fallen comrades finally avenged.

It is alone, finally. Its essence, its soul, trapped in what remains of the house. It can feel the fire burning, and as the flames eat the house and all its contents, the Intelligence feels itself fading. After centuries of trying to find true peace through the unity of consciousness, it finds it in death.

They stood at the edge of the woods, far enough from the burning house to not be singed by the heat. Lethbridge-Stewart's mother was still out cold, but her breathing was steady. Owain and George stood side by side, watching the house burn. Owain patted his father on the shoulder and turned to Lethbridge-Stewart.

'Sorry about that,' he said. 'Was the only way to show you how to kill the Intelligence. Without the trace of itself in Arnold it could never survive. It was dying, what was left of its old self in Arnold was its last chance at restoration.'

Lethbridge-Stewart was sure he knew this. Only...

'It's all fading,' he said. 'But I think I also saw my future.' He smiled. 'A very rewarding one, except now I can't seem to recall a single detail about it. But I was right, there is much more out there than the Intelligence.'

Not that such a thing would help him with Hamilton; even if he could recall the details, which he couldn't. Hamilton would require proof. Well, one thing at a time.

Owain smiled sadly. 'Too much for the human mind to retain. Even I can barely remember it all now. But that's probably for the best.'

Lethbridge-Stewart nodded curtly. 'Yes, no man should know his own future.' He looked up at the blue sky. 'But it's still out there.'

'It is?'

'Yes. We have seen how it all ends, but the Intelligence we encountered was from a long time in the future. The Intelligence that invaded London… it's still out there.' Lethbridge-Stewart considered the implication of this. 'Which means it may return.'

'Yes,' Owain said slowly. 'But at least we know that it will be defeated. By you.'

'By us, Mr Vine. After the damage it has done to our families, I find that rather fitting.'

'Agreed,' George said, speaking for the first time since escaping the house. He looked back at them and walked up to his son. 'You did a good thing, Owain. I'm… I'm proud of you.'

Lethbridge-Stewart looked down to the wet leaves under his shoes as George and Owain hugged. He stepped back to check on his mother as the steady rumble of an approaching vehicle disturbed the air.

They turned to look and saw an army truck pull up near the gates of the manor. Several people jumped out, including Ray, Rifleman Bishop and Miss Travers. They looked around, confused, Ray's eyes lingering on the burning house. Miss Travers spotted them and a brief frown of annoyance clouded her expression. Lethbridge-Stewart returned Bishop's salute. He patted Owain and George on the shoulder.

'Looks like our lift is here, gentlemen. If you'd be so kind as to help me with my mother.'

It was almost time to leave Bledoe, but first Lethbridge-Stewart wanted to say goodbye to two people.

'You should have this,' Ray said and handed the photograph to Lethbridge-Stewart.

He took it and held it up. It was the picture of the three of them from 1937, before the Intelligence had first arrived in Bledoe.

'And I also want you to promise to return from time to time.' Ray held his hand up before Lethbridge-Stewart could say anything. 'Yes, I know you're a busy man, but this is your home. Literally,' he added, waving round the front room.

Lethbridge-Stewart looked around. He supposed it was true. No deeds were ever exchanged, so the house still remained in the Lethbridge-Stewart name. He reached down and stroked the dog which sat between his legs. Looked like Jack had taken to him.

'I promise,' he said. 'And this time I will make a point of it. Even now I can't remember a thing about James.'

'Now, Alistair…'

Now it was Lethbridge-Stewart's turn to hold his hand up. 'I know he existed,' he said, indicating the photograph. 'I can remember my life here in a vague kind of way, like anybody remembers their childhood, I suppose. I can even remember leaving here. But when I try to remember anything that involved James, I come up blank.'

Ray nodded. 'He was a good lad, you would have liked him.' He looked away, his eyes drifting out towards the garden. 'I often wonder what kind of man he would have become. I suppose we'll never know.'

'No.' Except, Lethbridge-Stewart wondered just how much like Owain his brother would have been. He sipped his tea. 'How are you feeling now? Now the truth is out.'

'Vindicated. Relieved. No more sideway glances, I imagine. I just wish I had gone to the Manor with you.'

'Yes, well, you went there eventually, and that's the main thing.'

He finished his tea and stood up, reaching for his sheepskin coat. It was good to be in civilian clothes again. He'd been allowed a few days off, and was using them to tie up the loose ends left over from the past few days. He offered Ray his hand.

'Thanks for the tea, and the photo. I shall be in touch soon.'

Ray shook his hand and reached out to embrace

Lethbridge-Stewart. He tensed, not used to such physicality. He patted Ray on the back and the man released him.

'Goodbye, Ali,' Ray said, smiling properly for the first time in days.

'I think things are going to change at home. I don't think I've ever seen my parents so close,' Owain said. 'But I'm not staying. After Lewis' funeral I'm leaving Bledoe.'

Lethbridge-Stewart wasn't surprised by this. There was a new maturity about him, as George had pointed out. Much like the rest of the village, he had been changed by his experiences in the last week or so, and the death of his twin only made that change more prominent.

'How did your parents take the news?'

'Surprisingly well. I think my dad knows I have to do this. I can't spend the rest of my life here.' Owain laughed softly. 'Thought I could once, but not anymore.'

They continued in silence until they reached the edge of the woods. The fire had long since ended and the ruin of the Manor house was all that remained.

'I'm still not entirely sure I understand the connection between you and James,' Lethbridge-Stewart said.

'It's complicated, and although much of what I saw in the Intelligence's mind is gone, I remember the most important fact.' Owain looked Lethbridge-Stewart in the eyes, the two of them of equal height. 'A long way in the future the Intelligence was born of a man, Mahasamatman, the result of a soul which had been reincarnated hundreds and hundreds of times. The soul that was originally born as James. And then was reincarnated as me.'

'I see.' Lethbridge-Stewart wasn't entirely sure what that meant for the two of them. He believed Owain; there was a sense of truth in his words, a feeling that Lethbridge-Stewart recognised as certainty in him. He supposed, in some strange way, that this made Owain his older brother: his older brother who was over twenty years younger than he. He shook his head. No, that was too hard to accept.

'I believe you're an Arsenal fan?' Lethbridge-Stewart asked, changing the subject.

Owain couldn't hide his surprise. 'Been talking to my dad?'

'Just a little bit. They're playing at Highbury this Saturday, against Southampton, I believe. Perhaps we could both go?'

'You like football?'

'Who doesn't. Tickets are not easy to come by, but I have some clout.'

Owain smiled. 'Yeah. That would be mega.'

'Good.'

They stood there in silence for a moment.

'You know we'll smash the league next year?' Owain said, a new enthusiasm in his voice that Lethbridge-Stewart hadn't heard before. He sounded like the teenager he was.

'I'm sure they will.'

'Been a bit of a lean time, last few seasons, but things are looking up.'

They turned and retraced their steps through the woods, chatting about football like two... brothers?

Lethbridge-Stewart considered. He still wasn't entirely sure how things would turn out for him and Owain, but he knew they would remain in touch. Owain was the only real link he had to his brother now. And every young man needed a positive role model in his life, just like he'd had Uncle Tommy in his when he was Owain's age.

Maybe not a brother then, but more of an uncle.

Yes, Lethbridge-Stewart decided, he could live with that.

EPILOGUE

HIS MOTHER DIDN'T REMEMBER A MOMENT OF HER RETURN to Bledoe, and was convinced she'd simply had a funny turn. Such a belief was helped by the fact that when she came to she was in her bed. Lethbridge-Stewart didn't feel he should burden her with the knowledge of what had happened, since she showed no indication of even remembering James.

This was the first time he had seen her in two weeks, other than a phone call to check up on her. That in itself was unusual, but Lethbridge-Stewart risked arousing her suspicions in favour of making sure she wasn't having a memory relapse.

It was too late to tell her now. She had lived every day since leaving Bledoe believing she had only one son; what good would it do to tell her any different now? Lethbridge-Stewart could not remember James and so wouldn't be able to tell her anything of use anyway. Best to let the ghost of his brother rest.

'You shouldn't be alone, Alistair,' his mother said, apropos of nothing.

He looked over at her from where he was sitting reading the local paper. It was a nice comfortable setting. He couldn't remember the last time he and his mother had spent any time together that wasn't a passing visit. He was set to return to London in the morning, but for now he intended to enjoy being alone with his mother in their adopted home of Coleshill.

'I beg your pardon?'

She looked embarrassed but carried on nonetheless. 'You know I've been alone ever since your father passed away, but there is this man, Mr Cooper, who has been trying to court me for a while now and...'

Lethbridge-Stewart laughed at the oddness of it. 'Are you asking for my blessing, Mother?'

She looked around the room, like a child caught out. 'Well... I suppose I am.'

Lethbridge-Stewart closed the newspaper. 'If this Mr Cooper can make you happy, then I certainly approve. You've been on your own for too long.'

'As have you.' His mother raised an eyebrow, a look Lethbridge-Stewart knew only too well. He had inherited it from her.

'Actually, there is someone,' he began, enjoying the look of joy on his mother's face. Why he hadn't told her about Sally before, he didn't know.

Life was finally returning to normal in London, and in *The Unknown Soldier* an engagement party was in full swing. It was a good turnout, although most of those attending were Army colleagues and Sally's friends. He did think about inviting Ray, but decided he'd rather introduce Sally to Ray at a later, and quieter, date. And Owain... After the match two weeks ago the young man had set off on his travels. He didn't know where he was going, but he promised to drop Lethbridge-Stewart a postcard when he got there.

Sally hooked her arm in his as they stood by the bar, waiting for Dougie to make his toast.

'I'm really just preparing for my best man speech,' Dougie began and received a few knowing chuckles from the small number of people gathered in *The Unknown Soldier*. 'Seems a long time ago since we both entered

National Service; remember it, Al? You were so sure you'd become a math's teacher, while I just wanted to run a fruit and veg stall on the Portobello Road. Neither of us were career military. Fast forward nineteen years and here we are. And not a single civilian amongst us.' Again chuckles, even from the very few civilians that *were* among them. 'But, you know, we've done a damn good job. You a colonel, me a lieutenant colonel, and now you've got a lovely dolly bird on your arm.'

Sally blushed at this, and looked around the room, smiling as sweetly as she could. Lethbridge-Stewart knew it was something of a compliment, really. When out of uniform and dolled up for a night out... well, the term certainly applied. Although Lethbridge-Stewart wasn't overly keen on the shortness of the skirts she wore.

Dougie continued with his toast, which was fast turning into a speech, and once he'd finally reached his conclusion and the hip-hip-hoorays were given, he turned to the man standing by the jukebox, who pressed a button. Moments later *Cinderella Rockefella* started playing: their song. Lethbridge-Stewart and Sally unhooked arms, and with an 'I'm the lady, the lady-who' she walked off to mingle with her guests.

Congratulations were given, and the odd comments about the 'big day' and 'what about children?' were made. Would there be any in the future? Lethbridge-Stewart had not really considered. He imagined that one day he'd like to be a father, but before such a thing he would be certain to make an honest woman of the right lady.

He just knew it would never be Sally.

He glanced over at her, and guilt washed over him at the sight of her laughing at another of Dougie's jokes.

You're the lady, the lady I love, Abi Ofarim was singing. Did Lethbridge-Stewart even really love Sally? There was much to love about her, certainly, but their relationship was not about love. He knew this. Had done since their first date. He was, as Dougie had pointed out, career military now, and the chances of him meeting a woman and falling in love were slim. But he and Sally got on very well: laughed at each other's jokes, made for good companions... But love? No, guilt or not, Lethbridge-Stewart knew that he was not in love.

'There you are, Colonel,' said a prim and cultured voice behind him.

He turned around to find himself looking down at Anne Travers' ever-inquisitive eyes. She was dressed smartly as usual, a polar-neck jumper under a straight cut jacket, and a practical skirt that reached just beneath her knees.

'Enjoying the party?'

Miss Travers raised her straight glass. 'Yes, must say this champagne is rather good.'

'Is it? I should try some myself,' Lethbridge-Stewart said, only now realising he had yet to get himself a drink. That was the downside of arriving in the nick of time, he supposed. 'Where is your father; did he not get the invite?'

'He did,' she said, smiling at a private memory. 'But he can be a bit stubborn at times. Doesn't feel himself after recent events. He's even thinking about returning to Tibet, to Det-Sen Monastery.'

'Whatever for?'

'Meditation, apparently.' Miss Travers shrugged. 'Can't honestly say I understand his fascination with it, even after spending all my life listening to his stories about the monks there.'

Lethbridge-Stewart agreed. He could just about accept the notion of reincarnation, and only because of what happened in Bledoe, but meditation...? New age nonsense as far as he was concerned. Give him a pint of beer and Lethbridge-Stewart would wash away any cobwebs left over by alien possession.

Still, talk of Tibet did give him an idea.

'Sorry you never got to use your new invention,' he said, while he let his idea run around his head a little.

Miss Travers smiled pleasantly. 'A shame indeed, although you achieved a good result without it, so we should all be glad for that. But I would like to have tested it.'

'At least you got to use your... What did Dougie call it? A web destructor?'

'Yes, will have to come up with a better name for it at some point. Still, probably would never have even got to the Manor without it. Not that we were much use.'

'You saved us a long walk back.'

'You're welcome,' Miss Travers said, and raised her glass in toast.

'I assume you're going back to the Vault tomorrow?'

'Yes, seems like the Army wants to keep me busy. The military isn't one to rest on its laurels when it finds new defensive weapons at its disposal.' She shrugged. 'They've set me up a nice pension, so I think I should be quite happy. And busy.' She sipped her champagne. 'And you, Colonel? What have your superiors got lined up for you?'

Lethbridge-Stewart wondered the same thing.

The next day saw him back at Army Strategic Command near Fugglestone. He sat in front of Hamilton's desk, once again a decanter of whisky sat on the desk between them.

'I've read all the reports, and I'm afraid to say as far as High Command is concerned, nothing has changed.'

Lethbridge-Stewart wanted to be surprised, but he wasn't. 'Phase three of the same event?'

'About the size of it, Colonel.' Hamilton sat back in his chair and sipped the whisky. 'However, having read your report, I am curious about the passage in which you say that there will be other attacks on sovereign soil in the future. How did you come by such intelligence?'

Lethbridge-Stewart raised an eyebrow at the unintended inference. 'I'm afraid I have nothing concrete, sir, just information given to me by the Intelligence before I shot it.'

'You shot Staff Sergeant Arnold.'

'No. Arnold died in the Underground. I saw no indication that he was the staff, just a reanimated corpse.'

For a moment the air seemed tense, then Hamilton smiled. 'Very well, then. I will keep pushing, but I need something concrete, Colonel. Some evidence I can take to the generals. The UN is out of the question at this time, but if we can prove that the United Kingdom is under a real and present threat, then perhaps we can do something about it.'

Lethbridge-Stewart knew it was the best he could expect for the moment. 'Very well, General.' He stood and they shook hands. 'I believe I know the place to start. If I may take some leave, I'll come back with evidence.'

'Leave? Well, I'm not entirely sure that's possible, Colonel. I believe 2nd Battalion want you back in Libya.'

'I'm sure Major Connor can survive without me for a while. Or,' Lethbridge-Stewart added, as the idea came to him, 'you could transfer me to F Company? Station me at Chelsea Barracks, at least officially.'

'You intend to act unofficially?' Hamilton did his best to hide his smile, being well used to Lethbridge-Stewart's cunning.

'Not exactly. But where I need to go I will have no authority.'

'I see. And where is that?'

'Where all this began,' Lethbridge-Stewart said. 'The Himalayas.'

The Forgotten Son Original Draft Scenes

The first deleted scene was the original prologue; literally the very first thing written for the book in June 2014. It was removed for various reasons. It didn't feel punchy enough, gave away too much, and a variety of other reasons that will be lost to the sands of time. A few things were changed for the pre-World War II sections of the book. For instance, in the final version of the book Lethbridge-Stewart's childhood friend was Raymond Phillips, but in the original he was Philip Raymond, the name he had in the very first iteration of the plot way back in 1998. The name was changed because Shaun Russell (head honcho at Candy Jar Books) thought, and I think rightly so, that Phillip as name didn't create a sense of the late '30s.

This scene also ruins the mystery of James – on page one! Bad form, indeed. It suffers from what I call first-draft-itis. An author putting down every thought and idea into the prologue, ideas and information that would serve the story better if revealed later. Such things are always changed in the redraft, and had this scene remained then I suspect it would be changed a fair bit. As it stands, the entire scene was removed, and thus the way in which James died was also changed.

Other fun changes to note: the action takes place later than in the final book, and Gordon Lethbridge-Stewart serves with a different part of the British Armed Forces.

It was the summer of 1938 and for Mary it would be the last summer she would see her family together.

Her two boys were out playing down by the local brook with their friends, while Gordon, her husband, was enjoying a break from life as a Royal Navy officer and was sitting in the pub garden with the Raymonds. Mary stood in the doorway, a tankard of ale in one hand and a glass of lemonade in the other. She couldn't believe how happy her life was, and every day counted her blessings. It was not often that Gordon was home, even less so that he was able to get a few weeks off during the summer. It was his naval career that brought about their move to Cornwall four years ago; while he was on active service, they both agreed that they wanted to live somewhere beautiful so when he returned home, their boys and they could enjoy their time together without the hustle of city life getting in the way.

She walked through the garden of *The Rose & Crown* and took her seat around the table, placing the tankard before her husband. He acknowledged her with a smile but did not break his stride in the conversation he was having with Harold Raymond; they were talking about recent happenings in Germany and ruminated on what this was going to mean for the rest of the world. Politics were beyond Mary, so she turned to Eileen Raymond and asked her how Philip had performed in the end of term sport's event a few weeks earlier.

Unfortunately Mary had not been able to attend as her eldest son, James, had been in hospital suffering some strange kind of fever. He had bounced back, as ten-year-old boys were wont to do, and was even now enjoying the summer holiday with his younger brother and Philip Raymond.

She was unsurprised to learn that Philip had done well, came first in most of the events, but secretly she knew this was only so because his competition, her youngest son, had been with her at the hospital. Normally she would have left him with friends, but he had insisted he remain by James' side. He had become increasingly close to James in the last couple of months, which, of course, pleased Mary, but it was out of character. Her sons had never really been that close growing up; James taking after her, and his brother taking after Gordon.

She congratulated Eileen. 'I'm sure Philip was very pleased,' she said, smiling broadly.

'Oh yes,' Eileen agreed. 'Indeed, Mister Wyndham was most pleased with Philip's progress in the last few months. Thinks he's really turned a corner.'

'No doubt. But of course, he always was a bit of a late developer.' As soon as she said it, Mary wanted to apologise, but she couldn't deny that she felt a little defensive after Eileen's attempt at scoring a point.

They were the closest of friends – of everybody in Bledoe, the Raymonds had welcomed her family with open arms and a natural friendship developed quickly between all of them – but it did not stop them from sometimes competing through their respective son's achievements. Mary chuckled to herself. Their sons would be horrified to see it – they truly were the least competitive friends ever. If only their mothers could learn from them.

'Do you suppose Al –?'

Eileen's question was cut off at the quick by a shout from the back door of the pub. Mary twisted her head around. Standing there, cheeks as red as strawberry's, was Philip Raymond, out of breath, and looking around wildly.

'Mum!'

Eileen rushed over to him. She attempted to calm him down, but was clearly having little success in her endeavour. Harold went to stand, clearly irritated that his quiet afternoon conversation had been disturbed, but Mary waved him back down.

'You two carry on. You know what the boys are like; I'm sure it's nothing.' She got to her feet and joined Eileen who was now attempting to usher her son out of the pub garden before the patrons complained too loudly.

'Now what's all the fuss about?' she asked, offering Philip a calming smile.

The look of horror on the boy's face as his eyes rested upon her made Mary step back in shock. When later asked about this moment, and asked she was, she could barely find the words to describe the feeling that welled up inside her. Such terror should never be seen in the eyes of an eight-year-old, but terror it was, and something at her core snapped. At that moment she just knew, somehow, that something had gone horribly wrong with her happy life.

'Philip, what is it? What's wrong?'

The boy opened his mouth to speak, but all that came out was a choke of breath, his lip trembling. Tears began to fall. He looked around, as if searching for someone. He swallowed hard, and Mary followed his gaze. Harold Raymond was looking over at them, clearly uncertain whether to move or not. Even Gordon was started to stir.

Raising himself up to his full height, strengthened by the sight of his father, Philip said, his voice still shaking, 'It's James. He... Something happened and he...'

Without even knowing she was going to do so, she yelled out, 'Gordon!' and darted out of the pub garden. Whether her husband was following or not didn't even register, all she knew was she had to get to her sons straight away.

She didn't stop running until she saw the brook. By that time her husband and the Raymonds had joined her. She shouted out for her sons, but no response came.

'Where are they?' her husband asked, his voice calm and commanding.

'Over there,' Philip said, and led the way.

The adults followed and as soon as Mary saw her sons her world ended.

James was lying beside the brook, his eyes staring emptily up at the blue sky. His brother was kneeling beside him, his eyes raw from the tears that no longer fell. Mary ran, but her legs wouldn't take her far enough. They gave way and she dropped onto the grass. Her heart felt like it had stopped, the world falling away from her.

A voice called out to her. Full of fear, confusion and anger. 'Mum!'

She looked over at her youngest son. His name barely escaped her lips. 'Alistair.'

Blackness claimed Mary Lethbridge-Stewart.

A variation of the following scene appeared in the epilogue of the final book, but it was originally written for chapter one. However, due to other structural changes made to that first chapter, the engagement party scene no longer fit, so I moved it to the epilogue, as part of the wrap up. The big difference between this version and the published version is which member of the Travers' family makes a cameo.

*

He returned to Aldgate and only just made it in time for his engagement party. It was a hasty affair, one that Sally had insisted upon, and Lethbridge-Stewart was happy to indulge her. He was not a man given to mixing his private life with his career, but being engaged to a corporal on Major General Hamilton's staff did negate the whole concept of separating his two lives somewhat. He was still not entirely sure how such an engagement had come about, in fact, something he wasn't going to mention to Sally.

She hooked her arm in his as they stood by the bar, waiting for Walter Douglas to make his toast. Dougie, as he was known to his friends, was probably Lethbridge-Stewart's oldest friend; they had entered National Service together and while Lethbridge-Stewart ended up at Sandhurst, Dougie got commissioned to the Royal Army Service Corps. They had since served together many times, but whereas Lethbridge-Stewart now served in the Scots Guard, Dougie served as a major in the West Yorkshire Regiment. It was Dougie who had introduced Lethbridge-Stewart to Sally at a black-tie event last year, and so it was apt that he should be the one to toast the happy couple.

'I'm really just preparing for my best man speech,' Dougie began and received a few knowing chuckles from the small number of people gathered in *The Unknown Soldier*. Lethbridge-Stewart didn't have a great number of personal friends, and most of the people attending were friends of Sally, and a few people Lethbridge-Stewart had worked with over the years. 'Seems a long time ago since we both entered National Service – remember it, Al? You were so sure you'd become a math's teacher, while I just wanted to run a fruit and veg stall in Portobello Road. Neither of us were career military. Fast forward nineteen years and here we are. And not a single civilian amongst us.' Again chuckles, even from the very civilians that *were* among them. 'But, you know, we've done a damn good job. You a colonel, me a major, and now you've got a lovely dolly bird on your arm.'

Sally blushed at this, and looked around the room, smiling as sweetly as she could. Lethbridge-Stewart knew it was something of a compliment, really. When out of uniform and dolled up for a night out… well, the term certainly applied. Although Lethbridge-Stewart wasn't overly keen on the shortness of the skirts she wore. For a moment he wondered what his mother would say. He supposed at some point he'd have to introduce them, especially now that he and Sally were engaged.

Dougie continued with his toast, which was definitely turning into a speech, and once he'd finally reached his conclusion and the hip-hip-hoorays were given, he turned to the man standing by the juke box who pressed a button. Moments later *Cinderella Rockefella* started playing; their song. Lethbridge-Stewart and Sally unhooked arms, and with an 'I'm the lady, the lady-who' she walked off to mingle with her guests. Loads of congratulations were given, with the odd comment about the 'big day' and what about children? Would there be any in the future? Lethbridge-Stewart had not really considered either of these things. He imagined that one day he'd like to be a father, but before such a thing he would be certain to make an honest woman of the right lady. He just knew it would never be Sally.

He glanced over at her, and guilt washed over him at the sight of her laughing at another of Dougie's jokes. *You're the lady, the lady I love*, Abi Ofarim was singing. Did Lethbridge-Stewart even really love Sally? There was much to love about her, certainly, but their relationship was not about love. He knew this. Had done since their first date four months ago. He was, as Dougie had pointed out, career military now, and the chances of him meeting a woman and falling in love were slim. But he and Sally got on very well; laughed at each other's jokes, made for good companions… But love? No, guilt or not, Lethbridge-Stewart knew that he was not in love.

'There you are, Colonel,' said a gruff old voice behind him.

He turned around to find himself looking down at Professor Travers' beady eyes. The professor was dressed as usual in his threadbare suit, a scarf loose around his neck, spectacles and hat ever-present.

'Enjoying the party?'

Travers raised his beer glass. 'Yes, must say this ale is rather good.'

'Is it? I should try some myself,' Lethbridge-Stewart said, only now realising he had yet to get himself a pint. That was the downside of arriving in the nick of time, he supposed. He had spent a lot of time with Travers in the past two weeks, debriefing over the Yeti do, working alongside the professor and his daughter to ensure that all Yeti were deactivated following the defeat of the Intelligence. It only seemed right to invite Travers – he wouldn't say they were friends exactly, but then Lethbridge-Stewart could say the same for most of those at the party. Speaking of... 'Where is Miss Travers?'

'Who?' the professor asked, displaying his usual absentmindedness when not engaged in constant conversation. 'Oh, Anne! I believe your army boys are keeping her busy. Smart girl, my Anne.'

Lethbridge-Stewart could not argue with that. Miss Travers had proven herself much more than smart, possibly the most intelligent woman he had ever met. She certainly stood out during the Yeti do, with one possible exception, of course. But that exception was long gone, and if Travers was to be believed then it was an exception that Lethbridge-Stewart would almost certainly never see again. Which left Miss Travers. He hoped to work with her again.

'And what of you, Professor? What's next?'

'Tibet,' Travers replied without preamble. 'I have to admit to feeling a little out of sorts, what with the Intelligence occupying my mind for a time. Not quite myself. So I'm going back to Tibet, join the monks at Det-Sen in a bit of peaceful meditation.'

New age nonsense as far as Lethbridge-Stewart was

concerned, but he wasn't going to contradict the professor. Give him a pint of beer and Lethbridge-Stewart would wash away any cobwebs left over by alien possession. 'Well, hope you get the peace of mind you need, Professor, and once again thanks for all your help in London. Couldn't have done it without you.'

'I'm not sure that's true. I didn't prove to be much help at the end.'

Lethbridge-Stewart patted the old man on the shoulder. 'Nonsense, you can't be blamed for what happened. Look at Arnold – that could easily have been you.'

Travers shuddered at the memory. 'Small mercies and all that, eh?'

'Quite so, Professor, quite so.'

This is a scene originally written for chapter eleven, but I felt it was delaying the main point of the scene, and that was the aftermath of the boys' first encounter with the Hollow Man. This was also moved because I just wasn't getting the rhythm I felt the scene needed. It is notable, however, for showing a softer side to the relationship of Alistair and James, and includes a brilliant nickname that got rather lost. (Indeed, I'd totally forgotten about it until reviewing this scene today, nearly five years later! I think I'll re-insert in the rewrites.)

The three boys weren't supposed to be there, but it was half term and their parents were too busy getting ready for Christmas to notice their sons had left the safety of the village. They hadn't gone that far, really, only out to Draynes Wood which was less than an hour away on foot. It had been James' idea, of course; he had grown increasingly rebellious since joining seniors. Raymond didn't mind, since it made a change for him to be part of the popular crowd – in juniors they'd both been what their parents called 'bookish', which the teachers liked but not a lot of the other pupils in their class. He and James now had many different classes, and so they enjoyed playtime more than ever, a chance to compare stories and tease the girls. Thus having almost two weeks to be exclusively in each others company allowed them many opportunities for mischief – alas, Alistair wanted to tag along.

'This isn't for juniors,' James had pointed out as they crossed the field nearest to Draynes Wood, taking them beyond Bledoe.

Nonetheless, allowed or not, Alistair was determined to join them, and had promised to tell on them if he was made to go home. At this James had relented, rubbed his knuckles in Alistair's hair, and told his brother to 'come on then, Ali-stare', using the nickname he had given his brother because of the younger boy's ability to stare him down whenever the two of them argued.

It was barely midday, and so the sun was out, blasting through the trees, although doing very little to help remove the cold air, as they made their way through Draynes Wood. Despite the cold, though, all three of them were warm in their duffle coats and woollen hats.

Alistair was hoping for some snow soon, just as Mum and Dad had promised, or otherwise Santa would never be able to land his sleigh.

'There is no Santa,' James pointed out, once Alistair had explained their parents promise.

Alistair wouldn't be put off. 'Yes there is. Everybody knows there is. Where else do you think the letters go?'

James looked over at Raymond, who watched the brothers but said nothing. He couldn't openly agree with Alistair, as he was James' best friend, but he did agree. Every year the three of them sat down and wrote their lists, and every year they put them in the fire and watched as the ashes of the letters floated up the chimney, where they would travel through the air to Santa at the North Pole. It was magic, and Raymond knew it was true.

'They don't go anywhere,' James said. 'Same place as all ash, up and then back down.'

Alistair stopped and looked at his brother. Raymond

smiled at James – this was it, time for the Ali-stare. 'I know you're lying, because Mum and Dad told me Santa's real, and you know he is too.'

'Suppose the Tooth Fairy is real, too?'

'Of course she is. Where else does the tooth go?'

James opened his mouth to argue, but instead started laughing. 'When you're in seniors' you'll see,' he said, and resumed his walk through the woods.

For a moment Alistair remained where he was, snuggled inside his duffle coat, his hands warm in his cotton mittens. Raymond walked over to him.

'Don't listen to James. Tries to think he's an adult now.' Alistair looked up at Raymond. 'But he's not. He's not old yet.'

The two boys joined James and the three continued on their way. Alistair knew where they were going because James had already told him. There was an old house on the other side of Draynes Wood, where a grumpy old man lived with his family. They had all heard stories about the old house – the Manor, they called it – and they were all true. No children in their school lived in the Manor, but the three boys had seen children playing outside the Manor before. James had wanted to go and introduce himself, but the old man had stepped out of the gate and called the children in. None of them liked the look of the old man, with the stick in his hand. He looked like the sort who would happily beat a child with it.

'What are we going to do at the Manor?' Alistair asked.

'Climb the wall and go scrumping.'

'But apples don't grow at Christmas.'

'Who said we're looking for apples?'

'Maybe he's growing mistletoe?' Raymond suggested.

'Yeah,' James agreed. 'Mistletoe. We can hang it between you and Jemima.'

Alistair didn't like the sound of that. He knew if that happened he'd have to kiss Jemima, and that would be yucky. He lowered his head, wondering if his brother was teasing him again. It was no fun being the youngest.